RED LINE BLUES

THE PASSION OF OWEN CASSELL, CLOSET CONSERVATIVE

a novel by
SCOTT SEWARD SMITH

LIBERTY ISLAND
LET YOUR RIGHT BRAIN RUN FREE

A LIBERTY ISLAND BOOK

ISBN: 978-1-947942-70-7

Red Line Blues: The Passion of Owen Cassell, Closet Conservative

Cover design by Logotecture.

Liberty Island

Libertyislandmag.com

Published in the United States of America

To my mother, who taught me the difference between right and wrong, and between literature and just writing.

CHAPTER 1

Rain On Monday

Had it not been for the Kissinger bollocking, Owen Cassell would have made the 5:23 MARC train to Baltimore. As it was, Dean Cernic didn't dismiss him until shortly after five. Owen thought he still might make the train as he left the 1930s mansion now occupied by Cernic's Institute for Geopolitical Statecraft on Seventeenth and Q Streets. He descended the old, creaking stairs two at a time. He passed the empty reception desk and exited into the early-summer sunlight. He walked briskly from the Institute to the Metro station at Dupont Circle. The sun was still high, and heat came up from the sidewalk through the leather soles of his shoes. He had taken off his oyster-colored poplin suit jacket and held it slung by one finger over his right shoulder, but still the summer sweat pooled under his arms and where the strap of his leather briefcase tamped his white, worn Brooks Brothers' shirt onto the skin of his shoulder. It was Washington, and summer, and hot, and humid, and he wanted to get home and have a drink. He was not in a good mood. Dean Cernic's labored Mitteleuropa-accented criticisms echoed with the slap of his leather soles on the pavement. All he had done was to mention in class the previous day that Kissinger had been the last grand strategist of American foreign policy. Cernic

1

pedantically had explained that such a thought would not sit well with Chilton Stiles, the institute's primary benefactor. Owen hated to be reprimanded and found Dean Cernic's dipthonged explanation to be petty and trite.

He descended the steep diagonal shaft into the Metro, almost running down the steeply descending escalator. He could still make the 5:23, he thought, if the Metro arrived almost immediately. On the platform the digital sign said the next train was one minute away. He loosened his tie and unbuttoned the top button of his damp collar and looked at his watch. The round scuffed lights on the floor of the platform edge began to blink, signaling the arriving train. Sweat still pooled under his arms and on his neck.

An unexpected halt in the tunnel between Dupont Circle and Farragut North lasted far too long. It was 5:24 when the Metro pulled into Union Station. He walked slowly up the escalator to the departure hall. The electric schedule said the next train was at 5:50. That was time enough for a glass of wine at the Center Cafe in the vast vaulted area in the middle of the station.

It was the same bartender as the last time. He told the same joke, as he slapped a coaster onto the bar. "A guy walks into a bar carrying a piece of asphalt. One for me, he says, and one for the road." The bartender laughed. Owen smiled and ordered a Malbec. It was cool in the high-vaulted space and he felt the sweat on his clothes begin to dry. From his briefcase he pulled a printout of the article he was hoping to publish in an academic journal. It was the seed of what he hoped would be his second book. He would need Cernic's help and maybe even Stiles's to find a conservative publisher, because he doubted any mainstream press would take it. That made Cernic's complaint all the more annoying. The working title was "Leviathan in Knots." It was hard to work because the light at the bar was weak and muddy yellow. Also, he kept glancing at his watch, his father's old Patek Philippe. It was too hard to work, so he stared at the bottles behind the bar instead, looked at his watch again, then addressed his Malbec with several large sips. He didn't want to miss the 5:50 now. Even so, he wouldn't get back to his mother's apartment in Baltimore until after seven.

There was no real urgency to get back to Baltimore except to get out of DC. He needed to buy shaving cream at the CVS and a pack of cigarettes. He also needed a bottle of Cutty Sark, but the liquor store a block from his mother's apartment didn't close until nine, so there was time even if he did miss the train. The CVS was open all night. He would have a drink, a few smokes, and put a bit more work into "Leviathan in Knots" once he was home. He would sleep early because he had woken early to catch the morning train. He took another large sip of his Malbec. He was tired. He looked forward to dozing on the train, listening to his iPod. With any luck a pretty girl would sit next to him. He would not say anything to her, but he would enjoy her being there, sneak looks at her through the reflection of the dark window, listening to ballads on his iPod, trying to doze off. He liked having beautiful things around him, even if they were temporary. Everything around him was temporary. The glass of wine was temporary and nearly empty. He packed his papers and went to the platform. It was nearly five forty-five and the herd of commuters was already streaming onto the platform. He made himself a part of them.

He chose the upper deck and reached into his briefcase for his iPod. He plugged in the earphones and turned it on. Nothing happened. The screen said the battery had drained. He must have accidentally left it on after the morning ride in. He sighed, pressing his head back into his seat just as a heavy, older lady lowered herself onto the seat next to him; the panting odor of women's faintly deoderated sweat briefly reaching him as she adjusted her buttocks and pulled out a copy of *Fifty Shades of Grey*. The train pulled away and he tried to doze off, sans ballads, sans pretty companion. He could not sleep now, and the expected depression came over him—the one he had hoped the ballads would ward off, a sort of dread of something unknown and unforeseeable. Nearly forty, what was left of his life sans wife, sans career, sans home, sans direction? And Dean Cernic, fossil director of this two-bit institute that had just recruited him from Columbia, bollocking him for merely pointing out that Kissinger had been the last real strategist of American foreign policy.

"I know that you're new here," Dean Cernic had said. ("Dean" was a title, not a name.) Cernic always used two or three words when one would do, as if triangulating towards his meaning. "You are a neophyte, a 'newbie' as they say, somewhat green, and also fresh to the institute. And of course we stand for free speech and open opinions like any accredited, licensed, inspected institution of higher learning and also education. But there are reasons you perhaps are not aware of, that you might not fully realize yet that are important to Mr. Stiles, reasons why we generally avoid praising and elevating Henry Kissinger too...fulsomely, excellently, admiringly. You should know this and understand it as well." The memory of that voice bothered him but also put him into a light and unexpected sleep.

Owen woke up when the train stopped at Odenton and the conductor's voice screeched through the overly loud speakers. The clouds were darker here, and he worried that it was going to rain. He now remembered that he had left his umbrella at the office. He stared out the window at the chipped asphalt, steel railing, and chain-link fences that seemed to barely string civilization together in a series of very weak links. He stared at the yellow-lit windows of the cheap track-side houses, the emptied factories, the barbed wire, and imagined the ballads on his dead iPod. What is love, anyway? Love. This heart. I never dreamed. It was all pale echoes. He dozed again and woke up when the conductor screeched that the train had arrived in Baltimore, Penn Station, and it was the last stop.

The walk from the station to his mother's apartment on Mount Vernon Square was fifteen minutes, straight down North Charles Street. His mother was on her annual summer European tour: friends in Paris, the Mozart season in Salzburg, a detour to Istanbul to visit former Foreign Service colleagues of his father's. It was better she was away; he would not have been able to do it if she had been at home. He needed her apartment until the one he just signed a lease on in Washington was ready. If she had been there they would only have fought. The Washington apartment would be ready in two weeks, long before she would return. He had swallowed his pride to ask her if he could stay there temporarily and, he supposed, she had swallowed her pride to say that he could. He doubted it was the beginning of a reconciliation, merely the extension of a truce, but it would surely bring its complicating details.

The first drops of rain began to fall just as he was passing the new University of Baltimore law school that was being built. An hour before, there had been no hint of rain in Washington. But the skies were dark and inky in Baltimore and the drops were coming heavier and faster. He reached into his briefcase for his umbrella and remembered again that he had forgotten it. He would buy another one at CVS. He turned right on West Eager Street as the drops seemed to pursue him, slapping harder, seeping through his suit. The dark clouds seemed to have been pulled across the dusky sky like a tarp. The air felt damper and more humid with each step. When he crossed the parking lot at CVS, the rain had splotched his light jacket with dark, messy spots.

He was soaked by the time he made it across the parking lot to the drugstore entrance, rain dripping annoyingly from his hair as he entered the vast, brightly lit, soap-smelling space. It took him some time to find the umbrellas—they were half-hidden behind a magazine rack. He had wandered every aisle by then, catching himself in various mirrors and almost jumping in surprise: his suit splotched, his hair tamped down by the rain, his gaze tired, his face jowly. The depression he had felt on the train returned. He did not trust the man he saw in the mirror. He asked for a pack of Marlboro Lights at the counter, where he set down the umbrella and the shaving cream, and where the pretty young black cashier smiled at him with a sort of pity.

The rain had stopped when he left the drugstore. The conical cast of the streetlights gave the suddenly dark city a movie-set feel. His dampened suit felt soggy against his skin. His socks sloshed in his shoes, the new umbrella dangling pointlessly from his wrist. The sidewalks had emptied, and cracked streets felt menacing. Baltimore, to him, had always had a meanness to it.

Charles Street was nearly empty when he turned on it, taking a right towards Mount Vernon Square. A block before the square, on the opposite side of the street, half a story below street level, was the dingy liquor store. He asked the Sikh for a liter of Cutty on the shelf behind him, remembering that two nights before he had bought a liter as well. The Sikh, he thought, remembered him but tried not to judge.

The bottle would not fit in his briefcase, so he carried it in the paper bag the Sikh had put it in. On the corner of

Charles Street and West Madison there was a red light for pedestrians but no car traffic, so he crossed. He looked up and saw, coming towards him from the Washington Monument, the silhouette of a pleasing shape some fifty yards away. The closer it got, the more attractive it became: long, slim legs in blue jeans; tight, erect shoulders; light hair swept to one side; hair framing, from what could be discerned behind the intermittent flashing of yellow streetlight, a face that he imagined to be pretty. As he approached the entrance to his mother's apartment, and slowed to give her passage on the sidewalk—an act he thought of as non-threatening gallantry—she seemed to slow as well, as if wanting to meet him, as if she recognized him. He slowed; she slowed as well. He had intended to let her pass, but she stopped in front of him. Suddenly they were face-to-face under the awning of the building's entrance, and he wondered if he was supposed to know her, his mind searching memories of former students, ready to be polite or to pretend that he remembered her. She stood quite close to him, and he could smell her perfume. Now he could see she was very young and very pretty, though her eyes seemed to flare up at him and her jaw tensed as he stared at her, still trying to place her. He could not remember her at all, but she was so young, she would have to be from a recent class.

"Hello," she said, again as if he ought to know her. Her tone was cold, her face firm, but the fact that she had spoken to him took him by surprise.

"Hello," he answered hesitantly. Why had she stopped? Why had she spoken to him? Why was she standing so close to him? His heart beat faster. He really could not place her.

"Can I help you?" she said, in that tone that actually meant the opposite.

"Not really. I'm just going in."

"Well, go in then."

Now he realized why she had slowed, why she had stood so close to him. He glanced up at the security camera above the door; she was standing within its range should he do anything to harm her. He stepped away from her and rang the buzzer at the entrance.

"Don't you have a key?" she asked.

"I don't have a key to the outside door," he said, staring through the glass into the lobby. Then he realized how suspicious his actions must have seemed to her: he, without a key. He turned to look at her. She stood, pretty, in the amber glow of the awning, a foot back on the sidewalk and still squarely in the range of the camera. He peered inside the door to the entrance hall. The night concierge was still not at the desk, though. She was probably driving one of the ancient elevators in this old building, where the elevators couldn't drive themselves. It had happened before that the concierge wasn't there while he waited at the entrance. He waited.

"Do you even live here?" the girl asked, her voice edged with a sharper suspicion. He had stared at her all along the sidewalk—his fading long-distance vision had probably made his stare more intent than it should have been—and he was holding a bag that clearly contained a bottle of liquor, and his hair was soaked from the rain and plastered to his head, and his suit was splotched and crumpled.

"My mother lives here," Owen said. "I'm staying at her place temporarily. That's why I don't have an outside key."

"What apartment does your mother live in?" This was a confident girl, confident and quite afraid. This made him sad, and he felt the bag holding the bottle in his hand, the weight of the rain on his suit, the thinning hair plastered against his forehead. The hangdog look that he had seen reflected in the

CVS mirrors. He felt his shoulders droop and realized that it did not help the situation.

"Five D," he said, mustering an air of confidence. "Do you know her? My mother? In 5D. Mrs. Cassell."

"Well, I just moved in a few weeks ago."

"I'm sure Marisha is just driving the elevators. She'll be back in a moment." He was glad he had remembered the name of the night concierge. "Do you have a key?"

He turned to face her and could not find a flaw. She had relaxed a little, and even, he thought, looked almost sheepish.

"I have it here somewhere," she said, lifting her right knee to support her large handbag and searching inside for her keys. Her head bent gently down and her chestnut hair gleamed in the light.

Behind him the door opened and Marisha said, "Good evening, Mr. Cassell. I'm sorry I wasn't here when you showed up. I was taking Mr. Connor up in the elevator." She opened the door and greeted him with her flirty smile. The last time he was there, his mother had said she had a little crush on him and was always asking when he was coming back. "You got caught in the rain. I would have lent you an umbrella if you had asked this morning." She ignored the young lady who followed them in; she did not even greet her.

"Thanks, Marisha. But there were clear skies this morning. I wasn't expecting rain."

"Oh, you know the Baltimore weather, Mr. Cassell. In the morning it's sunshine; in the evening it's rain. Or the other way around."

Still ignoring the girl, she said to Owen, "Should I take you up in the elevator?"

"I'll take the stairs," he said. "I need the exercise."

"Oh you look fine," she said. "And I like that suit, except you got caught in the rain. Do you need me to take it to the cleaners for you?"

He smiled at her. "That's all right," he said. "But thanks." Then he turned to the young lady. "Good night," he said.

"Good night," she replied and gave him what he thought was a smile of minor embarrassment. She turned towards the south wing, opposite from where his mother lived, and he watched her walk away. Marisha waited for her to walk a few steps before saying, with that cold and diffident tone that only the masters of the universe and the forever downtrodden can muster, "Do you need the elevator, miss?" The girl turned her angelic head and replied, "No thank you." As she turned, her gaze caught Owen's, magnetic to each other for a moment, and then she turned away and went around the corner.

Upstairs, he opened the bottle and filled a glass with the heavy ice cubes he had made (not the little ice pellets that the refrigerator made) and poured in the whiskey. He took the cellophane off the box of Marlboros. He found the empty can of nuts that he used as an ashtray and took that and his drink out to the fire escape that led from the kitchen and overlooked the interior court of the building. He lit his cigarette and thought of the pretty girl. He thought of all the accidents of that evening: from the class's going long, to the Kissinger bollocking, to the missed train, to the long hunt for an umbrella at CVS, to the decision to buy a bottle of Cutty Sark. All the accidents that had so annoyed him earlier, they now seemed like nothing more than fate's tricks to get him to slow down so that he would, at precisely the right moment, come face- to-face with her.

CHAPTER 2

The Kissinger Bollocking

O n the fire escape, in the cooling quiet night, Owen smoked and drank his whiskey. He had thought about the girl, which was pleasant thinking when it came to her looks but less pleasant when it came to her suspicion. He thought about meeting her in another way, in an unblotched suit, in a lecture where he might impress, or during the intermission of an opera at the Kennedy Center, where they were waiting in line for a drink. Then the fantasy faded and he thought about the Kissinger bollocking.

The only thing that Owen had said in class was that the last time the U.S. had acted upon grand strategy principles was when Kissinger had engineered the opening to China. Since then, all foreign policy had been management, global housekeeping of an increasingly lackadaisical manner. What about the invasion of Iraq? an attentive student had asked. That had been a radical policy, Owen agreed, but not a geopolitical one. It had been a continuation of a policy that had begun in 1990, with the first invasion of Iraq, followed by the no-fly zones. It was more the logical culmination of a policy that had exhausted itself rather than a new calculation. A lively debate had followed among the students. For the first time, Owen appreciated the intelligence of some of them. But one of them had apparently relayed his Kissinger comment to Dean Cernic, and the old Bulgarian had summoned him.

Dean Cernic's office was in a room formed by the turret of the old mansion that had once been the embassy of an African country, bought by the institute's benefactor, Chilton Stiles, former CIA agent who had made a post-9/11 fortune in security services. Dean Cernic's desk was in a corner, set diagonally in front of the curved turret window. When Owen had entered, the room was speared by a semi-circle of late-afternoon sun, the shaft of light falling squarely on Dean Cernic's peculiar golf ashtray. The Dean himself had his head bowed over his papers, his pen twirling absently through his fingers, his semi-bald head receiving an edge of the evening's dying rays, like a background figure in a Caravaggio painting. When Owen had knocked on the doorframe, the ponderous head lifted. Dean Cernic motioned him in, indicating more with his chin than his hand one of the two leather armchairs set on the fraying Oriental rug fronting the chipped desk. The room still had the stale smell of the cigars that Dean Cernic had reportedly stopped smoking during the second Clinton administration. The dean, despite the heat—even with the old air conditioner droning and wheezing—wore his double-breasted navy blazer buttoned and his tie squeezed up against his too-tight, yet unstayed, collar. A button on one of his suit sleeves, Owen noticed, was dangling from a dark, coiled thread, threatening to jump forever from his sleeve but perhaps lacking the courage. Owen tried not to look at it; it made him want to tear it off and sew it back on again. He stared instead at the unused ashtray, bathed in light, that held the torso of a tiny ceramic golfer on the rim, in a putting stance, as if the ashtray were the green. The head of the golfer had been snapped off long ago by some overzealous cleaning lady, but miraculously, the tiny golf club shank was still intact so that one could imagine the putter, sans head, still optimistic about the putt.

He had sensed from his first day at the institute, two weeks earlier, that Dean Cernic did not like him. Yet it was Cernic who had written him a letter inviting him to join the institute's faculty, and Cernic—and Cernic alone—who had interviewed him; and Cernic again who had offered him the job. He had been surprised to receive the offer, since he had already sensed, during the interview, Cernic's antipathy. But Cernic's offer had come at precisely the right time, shortly after Owen had been denied tenure at Columbia (despite excellent evaluations and a decent record of publications). Owen was fairly certain he had been denied tenure because he was viewed as too conservative—a stray comment about Iraq had left a permanent stain—and suddenly this offer had come from this non-prestigious but known conservative institute. He had taken it because he had nothing else. He had, in fact, felt grateful, no matter his distrust of Cernic.

The wheezy air conditioner gasped gusts of semi-cold air, stirring the musty smell of ancient cigars. The carpet was worn and even the photos of the dean with Ed Schultz, Al Haig, Grover Norquist, and Lyn Nofziger looked as if, and in fact were, from another century. The suits and ties, Owen thought, were so much more colorful and varied than those of politicians today. The evident laziness of the current president himself, Owen had once thought, seemed to begin each morning before his wardrobe: What should I wear today? What the hell, the old black suit, a solid tie, and a white shirt. (Then again there was something fitting in these days that each morning the leader of the free world should dress like an undertaker.)

"I understand your position," Dean Cernic had said patiently to him, as Owen had glanced at his watch, wondering if he would make the 5:23. "Your essential thesis, your design, your argument. You will talk about free speech. I understand it is in many ways a conservative point, true, somehow perhaps valid, and of course liberal in the classic sense. I understand that we Americans value the freedom of speech and that is above all else, of course, though there are other things to take into consideration. I understand all the arguments you'll surely make against me before you make them. But we must deal with political realities. Chilton Stiles, who is our major benefactor, as you must know, had important issues, differences I should say, with Mr. Kissinger during the Ford administration, when they were at similar levels. Things were done that were painful and perhaps unfair to Mr. Stiles. And to be clear, open, candid, Chilton Stiles would never tell you to not praise Kissinger, if you feel that that's where your intellect brings you. Chilton Stiles is not a censor. However, I'm just suggesting to you as an unwritten rule that it might pay to be...diplomatic, and perhaps delicate and even nuanced in this regard and on this particular point."

The scene was pathetic to Owen as he replayed it in his mind on the metal stairway. Cernic, a young rising star in the Cold War Bulgarian foreign ministry, had defected while accompanying an official delegation to Geneva. He had devoted the rest of his life to the advancement of freedom, the Reagan doctrine, the collapse of the Soviet Union. Yet now he faced Owen like a Stalinist apparatchik sputtering the party line. Dean Cernic, it was well-known, listened to Sinatra during the late hours he stayed at the institute, working on a manuscript about which there was much speculation but little knowledge. Dean Cernic, it was rumored, had taken up golf with an American bourgeois vengeance as soon as he was cleared as a defector and got his first job at the State Department. Owen realized that he himself did not care enough to muster the case for his own defense that the dean expected him to make. Perhaps Cernic was just an old man who wanted company, and was blowing this issue out of proportion. Owen was still more concerned about making the 5:23. Still, he accepted the ritual of this miniature show trial. A tactic of total insouciance would have seemed insincere, and he would have been judged badly for it. He tried to look concerned, contrite, as if he cared. In party politics, left or right, a pretense of sincerity is valued coin. The dispassionate observer—the very trait that had made Owen a conservative—was wholly untrustworthy to the faithful of whatever camp. "I was only quoting Paul Johnson," Owen said in defense, "who wrote that Kissinger was the last real grand strategist in American foreign policy. It was something for the students to think about. It led to quite a discussion, a worthwhile discussion I would say. Somewhat unusually worthwhile, I would add."

"I understand, of course, yes." Dean Cernic suddenly gripped his pen with a vital force. "But if you ever work in diplomacy," he lectured, "you will understand that there are sensibilities that must be respected. And we are teaching these students diplomacy." The dean's proudest moments, to judge by the photos on the wall, had been the few years he had spent in the State Department under Reagan. But he had in fact not been working for the Reagan *administration*. He had had a non-political position in the State Department, had been a diplomat, a bureaucrat—had been, in fact, exactly what he would have been had he not defected. Either way, he was on the losing side.

"And statecraft," Owen added.

"Statecraft, of course," Cernic said, annoyed. "But what is diplomacy without statecraft?"

A highly interesting question, Owen thought. Perhaps the very definition of American foreign policy, he suggested to himself. Perhaps there was a possible monograph in that. He looked at his watch. There was time, he thought, to make one more fake defense and still make the 5:23. "The larger point I wanted to guide my students towards," he said, "is the paradox of how big government cannot do grand strategy. It ties itself up. It lacks the nimbleness required. This is even more the case when big government is democratic. I think this is fundamental to our assessment of American foreign policy today. Not only can we not define our aims because those charged with defining them put their bureaucratic interests above their national interests, but we cannot achieve them even if we know what they are."

"Try to find other examples," Cernic suggested. "Perhaps not Kissinger, because of the sensibilities. Maybe Monroe. Yes, Monroe and his doctrine," said the dean, pronouncing the name slowly the second time. "Monroe is in fact a better example, because in 1821 our government actually was small. Monroe's doctrine was far more significant, and longer lasting to our foreign policy, than the opening to China, which has really yielded very little except one additional vote in the United Nations Security Council—which is generally against us."

Owen sighed and silently retorted: Then please admit to this institute students who know who Monroe is. Instead he lowered his head deferentially, sneaking a look at his watch again, and said, "I'll look of course for other examples."

"I think we have reached an understanding," Cernic said, as if he had just concluded the Helsinki Accords. "And of course we stand for free speech and open opinions like any institution of higher learning, but there are reasons, as I have discussed, why we generally avoid praising Henry Kissinger too...fulsomely, excellently, admiringly..." Owen nodded and said he understood. "I too..." Dean Cernic began to say, as if apologetic. He didn't finish his thought, raising his eyebrows instead, indicating that Owen could leave.

He had not made the 5:23 but he had bumped into the girl. That, more than the chaos of the world and the hiring processes of the institute, was something to think about. You see beauty every day, on the street, in the classroom, on the MARC, but some beauties affect you more than others. What bothered him most was that she had not seen him as he was. He was something else, he wanted to believe. Yet in her first impression of him, he was a degenerate bum. Then it bothered him that he thought so much of her, and he remembered he had to recharge his iPod.

The night air had turned pleasant; the skies had already cleared and the dampness had lightened. He poured himself one last drink and lit one more cigarette and decided not to think any more about Dean Cernic or Chilton Stiles or Henry Kissinger or even about that girl. He tried instead to remember the details of Renaissance paintings, a game his grandfather had taught him. What are the objects in front of Tintoretto's Magdalena? (He remembered that with her bare breasts and fiery hair she was, even penitent, an insanely hot Magdalena.) As he lit his cigarette, his eye caught a light suddenly turned on in the fifth-floor apartment across the courtyard. He turned towards it and saw what might have been a silhouette, in a white slip, holding a glass of wine, a slim silhouette. He inhaled his cigarette and watched the silhouette, the silhouette that seemed to turn towards him. It was her, he was sure. He recognized her and wondered if she recognized him—if she was even watching his own silhouette framed against the light of his mother's kitchen, his features lit perhaps by the faint glow of his cigarette. He sensed across the darkness that they were looking at each other without realizing it. He felt her gaze finding his across the black chasm between them. They were far enough apart and shrouded in sufficient darkness that they could pretend they never knew it was each other they were looking at. It was a curiously safe sort of intimacy, and all the more thrilling for being so safe. She drank; he watched her; he smoked and sipped. They were alone together, pretending that they didn't exist to each other, yet he could not turn away from what he thought were her eyes finding his.

He kept drinking and thinking long after she had turned out the light and taken her slip to bed—alone, he hoped. It is really only when you are drunk that the idea of destiny becomes rational; and, he realized, standing up and suddenly grasping the cast iron railing, that he was drunk.

CHAPTER 3

The Baccarat Tumblers

Owen Cassell's mother never had forgiven him for being the inheritor of her father's five-room, Upper West Side apartment overlooking Central Park. Neither had she forgiven Owen for becoming a conservative or, as she mostly put it, a fascist—"just like your grandfather." Those two things had ruined their relationship long ago. She had not forgiven Owen for either of them, and she blamed her father for both. Her father was Silas Stone, the famously self-exiled writer who had lounged during his declining years at his villa on Lake Como. Stone had named names in his time—or named one name in particular, but that had been enough—and then had left America. He had declared publicly at the airport upon leaving that he would not return until his government offered him an apology for putting him in an impossible position—a position impossible for a government of free men. Governments don't apologize. A few years before dying, he had ruined what was left of his public reputation by writing, after decades of silence, an unfortunate article that, as a side effect, reminded people that *Vanity Fair* still existed as a literary publication. The right claimed he had become anti-American, the left that he had become a fascist. The article had been published around the time that Owen was beginning his political conversion away from liberalism. "He turned you into a fascist, just like he was himself," his mother had accused at the time. "And look at him now. Disgraced!"

His mother had stopped speaking to her father long before he'd died, and even before the infamous article, but she *had* expected to inherit that apartment: three bedrooms, a large living room facing Central Park, a spacious study and library, a full kitchen with a breakfast nook. And if you didn't like living in Manhattan, it could be sold for at least two and a half million. Along with the apartment, his grandfather had also left Owen ownership of the rights to his novels, which had significantly dropped in value after the unfortunate article but which still brought Owen enough money to sustain the costs of the apartment. All that, along with a somewhat generous trust, had made Owen Cassell a rich young man. His mother, though rather well-off herself, thanks to the death benefits of her late husband, still resented it.

She lived in Baltimore, in the apartment Owen's father had bought the year he had retired from the Foreign Service, which was the same year that he died. That was before Owen's own political conversion, when he and his mother had things in common. Owen's father had died in that same apartment, collapsing in the study one evening after dinner, surrounded by photocopies of articles from the *Annals of West African History*, *The Journal of the Royal Academy of Anthropology*, and the *Harvard Review of African Ethnography*, while about to continue working on one of his endless and unpublishable articles about a minor West African tribe, having just had dinner and an after-dinner drink. He had died in November, with Christmas already in the perfumed air of the department stores and the abbreviated family trio making plans for being together with Owen home from Princeton, and wood being bought for the working fireplace in the grand Baltimore apartment. The day they buried him, after the mourners had left, Owen had paced the hardwood floors of the suddenly empty Baltimore apartment, the dead phone that had just rung with yet another condolence in one hand and one of his father's crystal tumblers in the other. The thick ice made soothing wind chime sounds against the old cut crystal. He was drinking the Cutty Sark that his father used to buy by the case. He had dug the bottle from one of the cases in the pantry. He replaced the phone in its charger and then sat at the bar of the kitchen his mother had just remodeled, a cold evening, the glass cold in his hands that night, and not much to say. The mourners had gone, leaving behind piles of food on loaned plates and an ice-cracked silence, his mother busying herself with putting food into Tupperware containers. After a while Owen asked if he could have as a memory the set of four crystal glasses and the decanter that went with them.

"There are only three glasses," his mother had said. "It was a set of four once. Your father dropped one earlier this year. He wasn't well, you know. He didn't want you to know how ill he was, of course. And I didn't agree with his not telling you, but I respected what he wanted. He wanted you to remember him in a certain way. Not as an invalid."

Owen sipped from the crystal, his tongue tracing the cut rim, his eyes staring at the clipper ship on the yellow label on the bottle. "I remember him like I remember him," he said. In my way, he thought, a way that you will never be able to change.

"I should have seen it as a sign," she continued. "His not telling you. Maybe even I didn't realize how ill he was. He didn't tell me everything either. He was always like that, you know. A little bit secretive. Oh, he had his secrets." Owen guessed that she wanted him to ask what those secrets were, but he wanted to remember his father in a certain way, without secrets. His father had been a gentle man, with an old-fashioned reserve, yet sly in his own way, especially when it came to dealing with his wife. He stared at the bottle. The Cutty was a mild whisky, almost yellow rather than amber, quite gentle when diluted with the sweat of a few rocks, perhaps better to consume in one's older years, especially when one has a heart condition and is retired and has not much else to do to pass the time (except write unpublishable articles about minor West African tribes) and therefore drinks too much and starts too early. He remembered during his youth the strange illnesses his parents used to develop late at night, after their parties, where they would bump into things, and then he would hear them scream at each other in what he thought was some sort of diseased pain. He would almost go to check on them, but they had always returned to normal before he'd had the courage to open their door.

"They were a wedding gift from my father," his mother said, now shifting to a different tack. "We carted those four glasses all over the world, packing them carefully. The foreign minister of Bolivia drank from one of those when your father was posted in La Paz." She carefully packed a couscous salad into a Tupperware container that was almost too small for the salad that remained. "Over four continents, you know. And then he finally goes and breaks one here in Baltimore and then dies a few months later. I should have noticed that he wasn't well, and I tried to tell him not to drink so much. He was stubborn, though. He always was. He might have seemed to you to be a mild man, but oh he was stubborn. Especially about that."

"So can I take the three that are left?" Owen asked.

"Go ahead. Take them. It will all be yours eventually, if *you* don't die of alcoholism."

Once, when he was a bit tipsy, visiting Owen at Princeton, his father had said: "Your mother is one of those who thinks she's dancing with seven veils when in fact she discarded six of them long ago." Owen had been too young to understand what he meant but old enough to remember the image, and much later surprised to encounter the phrase—dance of the seven veils—later in life. He had, until then, thought that the dance of the seven veils was something his father had invented.

"Yes, I suppose that broken glass was a sign that he was on his way out," she said, more to herself than to him.

Owen stared at the bottle, because he couldn't bear to look at his mother. He had had his occasional annoyances with her: her tendency to tantrums, her moral certainties, and her almost oppressive cosmopolitanism. She took an almost cruel delight in correcting people's mistakes about places and culture. She had more than once intimidated the few girlfriends from college that he had brought home, and who had been insufficiently cosmopolitan. "The Hermitage is in Saint Petersburg, not Moscow," she would say with gentle pity. But he had never confronted her. In this he was like his father, a diplomat to a fault. A Munich every week for the sake of peace in our time. Now, with his father consigned to the Maryland soil only hours ago, he was afraid that if he looked at her he would lose control. Someone might have told him that his father was close to dying, he thought. *She* ought to have told him. He deserved a goodbye. Since when did she ever listen to his father when she thought that she was right? If he weren't so angry, he would have wept right there. So he said nothing for a while, staring at the yellow whiskey label as she continued to clear the counter. He listened to the clacking of drawers and the clinking of glasses as they were returned to their places in the cupboards, lost in his own sad and bitter thoughts. After a while he realized that he could not continue staring at the clipper ship on the label of the bottle of Cutty Sark much longer; he had memorized the riggings. So he looked up at her and said, "They're Baccarat, right?"

"Of course. My family was from there—on my mother's side. You might as well know, he didn't really die from a heart attack. He was drunk, and he fell, and he hit his head, and that set off the heart attack." She slapped down the last Tupperware cover and said, "Well, that's all the food." There was a silence that neither knew what to do with. Then she said, "Of course, there's plenty more *whiskey*. But I'm going to bed."

You bitch, he thought. But when she offered her dry, powdered cheek on her way out of the kitchen, he pecked it obediently. Once he heard her bedroom door close, he popped some more ice cubes out of the tray and filled the Baccarat tumbler again.

CHAPTER 4

Happy Hour

At the institute, where his phone hardly ever rang, Owen was surprised to receive a voicemail from Jill Gervais. It took him a moment to remember who she was. She would be in her mid-forties now, he realized. Her voice on the electronic recording system was smoke-scratched, yet his last memory of her still roused him more than momentarily. She said on her message that she had heard he was back in town. She suggested they go for a drink. He did not call her back immediately.

Jill Gervais had been nearly ten years older than Owen the year he worked as a junior speechwriter for Senator Morgan Douglas, Republican from New Hampshire. Jill had then been a strikingly gorgeous thirty-five-year-old, dazzling in a miniskirt, turning heads even in the large Hart building lobby, which did not lack for stunning young staffers looking gorgeous in their miniskirts. Jill was not a New Hampshire girl. She was from Georgia and had been transplanted to northern Massachusetts by her divorced mother. Jill had kept much of her Georgia charm despite spending high school in New England. She had a genuine smile and an easy courtesy towards almost everyone. She had hair the color of gold and honey, a bronzed sheen of silkiness that always smelled of shampoo. She treated Owen in the office as if he were a younger brother, with a warm but false intimacy that nearly drove him crazy. He tried to avoid staring too long at her breasts that seemed so full and fruity, her tanned and smooth and shaved legs, with that gorgeous bump of bronzed calf muscle pushed up by her high heels. "The senator likes this draft a lot, but wants a bit more on the folly of our intervention in Bosnia," she said to him, leaning beside him at his desk. "How long will we end up being there? Does Clinton have an exit strategy? You know, those things. Insist on Congressional approval. Look at George Will's recent editorial. The senator said he couldn't have written it better himself." Her honey skin almost dripping onto his, her shampoo smell making him want to reach down and touch that calf muscle, the tendrils of that soft and fragrant hair teasing his forearms.

She belonged to the senator. Even the senator's wife knew that. Everyone knew that "at home" things were getting complicated for the senator. It was never spoken of openly in the office, but if there had been a betting pool, no one would have bet against Jill Gervais's becoming the senator's third wife.

Owen had deep reserves of decorum. He had learned a few things growing up in a diplomatic environment and, like his father, he was naturally cautious. He met Jill's natural warmth and friendliness with a cold armor of caution. Mistrust of others came easily to him. But the gravitational pull of a beautiful woman was something else, and he pretended to ignore her, though she was really quite impossible to ignore.

The senator's second divorce was reported in the *Washington Post*. For a liberal paper like the *Post*, it was a great thing for a Republican politician to divorce. It offered an endless mine of stories about family-values hypocrisy to be exploited to the last vein. It did not matter that the senator's social views were quite liberal for a Republican. These were complicated days for the senator, who decided to spend the Congressional recess alone at his lake house in New Hampshire to let the story die. Jill remained at the office for the illusion of propriety for a short period after the divorce. The senator could not immediately be seen with her. She seemed melancholy during those days, in the middle of the hot Washington summer. She knew she was the cause of these complications and perhaps sensed that the senator who would wed her would be a different man from the senator who had wooed her. This melancholy was a decaying emanation of her otherwise cheerful floral perfume. The senator's self-imposed exile was a bad omen. Ann Boleyn was never an easy part to play, in any century. One should always question near-victory; victory has all the answers, even if they are not the ones expected. But near-victory is full of traps. Jill was too shrewd for them, but perhaps had an intuition that the fruits of victory were not quite perhaps what she had imagined. Imagination, too, is a shrew.

Nobody believed that she pitied the wife she was about to replace, a woman reviled by the senator's staff for her imperiousness. None had escaped her humiliating caprices. Most enjoyed knowing secretly that the senator frolicked, behind her back, between the lovely peach-skinned legs of Jill Gervais. Everyone desired the humiliation of the shrew; it was a sort of justice.

It was during the senator's lakeside exile that it happened. Jill, during that hot summer torpor, had one day looked at Owen, whom she called "Meany" for obvious reasons—reasons that annoyed him (the only thing about her that annoyed him). "Meany," she said, "why don't we go get a drink somewhere?" Owen had been surprised at the melancholy note in her voice; surprised in fact at being asked to go out.

"Just you and me," she said, quieter, leaning towards him so that he could smell that clean floral magical perfume dancing off her neck, playing with the smell of her shampoo. "I'd like," she whispered wistfully but not sensually into his ear, "just to spend some time with someone a little closer to my age." It was the wistfulness that got him.

They agreed to meet at Millie and Al's, a pizza dive near the group house in Adams Morgan where Owen then lived. The food and beer were cheap, sometimes the jukebox was good, sometimes there were girls who danced, sometimes he had picked them up. Mostly, though, it was far from the Hill and nobody who mattered was likely to see them. Not, he thought, that they were doing anything wrong, or would do anything wrong. But there was politics involved, and he was learning that noble intentions counted for little while a few unfortunate rumors could leave your head upon a stake.

He could not help the fact that, when she arrived, she agreed without hesitation to ordering the pitcher of Rolling Rock on special suggested by the waitress with the tattooed forearms, who then brought two frosted beer mugs and just afterwards the pitcher itself. Jill licked away the beer foam on her tight upper lip with a tongue that he could only imagine doing something else. For a while they talked about office gossip.

"The senator," she said, "he says you're a real writer. He likes you. He says you have talent."

"He's easy to write for," Owen said. "He knows his positions."

"He certainly does," she said.

And to avoid the conversation's turning in a direction he did not want, he blurted out a question. "Can I tell you something?" he asked. "A speechwriter's torment?"

"Sure. What?"

"I can never listen to him deliver speeches that I write. It's a problem I've always had. When someone else delivers my speeches, I become a director and an editor at the same time. Either I want to rewrite it, or I want him to say it differently. Or both. I simply can't bear to hear the speeches that I write being spoken. It has nothing to do with him. I just can't bear it."

"I'll tell him that."

"Please don't!" he said. "It's nothing to do with him. It's just me. Nothing I write ever seems final. Every time it's heard or read, I always find ways I would change it. It always makes me very nervous."

She smiled at his panic. *I'll tell him that*, she had said. When, he asked himself? In bed after coitus? Her peachy ass bare to the air as she lay back-up, propped perhaps on her thin slim arms, those breasts resting plump on high-ply sheets? He imagined the senator, his fifty-something stomach flab an insult to her taut, youthful flesh, listening with a yellow-toothed sneer as her pear mouth said: *Owen, you know, your speechwriter, can't bear to hear you read his speeches.* She had simply been smiling at Owen. He grappled for something to say: a new diversion. Her ankle under the table rested against his.

"What are your long-term plans?" she asked.

"I don't know. For now I'm happy where I am."

"You can't be a senator's speechwriter forever. What if he loses an election? You have to have your own plan. You're different from the other Hill rats. I'm not sure how, but you are."

He wondered what she meant, but she had in fact pried open thoughts he'd had recently along those lines. "I have been thinking about doing a PhD in international relations.

I want to write books. I think I would be a good teacher, if nothing else."

"You grew up abroad, didn't you?"

"My father was in the Foreign Service."

"Morgan once told me that he was surprised you were a Republican. Most State Department people are Democrats, he said. Always about appeasement instead of building American strength. It's rare, he said, for someone to come out of that environment as a Republican."

"My mother was devastated by my politics. My father died a few months after I graduated from college, before I became a conservative. He also was a Democrat, though, and probably would have disapproved."

"I'm sorry," she said. He realized he had sounded, when talking about his father, uncommonly wistful. It was uncomfortable, this sympathetic silence, and Owen tried again to change the subject: again, perhaps, disastrously. "And what are *your* long-term plans?"

"You mean after the wedding?"

"I guess. So it's confirmed?"

"Next summer. He bought a ring. He doesn't know I know it. He showed it to someone in the office. She told me about it. There are no secrets there. How could he be so stupid?" Owen flinched at her sudden vehemence.

"Will you keep working? After the wedding?" he asked.

"No. God no. Not with him at least. I can't work for my husband. It would never work out. No. I'm going to take a break for a while. Take care of the house in Virginia, and the other one in Concord, and the other one at the lake. Become a good senatorial wife. There are worse things."

"Is that what you wanted?"

"Out of life?"

"So to speak."

30

"Oh I suppose you will tell me that I could have had more. Are you disappointed in me?" She half laughed, and the ankle left his leg briefly, then returned. "We have a lot of fun together," she said, almost at the same time as he said, "I don't know you well enough to tell you anything." There was a short silence.

"But you're a romantic at heart, aren't you?" she said. "Aren't you the type who might want to save me?"

"Even if I were, I don't have anything to offer someone like you."

"Like me?"

"You know."

"I might, but tell me."

"Rather beautiful."

"Rather." She sighed as if it were not enough, and smiled as if she understood.

"Yes, very beautiful."

She suddenly seemed to perk up, setting herself straight, smiling and revealing perfect white teeth, her neatly plucked eyebrows suddenly lifting into the perfect arc, her mouth and delicious tongue fluttering anew. She was saying: "The romantic is a romantic because he doesn't know what he can offer. In the real world, someone like me knows you have to protect yourself. You choose people who can offer that protection. And I'm a traditional girl. That's why we're conservatives in the end, you and me. We're realistic about the world. And if you don't mind me saying, I've had enough of young men who don't know what they want or what they can offer."

"What am I doing here?" he asked, the question more vicious than he had intended. But the first pitcher had evaporated amid the gossip, and the second one had been placed before them several glasses ago.

She did not answer for a time, as if momentarily stunned by his tone but too worldly to let it show. She simply held her head beautifully cocked for him to contemplate. It was endearing, that face, neither petulant nor seeking drama. He believed in that face because it seemed not to seek any particular emotion from him. The moment hung between them, suspended between his fear of having gone too far and her fear of going too far. Then her other face returned, gathered now and composed, pretty and hopeful, Georgia and New Hampshire, peach skin and granite resolve. "I'm going to be a senator's wife," she said. She did him the favor of not explaining further, and saying it as deadpan as it could be said, the good and the bad, the pride and the passion, the end and the beginning, all laid beside each other like bodies in a triage tent, and all he felt was a doctor's emotion: stricken, tired, and sick of playing God.

"I think," he said, "that you're a woman who knows what she wants." The play of her ankle had ceased long before, though later in the evening it was held deliciously in his grasp, in her sheets, and she moaned like the hungry alley cats behind his building and he felt the peach-ass buttocks in his hands and thought he would never fuck anyone as beautiful—and as young—again.

Their divorce, eight years later, had been reported in the Washington press. Owen had noticed it only because he had once worked for the former senator and always recognized the name when it appeared in a minor news item. The news had left him indifferent. He was immersed then in his dissertation at Columbia, a task whose true test, he realized, was not scholarship but the endurance of a terrible loneliness, the loneliness of the library stacks, of the cramped desk, of hearing through the library walls the shouts of revelers on Broadway and longing to be among them, of sensing that this work in the end was probably for nothing at all, for the spectacled eyes of a few old specialists whose main fear was that his theory might one day replace theirs.

But at least, in those days, after the loneliness of the library carrels, he had Lisa waiting for him at his grandfather's Central Park West apartment. Lisa: the woman of his dreams, the queen of his loneliness, the mother of the children they were trying to have with punctual sex each morning when she was ovulating.

* * *

The next afternoon he called Jill Gervais, and they arranged to meet near Washington Circle around five. He walked, his messenger bag slung from his shoulder, heavy with his old laptop and several books, up P Street in the evening summer heat, slowly, trying to avoid sweating through his suit. He was wearing his poplin again. The sartorial rules of Republicans had always appealed to him: no light suits after Labor Day or before Memorial Day; always braces, never suspenders (and one of course had to know the difference); never cuff non-suited slacks; never button the lower button of a blazer; never button a blazer when sitting down. They were not, perhaps, conservative rules, but like most rules in this age, only conservatives followed them.

She had chosen a restaurant that hadn't existed when he had last lived in DC. It had an Italian name but unusually was only two syllables. The décor was also duosyllabic: flat lines of polished dark oak and a great deal of frosted glass. It was a little past five and the restaurant was nearly empty. The air conditioning was mercifully high, and he felt the sweat that had begun to seep through his shirt begin to dry. He saw her as soon as he entered. She was sitting at the bar and rather alone. From just that first glance he noticed how she had aged from the fresh, sexy youthfulness of his memory. She sensed his arrival and turned to face him, slipping from the barstool as he approached. He noticed first her low-heeled shoe and a wisp of varicose on her leg, then the filmy white camisole that she wore, he realized, to cover her sunburnt and ampler shoulders, then her face—a still-decent but somewhat worn face that would not have seemed so unattractive now had it not been for his memory of how attractive it had once been.

Did he conceal, he wondered, his surprise at her deterioration? Yet he smiled and bent to kiss her offered cheek. He smelled her old perfume, remembering it from before and wondering if she had deliberately worn the same scent or if she had simply become a woman of habit—the habits of her youth. He smelled too the second or third Chardonnay on her breath. Had she, he wondered, turned her cheek a bit too abruptly, so that his Gallic peck actually caught the edge of her lip? It was moist. He felt embarrassed but she didn't seem to be.

"Well," she said. "Sir Galahad at last."

"It's nice to see you," he said, sitting down, and they navigated the awkward early formalities while he ordered a Manhattan, on the rocks, not shaken.

"I'm sorry about the divorce," he said early enough in the conversation, to situate themselves. It was no secret. She knew it was no secret. He might as well get it out of the way, as if it were a lumpy cushion between them.

"In his heart," she said, "he blamed his divorce from her and his marriage to me for losing his election."

"I wouldn't think, in this day and age, those things still mattered to voters. After all, it was the decade of Clinton. Knee pads were in fashion among the intelligentsia."

"Ha!" she laughed. "And you're right, they don't matter. Except in his imagination, which was where things really happened. It was easier to blame me than to accept that he'd lost touch with his voters. It was easier to see himself as a twice-divorced man than the bad politician he'd become. He was really not a very good politician, except in his first campaign as quite a young man, long before I knew him, with his first wife. I realized that too late."

Owen now remembered reading that the senator's first wife's father had been a grandee of the New Hampshire Republican party. But Owen, apart from that situating memory, was indifferent to the fate of the now-depleted New Hampshire GOP, and to that of Senator Douglas, and concentrated instead on what seemed to be the low-heeled shoe of the former senator's wife absently brushing against his pant leg.

"Not too early for bourbon?" she asked when his Manhattan arrived.

"I start the day early. It's about the right time for bourbon. My last train's at ten thirty, which means my night effectively ends at nine thirty."

"Train to where?" Jill asked.

"Baltimore. I'm living at my mother's place for now. Next week I'll move into my new place in DC."

"Stay with me tonight if you want." So direct. Her foot more insistent against his leg. "I live just across the river, in Arlington. A short cab ride. The settlement was decent. I own it." He tried to imagine the place—perhaps a two-bedroom condo from where the hum of 495 could always be heard: new appliances, a building from the seventies, with modern fixtures that a politician's alimony could provide. The drink, which he sipped as soon as it arrived, was clarifying. The first sip of a Manhattan, when served on the rocks, was almost always mostly sweet vermouth, no matter how well stirred. He liked to sip through it to get the bite of the bourbon.

"Are you working?" he asked.

"Not on the Hill," she said. "I'm doing PR at a conservative foundation. That's how I found out you were back in Washington."

How everything had changed, he thought. Now he was all nonchalance while she seemed eager to keep the conversation going. "How?" he asked absently.

"One of my partners was reading your book," she said. "He asked me to track you down and put you on our mailing list. You weren't easy to find, by the way. You hardly show up on Google."

"The book didn't sell that well." They talked about the state of the world. Her job at the conservative foundation had made her more conservative, but in a pedestrian way, he thought. She was backing Romney for the nomination. He agreed with her but with less enthusiasm.

"Remember when we had drinks at Millie and Al's that night?" she asked.

He nodded. How could he forget?

"Then of course I got married. We lost contact. Then Morgan lost his election and joined a law firm in New Hampshire. I got stuck in Concord for a while, watching the snow fall, until he decided it was time for a divorce. And here we are again. Not far from Millie and Al's. You and me."

Her shoe again. Not far and yet so far from Millie and Al's and those days and those desires. He looked at his watch and wished he hadn't. It was a sign he was drinking too fast, that he was already losing control over his instincts. That was what bar mirrors were really for: to gauge whether you could maintain the pretense of looking sober. When you stopped looking in the mirror, you were too far along to care. His watch had said it was a bit past seven. He would leave soon. Better a wine alone at the Center Cafe in Union Station than more forced chatter with this fossil of his erotic dreams. One more drink, he told himself, to be polite, for old time's sake.

"But," she said, and he could almost feel the sudden withdrawal of her foot from near his leg, "you got divorced too." That got his attention. His mind had been focused on getting the bartender's attention. Now the bartender appeared just as he was refocusing on what her comment meant. How did she even know he had been married? "Another Chardonnay?" the bartender asked Jill.

"A martini," she said. "It's getting late for Chardonnay."

"And another Manhattan," he said, not sure if he even wanted it, but curious enough to have it anyway.

"Grey Goose in the martini," she said to the bartender, looking at Owen. "No olives." He had met Lisa after he left the Hill. Unlike Jill's, his marriage and divorce weren't in the papers. "I didn't even know you knew I was married."

"Oh, nobody's anonymous anymore. Did I shock you?"

"A bit."

"Suddenly you're curious." She smiled coyly, now that she had his attention. In this different light she seemed more attractive. Perhaps it was just the smile in the light. It was dusk outside, and the world seemed softer.

"You want to know how I know?"

"I do."

"Well, I met your ex-wife."

"In Washington?"

"Yes."

He was thinking of Lisa again. He was trying to figure out where she and Jill might have bumped into each other and trying to avoid the thought that Jill was comparing her utilitarian marriage to the senator to his doomed but honest romance with Lisa.

"Don't you want to know where?"

"OK. Where?"

"At a fertility clinic."

"What were you doing there?"

"What does anyone do at a fertility clinic? Get sperm."

He had missed a beat. He was thinking of his wife at the fertility clinic and imagining her alone. "We started talking," Jill said, "while we were waiting. She mentioned she was divorced; I mentioned the same thing; the senator's name came up and then so did yours."

"I see. Was she...alone?"

"We are all alone. That's the point of these places. We don't really need you anymore." She smiled as her drink arrived and lifted it ironically. "Yes, that's liberation. We don't need you anymore," she repeated.

"But why?" he asked. He wasn't sure what question he was asking, but she answered the one she wanted to.

"Maybe because we don't want to die alone."

"That can't be it. The project is too big for that. It's a life!"

"In any case," she said, "I am too old. But not too old, if you know what I mean." Her foot was definitely on his ankle now, lingering, as if by old habit. "Why don't you stay with me tonight," she said again. "We can have some drinks at my place. I bought some scotch just in case. I never drink it but I know you like it."

His humiliation, he thought, was complete. She sipped her martini and looked at him over the rim of the glass. Now she was almost beautiful again, but he looked at her in horror.

"We can have some fun," she said. "Pick up where we left off so many years ago."

He bit the maraschino from the Manhattan at its stem and dropped the useless stem onto the napkin under the glass and turned back to the mirror. A pale and empty expression stared back at him from above a rack of ready bottles. The expression startled him. The pale and empty expression was suddenly startled. He saw, still in the mirror, her arm reaching for his shoulder and he stiffened before her touch.

"I think it's best that we don't," he said. "Not tonight."

"Not tonight," she said. "Of course not tonight. But ten years ago you didn't hesitate. Right?"

"Everything's changed." He turned back to the mirror and almost couldn't find himself among the bottles. "I hesitated," he said, "if you want to know, but not enough."

"Well you turned into a bit of a shit," she said. You were too beautiful, he thought. And then he thought of all the beauties who had expired long before they had died and admitted, to himself at least, that he had turned into a bit of a shit.

All he wanted was to be alone on the MARC, listening to his iPod, and thinking of the girl, and perhaps meeting her again at the end of the road. Or if not that, at least commune with his bottle of Cutty Sark and smoke a cigarette on the fire escape, tending carefully to the ashes and the stubs, and hope she might appear in the kitchen across the way and he could contemplate her silhouette again.

"I'm sorry," he said.

She had quickly composed herself. "I didn't mean that," she said.

"It's just a strange time for me." That was a sort of apology.

"You're not over her, are you?" He stared at her and realized she was staring at him. Then he realized she was talking about Lisa. He wasn't sure what to answer, so he nodded.

39

"She's a beautiful woman," Jill said. They finished their drinks and said goodbye like adults.

Outside, despite the sunset, the city had barely cooled. He descended the long escalator through the maw of the Dupont Circle Metro station, grateful for its darkness. He felt like Orpheus but in reverse, descending into hell, fleeing from Lisa, looking back constantly to make sure she was not behind him, hoping to freeze her to stone. In any case, he told himself, he was long out of love with her. It was just that he would rather not run into her. He had not counted on her moving from New York to DC.

CHAPTER 5

Divorce

He had been truly in love with Lisa. He had converted to Catholicism for her—a decision that further infuriated his mother, who had *left* the church in order to marry his father. Owen had married Lisa. And last year they had divorced. Now he could hardly recognize his own behavior during the decline and fall of their relationship. Caught between modern science's temptation to go the in vitro route to have children—which he would not accept (but not because of his new religion, because of something more primal)—and society's offer of divorce if they could not reconcile their differences, they had locked horns. She had wanted to try despite the long odds. He had wanted to give up because he did not believe in it. They were caught between two mortal sins, exhausted from a fight without end, sick of even seeing each other, presiding over what seemed to be the cold corpse of their love as unalive as the child they could not conceive. They *would* not, she would have corrected him. They *could* have if he had agreed. So he had accepted divorce. He did not want to remember those painful fights, those parodies of theological disputation whose goal for her was to bend theology to her deepest wants, to have despite not being given. It was not that he did not want children, it was that he resented her self-

41

ishness and what he then saw as a defiance of God. For his part, he simply had a deep and unexplainable aversion to the creation of life in a test tube, a visceral position that pre-dated his conversion to Catholicism, and perhaps a fear that the lab might make a mistake—especially in this era of generally diminishing competence in everything. And when he had been brought to masturbate into a plastic cup to test his sperm with the aid of a pile of porn DVDs clinically provided, he had been unable to do it. She had retorted that he had been unwilling. There had been something about the forced and clinical process that paralyzed him. Lisa had never forgiven him. She shut herself off. He brooded. The marriage was dying, and they fought against each other rather than together to save it.

In the end, he reasoned with himself during those turbid days when they both knew their marriage was ending, if she was not going to be Catholic enough to respect the Church's teaching on the creation of life, he was not going to be so Catholic to deny her a divorce. His own modernity in this matter disgusted him at the time, but he thought it was the lesser evil. Now he went to mass every Sunday, sat in the rearmost pew, off to the side, under the shadow of Saint Jerome, listened attentively to the homilies, recited the new liturgy, of course did not take communion, and prayed that at the final judgment God would be merciful to him. His grandfather—his father's mother—had attended mass like that. Owen remembered accompanying him to mass at Como one summer when he was very young, when his parents had left him there to go on one of their trips. Not knowing anything, and not having been raised Catholic, Owen had risen to take communion with the rest of the pew when they rose. His grandfather's hard, wiry hand pulled him back down to the old wooden seat with a force that surprised him. "Not me ever, not you yet," he whispered. But in the end they both became Graham Greene Catholics, believing *ma non troppo*—committing the irredeemable sins and casting themselves extravagantly onto the ultimate mercy of God.

Shortly after the divorce, towards the end of the fall semester at Columbia, where he was teaching, between Thanksgiving and study week, he was eating alone at a bistro. He was lonely and indulged himself: a martini to start, steak-frites with several glasses of good Burgundy. He had finished his main dish and was looking forward to dessert, an espresso, and a cognac. He had in front of him a book of essays by Hannah Arendt, who was a cheap date in that she required nothing to eat, but high-maintenance in the attention she demanded. It was, he thought, as perfect an evening as he could have hoped for during that bleak time. Since Lisa had left he had no interest in meeting anyone else. Most of their New York friends had been hers anyway, and she had taken them with her. He had few friends among his faculty colleagues. He was untenured and vulnerable. He sensed the beginning of a campaign against him after an unguarded comment he had made. "I understand the arguments the Bush administration put forward for their invasion of Iraq. In some ways to them it was over-determined." He had been told later by a colleague that this had been interpreted as being pro-war and even pro-Bush. After that he felt new and greater distances were being created. He was too tired from the divorce to try to fight his way into Columbia. He had become almost indifferent about tenure. He liked the area around 116th Street, though, and he liked this bistro. Between the first and second glass of Burgundy, he was distracted from Arendt by two young women, undergraduates, just seated at the table next to his. The louder, more talkative one, was telling the other about the upcoming visit of her father to campus, how she was looking forward to seeing him, and all the things she wanted to show him. The father was some sort of lawyer, and she talked about how she admired him and wanted to be a lawyer like him. It was not a particularly interesting story; she was not a particularly engaging speaker. But it moved him, this love she had for her father. This, Owen thought, was one way he as a man would never be spoken of on earth. He was the end of the line. He realized then how much he wanted to have children. He canceled the rest of his order, signed his bill, went home to his grandfather's apartment, and drank himself to sleep overlooking the darkness of Central Park.

CHAPTER 6

Lunch At The Metropolitan Club

Dean Cernic looked up from his desk and greeted Owen with a pained expression. He was fiddling with an electronic cigarette, not smoking it but twirling it between his fingers. "I wanted to avoid this," he said. "To prevent it from happening, to defuse it, one might say. But it has unfortunately become unavoidable and even inevitable. Someone, perhaps one of your students, must have leaked the issue, revealed it, I cannot say how, and now Mr. Stiles has asked me to inform you that he wants to see you."

"About the Kissinger thing?" Owen asked, hardly believing it. Things had reached the point with Dean Cernic that he almost thought everything the man said was part of a giant joke.

"The 'Kissinger thing' is more than a thing. This was what I tried to tell you. Mr. Stiles is a generous man, but in politics there is also passion, a lack of reason, blind spots. I wish you had taken more seriously and devoutly the advice I had given you. Mr. Stiles did not tell me why he wanted to meet you, but I cannot think of any other matter than the incident in class—the 'Kissinger thing,' as you say. Tomorrow, noon, at twelve, for lunch, at the Metropolitan Club. He is a member there. Do you know the address?"

"No," Owen said. Dean Cernic gave him the address. It was downtown, near the White House, walkable if it wasn't too hot. Owen left the dean's office and went up the flight of stairs to his own small office space, thinking that it was odd to be invited to lunch at a swanky club in order to receive a venting of displeasure. Kissinger thing or not, he was looking forward to meeting this eccentric benefactor whose general background he was, of course, familiar with. Chilton Stiles was well-known in conservative foreign policy circles, for his spymaster past, for his participation in most Republican administrations since Nixon, for his massive recent wealth, and especially for making people wonder what he would do next. Owen wondered, though, if it was Dean Cernic himself who had revealed to Stiles his Kissinger blunder. You could take the boy out of the Bulgarian Communist apparatus, he thought, but you couldn't take the snitch out of the Communist bureaucrat.

* * *

It was hot and muggy again the next day when he left the institute's decaying mansion for lunch at the Metropolitan Club. Owen was wearing his best suit: Brooks Brothers, navy blue, wool, conservative cut, theoretically year-round but in fact far too heavy for the Washington summer weather; but he thought that poplin or linen would have been disrespectful. He had, unusually, put on a tie. His mother had kept his father's ties even as she had gotten rid of most everything else of his. For some reason, instead of giving the ties to Owen, which he thought would have been natural, she had kept them in the Baltimore apartment, hanging from a tie rack in the closet of the guest room. She used to choose them for his father carefully, dressing him each morning before he headed off to the State Department or whatever embassy or consulate he was posted to. His father had no sense of sartorial combination, but because of her he was considered to be one of the more elegant Foreign Service officers. Owen had chosen, that morning in Baltimore, an Hermès tie that his father had worn for his official photo when he was appointed deputy ambassador to Ghana. Owen had tied it over his crisp white shirt, calculating the length properly in the mirror, so that the end lay halfway across the belt buckle as it should. It looked perfect, and he hoped that he might bump into the girl from across the courtyard on his way out of the building. He did not.

At a quarter to noon he left his office, carrying with him a signed copy of his mostly unread book, *The Clash of Histories and the End of Civilization*. He half expected to see Dean Cernic lurking in the lobby of the mansion, ensuring, nanny-like, that he was leaving on time for Mr. Stiles and that his hair was combed and his socks matched. But Dean Cernic was not there. It was too hot to walk, and so Owen hailed a cab.

Everything in Washington was fifteen minutes from everything else. The cab was air-conditioned and he felt fresh as he stepped from it and walked up the steps to the entrance of the Metropolitan Club. He knew, of course, what Chilton Stiles looked like. There was a discreet portrait of him in the conference room of the institute, known as the "ballroom," and obviously he had Googled him before taking the job at the institute. Stiles's face was everything it should be: ruggedly creased, ruddy complexion, intense blue eyes, short-cropped white hair—the portrait of a cold warrior.

The door from the street led into a vestibule, where there was a round table with a vase of chrysanthemums around which were strewn that day's papers and the usual set of journals—a bipartisan selection. In front of a fireplace were two settees and a couch around a table with more newspapers. One man sat in the settee, his back to the door, and when Owen walked around he saw it was not Stiles, but a young man of his own age with a more expensive suit than his. He glanced at Owen and then down again at his BlackBerry. Someone came out from one of the club rooms, but it wasn't Stiles either. Owen sat down on the settee opposite the young master of the universe.

The room was meant to comfort those in power and intimidate those without. To be at home in it was to know power. To feel unfamiliar and hesitant amid the polish, the tuxedoed coat-check man, and the portraits, was to reveal weakness. Owen was intimidated, but he was determined to act as if he weren't. He was the grandson, after all, of Silas Stone, and fuck them all. Owen picked up a copy of *Newsweek* that had a cover story of the dreary London Olympics, settled back into the plush lobby settee, and pretended to care what *Newsweek* had to say, while actually trying to think of how to deal with an angry Stiles, who was still responsible for his paycheck.

Stiles, he had learned from Googling, was one of those semi-dark figures that Cold War America had invented. It was no secret that he had been a senior operative in the Directorate of Operations. After rising as a young star in the Nixon National Security Council—when he must have begun his dispute with Kissinger—he moved quickly through the ranks of the agency in the 1980s. He had made his name at the nexus of Cold War and post-Cold War espionage. His job towards the end of the 1980s was hunting terrorists who everyone knew were funded and supported by the Soviet Union. Stiles the terrorist-hunter had one of the few Cold War skills not viewed as redundant in the post-Cold War world—while the Kremlinologists and missile-counters frantically retooled themselves into bureaucrats whose main job was to defend the existence of the agency. After his retirement he got into the business of supplying intelligence privately, then providing security privately, and was therefore perfectly poised to make tens of millions during the Iraq-Afghanistan wars. Being a generous fellow, he had taken over the institute, then half languishing under Dean Cernic and surviving on the interest of a few dwindling estates hit hard by the crash. For this, Dean Cernic would always be grateful to Chilton Stiles. The old operative had stayed in the political game and now was rumored to be among a close group who led the foreign policy apparatus of the Romney campaign. "Mr.

Cassell," the voice said. Owen stood up and shook the proffered hand. The man had come in stealthily while Owen had his nose stuck in *Newsweek*. He wished at that moment that it had been at least *U.S. News & World Report*. Stiles, conjured suddenly before him, was dressed in a seersucker jacket, off-white linen pants, and a bow tie with Princeton's colors. The BlackBerry boy, suddenly realizing who was there, almost stood up and bowed.

"Mr. Stiles," Owen replied. "Thank you for the invitation." Stiles bore himself like a man who had once been taller, and combed his hair—straight back across his domed pate—like it had once been fuller. It was as if, when shrinking, the muscle of his torso had shifted to his gut, which protruded. But his handshake was hard as steel.

"Have you been to the club before?" Stiles asked, leading him towards the elevator.

"Never. I am not really a Washington creature."

"More of a New Yorker, right?" Stiles's question was not a question, and Owen suddenly wondered how much Stiles knew about him.

"I suppose so," he answered cautiously. "My father was a diplomat. I grew up all over the world. But I've spent the last few years in New York."

"You should consider yourself very lucky." Stiles had pressed the button for the second floor, but the elevator was hesitatingly slow to get there. There was another man in the elevator when the door opened—tall, well-suited. He looked vaguely familiar and acted as if he should have looked more familiar. "It is a great advantage in our world," Stiles continued, "to know how to function in foreign cultures. Languages?"

"Several," Owen said, not naming them, embarrassed to recite his qualifications in front of the strange yet familiar tall man in the elevator.

"Good," Stiles nodded, as if understanding his discretion. "We'll talk about it later." Owen almost felt like he was being interviewed for his job again, but in the friendliest way. This surprised him; it did not seem that the Kissinger thing mattered. But Stiles was surely a crafty operator and Owen—despite feeling strangely warm to this man—tried to keep up his guard.

When the awfully slow elevator finally stopped on the second floor, Stiles led Owen to the right into a large dining room. The maître d' gave a short bow and with a broad smile and an Italian accent said, "Mr. Stiles. How nice to see you again. Table for two?"

"And you know which one, Federico," Stiles said. "I was here last night," Stiles noted to Owen. "A dinner for Oliver Pont-Murphy. Do you know who he is?"

"The British journalist?" Pont-Murphy was a well-known correspondent in the conservative world, a Catholic and an anti-Communist, a sprightly writer who would have been far more famous had he been a liberal.

"Exactly," Stiles said. And while Federico pulled out their chairs, allowing them to sit, Owen wondered if Chilton Stiles was verifying his conservative bona fides. He did not, after all, have a particularly conservative background, except for writing speeches for Senator Douglas a decade ago, but even Douglas had grazed at the border of RINO-ism. Was Stiles questioning Dean Cernic's judgment in hiring him?

They were seated at a two-person table next to a window. The space felt cramped, but from the narrow window there was a clear view of the White House through the trees, and of the Washington Monument beyond. The monument was sheathed in an unfortunate scaffolding, apparently being repaired after last year's earthquake.

"I brought you a copy of my book," Owen said.

"Signed?" Stiles asked.

"Of course—more than that, dedicated."

The old man seemed, to Owen's surprise, almost childishly pleased to receive the book. "I'll have to give my other copy to someone else," he said.

"You've read it?"

"Of course. It's very good. We'll get to that in a moment. In the meantime, do you know whose chair you're sitting in?" Stiles asked.

"No." Owen looked around as if he might find a name on it.

"Kissinger's!" Stiles guffawed. Owen began to feel trapped, as if it were the first move of a diabolical gambit, as if Cernic had set him up. It was going to be an uncomfortable lunch, and he suddenly hoped he might have a drink with it.

But noon was perhaps too early. Stiles was perhaps not the type. He steeled himself for the possibility of dealing with another bollocking with only an iced tea to refresh him, and both thoughts made him miserable.

"We were young guns, Kissinger and I, in the Nixon administration," Stiles said. "Of course, he went on to greater things."

"More public things, at least," Owen said, slightly disgusted at his own toadying. Yes, he wanted a drink.

"He was wrong about nearly everything," Stiles continued, ignoring Owen's veiled compliment. "But I can't stand the attacks against him now. That fool Hitchens and so forth. We're old soldiers, Henry and I, and were on the same side in the greatest sustained battle ever fought over the soul of the world. With time you forget the pettiness of our little quarrels that took place within the larger battle. The Cold War. That was the big one. And we won it. And old Henry was on our side all the way through it."

Owen relaxed cautiously. He began to suspect that Stiles knew nothing about his classroom blunder, and that if he were aware of it, he did not seem to care. The chessboard looked different to him now. "I mentioned Kissinger in my class recently," he ventured, advancing a pawn.

"Languages, I was saying," Stiles replied. "What do you speak? You said several."

"French and Spanish very easily. A bit of Arabic as well, which I can read, though with difficulty. Italian I studied for several years. It's rusty but would not take much to revive. I try to read something in Italian every few weeks."

"Italian," Stiles said. "You've spent some time in Italy?"

Owen was surprised that it was Italian, the least useful of his languages, that Stiles remarked upon. "Some time," he answered, "as a child."

Stiles nodded patiently. He himself was famous for the many languages he spoke fluently, and was less impressed at Owen's than most Americans might have been. Owen recalled the relevant chapters of the old man's biography. He had grown up in Louisiana, the son of a drunk grifter. He had worked his way through Tulane, studying by day and managing a hotel reception desk at night. He had skipped his junior year to work on a merchant marine ship, where he had discovered his quick ear for languages, including Chinese and Arabic. Along the way he had been recruited, then returned to Tulane, and then emerged at Princeton on a full scholarship for graduate school. "And one thing I always told them," Stiles said, presumably referring to the leadership at the Company, "if you just hire boys who look like they grew up corn-fed on an Iowa farm because those are the only guys you can trust, well then everyone in the world is going to spot them a mile away. Unfortunately that's still how we recruit." He took a sip of water and almost grimaced, as if he wished it were something else. "I would have recruited people like you, and they would have hanged me for treason."

"People like me?" Owen asked.

Stiles ignored him. "The other thing is," he said, "I'm telling you this quite freely but I'll never write it down. I can't stand those former agents who feel they have to write a memoir. That's what the State Department is for. The other thing I realized is that access to intelligence makes smart people stupid and stupid people stupider. They think that everything that's obtained by secrecy is by definition the truth. What does that say about us? Why do we even call it intelligence?"

He had, while talking, been looking at the menu. "I recommend the navy bean soup," he said. "This place is famous for it."

There had been hardly anyone in the room when they first sat down. Now it was gradually filling up, mostly with men, well-tailored and quite familiar with the place and each other. That, Owen mused, was what a club was, and he liked it. The waiter came and took their order. Owen was half hoping Stiles would have a glass of wine. A chilled white would be perfect on a day like this, but Stiles ordered a tonic water and Owen just ordered an iced tea. Then Stiles adjusted his cufflinks and stared at Owen for a moment. Owen realized that however old the man was, and however frail he might appear, he would not even now like to be at the other end of those eyes during an interrogation.

"I wanted to meet you," he said, "because I was the one who specifically asked the institute to hire you. You should know—you might perhaps have sensed—that Dean Cernic was not entirely onboard."

"Thank you," Owen replied. "I did sense that."

"I was impressed with your book. I haven't seen original geopolitical thinking like that for a while. I imagine it's not doing very well, though."

"I was hoping that it would be the big-idea foreign policy book of the year, but it hasn't really caught on."

"Nobody in this modern, progressive world of course can bear to be told that they are heading back to the dark ages, no matter how compelling the evidence. But as far as I'm concerned, you're right. Cernic is a decent administrator but is stuck in the past. I wanted someone forward-thinking at the institute, even if that thinking led backwards!" He guffawed again.

The first course arrived. Owen had ordered a salad; it was too hot a day for navy bean soup. Stiles, however, had ordered the soup. "There was another reason I wanted to meet you," Stiles said. "This one might surprise you."

"I'll try not to fall off of Kissinger's chair."

"Very good," he said, erupting again in his old-man laughter, then paused to sip a spoonful of soup. Swallowing, he looked up and fixed Owen with his warrior eyes. "Your grandfather was Silas Stone, wasn't he? The writer."

"Yes." The question had startled Owen. He had taken a startled moment to answer it.

"Of course I did a little background check on you. It's something of a habit."

"Everyone's background-checking everyone these days," Owen replied. "You would not be surprised to know that I Googled you before taking the job at the institute."

"No, I'm not surprised. I also Googled you, though I have other sources of information. Do you know what surprised me?"

"What?"

"How little there was! Your name is neither distinct nor common, but you were almost invisible." Owen did not know whether to be ashamed or not. In Washington invisibility was not a desirable trait. Yet his own age seemed sometimes to him to be a sort of hell: the triumph of the village gossip; the end of the city as a place for eccentrics to hide. He thought of his grandfather's last, unfortunate screed, and how left-wingers had accused him of being senile and syphilitic and the right-wingers had accused him of being a traitor. He was conscious, suddenly, of Stiles examining him.

"I suppose it helped to have my father's last name, not my mother's."

"I met your mother once. She must have been a teenager. Silas lived in Paris in those days, and she was visiting from boarding school in Switzerland. He wasn't much of a father, of course. Fatherhood is very hard on intellectuals."

"You knew my grandfather?" Owen asked, stunned for a few seconds by the natural way in which Stiles had introduced the information.

"That's why I wanted to meet you. That, in some ways, is why I hired you."

"How did you know him?"

"We worked together briefly in the sixties. My first job was as assistant editor to a magazine he had founded in Paris, *Remnant*. Have you heard of it?"

"It's been rumored for years that that magazine was funded by your former employer."

"Did you ever ask him about it?"

"He died before I became too aware of the issue. I spent some time at his villa on Lake Como when I was young and my parents were posted to faraway spots. I saw him infrequently after my teens. My mother didn't want me to be influenced by his politics, and he was then beginning his nasty phase."

"He should have stuck to fiction and literature—and film, of course. He wrote several brilliant ones. He was a good man. And as unpleasant as his way of putting things at the end of his life was, deep down he was more right than people can accept. He spoke truths that people did not want to hear. There is that similarity."

The comparison to his grandfather gave Owen a momentary thrill. He did not at all know what to say now. Stiles's eyes bored into him again. "I have a proposition for you."

Owen, curious, cocked his head. Like a well-structured essay, he realized, this luncheon had reached its main point, its thesis, between the appetizer and the main dish.

"I want you to write a speech for the governor. Write it as a major foreign policy address. But do it as if the governor had fully endorsed your view of the world. In a world where power is configuring itself increasingly outside of the shape of a nation-state, what should America's foreign policy be?"

"The governor?"

"Romney."

"I see. America: the last nation-state?"

"Or perhaps the only successful non-nation-state."

"Yes, that too, with our Tudor institutions still humming."

"Exactly. A bit at a loss during the Cold War but accidentally effective. Now coming into its own as the world returns to medievalism—as you argued in your book. But you must disguise your points so that they do not scare voters away. The world may be difficult but it must be manageable. Your ideas must be sharp but they must be understandable."

"I'll take a stab at it," Owen said. Without thinking, he was looking around the room to see if the young master of the universe happened to be there.

"I can't make any promises the campaign will use it, but a few of us around the governor feel we need something different on foreign policy. I've been urging him to make an address, a big-picture thing, but he hasn't because he hasn't liked any of the drafts and he says it's not a foreign policy election. I'd like you to take a stab at it. If it's good, I'll give it to him. He pays some attention to me."

Owen daubed his mouth with a starched napkin. "When do you need it?"

"Like a martini: as soon as you can as long as it's strong."

"I'll have it to you in a week."

"And when we win, I'd like to see you have a place in the administration. I find this foreign policy establishment is a little too established. Sit tight at the institute for a little while, until the election."

"Do you think it will happen in November? That the governor will win?"

"It's going to happen, and it's going to surprise a lot of people. America has already patted itself on the back for electing its first black president. Unfortunately he happens to be an unabashed socialist. Americans can afford this fling for four years, but they're not so stupid as to stick with it for another four. There's seething discontent in the heartland. You can feel it during the campaign. And for once those who make up the conservative center are organizing, and they're going to surprise a lot of people—a lot of these mainstream media people—who don't even recognize they exist. What do you want?" he asked abruptly.

"What do you mean?"

"What position do you want? When we win."

Owen hesitated. "I hadn't thought about it. I don't know."

"The next time someone asks you that question," Stiles said. "It will likely be serious. Have a specific answer." And for the rest of the lunch they spoke in generalities, generally agreeing with each other. Owen wanted to ask Stiles something more about his grandfather, but Stiles had just asked for the check, was looking at his silver Rolex, and said to Owen, with the courteous finality of an aristocrat: "Thanks so much for agreeing to meet me. Let's do it again. Write that speech, and we'll speak more about your grandfather."

After lunch, Owen decided to walk back to the institute, despite the heat. He had his iPod and an unexpected sense of purpose now. As he walked, he began to compose the speech for the governor and began to think about the position he might want when they won the election.

CHAPTER 7

Lonely Night

On Saturday morning he awoke to what he never liked to see: a whiskey tumbler on his bedside table. What had been left of the ice had melted into what he had not finished of the whiskey. That meant that he had drunk so much that he had poured more than he could finish. He could not remember that nor could he remember going to bed. His iPhone said it was nearly noon. He made a quick, unsteady breakfast of fried eggs while the coffee brewed; he told himself that in an hour, when his headache subsided, he would go for a run. He had not run in weeks and it showed in the paunch around his waist. He noticed that he had at least been aware enough to guard his cigarette ashes in the tin of nuts but that he had also nearly smoked them all. In the meantime, what? He lay still on the couch in the study where his father had died and stared for a while at the stilled fan on the ceiling and fell back to sleep.

When he woke up he got off the couch and stuck his hand out of the window. It might have been a hotter day except that it was overcast. Then he put on his shorts and tied his laces and left the apartment and did go for a run: down North Charles Street to South Charles Street, across Fort Avenue, up Key Highway along the waterfront, and then up Charles Street again to his mother's apartment. It was about three miles, with ups and downs that winded him. While he ran, there was a light drizzle along the waterfront. He took the ups at a slow, lumbering pace, and recovered on the downs. Between the drinks and the cigarettes, he thought, he did better than expected. Back at the apartment, sweating after having walked up the five flights of stairs, he showered. Then he went out again to the supermarket and bought some healthy things to make a late lunch with, pasta and summer vegetables. This was a good feeling, carrying the groceries back: legs aching but lungs clearer, hungry and looking forward to cooking something clean and light and fresh. The clouds had cleared, the sun poked through, tanning his face. The deodorant smelled fresh. He did not even feel like smoking a cigarette. It was rare, this feeling of brimming health.

After lunch he made more coffee and sat down at the desk in the study, his father's old books behind him—the few his mother had kept—and began working on the speech. He worked deliberately for four hours, drinking coffee and water only. Every hour on the hour he allowed himself a cigarette break on the fire escape. He had taught himself to endure the chore of rewriting. That was about the only thing he had learned while working on his PhD—that and how to endure loneliness. But this was a good way to work; it reminded him of the years of his dissertation writing, in his grandfather's grand old West Side apartment in New York overlooking the park, waiting for Lisa to come home after her long hours at Skadden Arps. The work on Romney's speech kept him concentrated like he had once been able to be, and he did not hanker for a drink. When it was over he thought about dinner. He went to a simple restaurant nearby on Ploy Street and had a sandwich and a beer.

When he got back to the apartment he reread what he had written. It was too soon to reread and so everything seemed wrong. It needed to harden a bit before he repoured his thoughts into it. So instead of fruitlessly rewriting what he knew he would change again, he watched a movie. It was a neo-realist Italian one he had been meaning to watch again, to keep up his Italian, to marvel at the filming, the faces, the shadows, the setting of the scenes. While watching the movie he had a few glasses of wine, practically the bottle in the end, but felt good because he had written for four straight hours. The alcohol distilled the thoughts into something stronger, more spirited, like burnt wine that, when left for years in barrels, turned into cognac. It was nearly eleven when the movie ended and he went into the kitchen and poured a whiskey and sat out on the fire escape again, now suddenly suffused with loneliness and needing the drink. His mind had unconsciously picked up where he had left things in the afternoon, and was turning over ideas about the speech, seeking rhythms, trying to imagine Romney saying his words. He had to write words for Romney, he thought, not words for himself. And Romney was a practical man, not given to soaring rhetoric. This was not easy, this speechwriting business. He poured another drink and carefully put out the day's last cigarette in the tin of nuts. He took one last look across the dark chasm between the two wings of the elegant old building, and thought for a moment that he saw her silhouette in the kitchen window, and in the darkness he imagined she had smiled at him.

He was not yet tired so he filled another glass with ice, pouring the light-colored drink at exactly the spot in the kitchen where he had done exactly the same thing the night before his father's funeral. He felt a sad and painful enjoyment when thinking of his father, especially when he was already tipsy and the memories were warm. They would say, Owen thought, if they ever bothered to write his biography, that he was an alcoholic. (He was still young enough to compare himself to George Kennan, who after all had done nothing of significance until his forties. Kennan, in his own memoirs, had spent six pages on his first seventeen years, two hundred pages on the next thirty years, and four hundred on the four years after that.) But Owen would not describe himself as an alcoholic. He would say that alcohol just happened to find him. It had even found him during his post-college year of globe-trotting in the high ramparts of northwest Pakistan, between Chitral and Gilgit, while he was visiting the nabob of Mastuj, tagging along with a homosexual British Persian scholar of unspecified but substantial means with a trailing retinue of servants to carry his carpets, china, and liquor. And when they found each other, Owen and liquor, they rejoiced at the unexpectedness of it all and celebrated. He always seemed to find the booze, like some men always seemed to find sex.

It was still so damned early—just past nine thirty. The memory of Mastuj made him think of his journals. He would have another drink in the salon area next to the living room, like a civilized man, and reread his journals. And like a civilized man he put on one of his father's old classical CDs. His father had been a decent piano player, and had built, in the early years of his marriage, a harpsichord from a kit. It had been a gift to his mother, and part of his attempt to impress her before they were married. The harpsichord still stood, never played (his mother's ear was tinned), next to the window of the salon where he was now sitting and drinking the last drink of the night, wishing that he dared to smoke inside. His father loved Chopin most of all, and that was what he had put on.

He was sometimes surprised at the quality of his youthful prose. It frustrated him that he had never been able to publish a novel, though he had written several. He selected the journal that included his father's death. He had written it while traumatized but knowing that he was writing to remind himself, to be able to remember it as it was. It was not a bad thing to read, now, while having perhaps the final drink, and looking at how the warm yellow light from the lamp bathed the sanded, lacquered wood of the harpsichord his father had built many years ago, years before he was even born.

He had almost moved himself to tears rereading that page and remembering that day. Then the doorbell rang, loud as a foghorn it seemed in the haze he had put himself in. He paused, tensed, wondering who would call at this hour. The old apartment door didn't have a peephole. But most people in the building left their doors open anyway. He went to the door and opened it. It was a dream or it was the girl. It could not have been a dream because of the strong, familiar, unexpected smell. Her hair had just been washed and she was wearing a pair of jeans and flat-soled shoes and a light sweater. The smell was not her hair. It was popcorn. She was holding a bowl in her hand as she stared at his startled face. Then there was another smell that filled him with sad memories.

"I made some popcorn," she said. "I realized that I made too much and I thought I'd bring some over." He noticed her glancing behind him into the apartment, sensing the soft lights, hearing the music. Then a glimmer of quick panic traversed her eyes. "I mean...I thought you might be alone," she said. "I saw you alone on the fire escape. But if I'm disturbing you..."

"I'm definitely alone," he said, moving out of the doorway. "Come in. I was just winding down." Like all practiced drinkers, he could compose himself when necessary.

"I like the music."

"Chopin." He offered her a seat in the salon and put his journal down next to his drink.

"Can I get you something to drink?" he asked.

"Oh, maybe some tea. Do you have tea?"

"There is every tea imaginable in this house. You're welcome to something stronger. I'm having," he pointed to the nearly full whiskey glass, "a little nightcap."

"It's too late for me," she said. "To tell you the truth I had some wine earlier. Just some tea would be fine, evening tea if you have it."

Evening tea, he thought. His mother, the tea connoisseur, would like this girl who knew the difference between an evening tea and a morning tea and presumably an afternoon tea. He went into the kitchen and put the kettle on and put a ginger tisane mix his mother liked into the pot and went out again. The girl was looking at the side table where his mother had strategically set her framed photos: her wedding, Owen's graduation from Princeton, a family picture of the three of them in Paris when he was around eight, the visit of Bill Clinton when his father was an acting ambassador to Ghana.

She sensed his return and turned around. "I really hope you don't mind that I came by."

"It just so happens that I had a craving for popcorn," he said and tried to smile without it becoming a leer. He was not very good at smiling nor, apparently, at reading women's cues.

"I'm Audrey," she said, holding her hand out.

"Owen," he said. They shook hands awkwardly. He sat down on the couch and gestured for her to sit as well. She sat in the mid-century modern accent chair opposite him. He took a handful of popcorn and a sip of his drink. "The water's on the boil," he said, feeling impolite for having his drink but not wanting to let too much of the ice melt. "You sure I can't get you a wine?"

She shook her head. The silence then was painful.

"I know your perfume very well," he said; his own words surprised him, and he told himself to drink slowly now. But Lisa used to wear that perfume. That had been the other smell.

"Really?" she asked, gently playful. "Then what is it?"

"Amarige."

She looked disappointed. He realized that he should have dragged out this guessing game. "You're right," she said, as if there were no mysteries left in the world. "It's actually my great-aunt's. I used a bit of it."

"It smells good on you," he said, wanting to forget the reason he knew the scent.

But as he had begun speaking, she had as well. "The truth is," she had said, talking over him, "I felt bad about the other night. It was bothering me. And I kept seeing you on the fire escape."

"No, you shouldn't feel bad. It was a little misunderstanding. You did the normal thing."

"Watching you smoke on the fire escape, I just thought you seemed a little lonely, and between you looking lonely and me feeling bad, I just felt the impulse to come over. I thought I had never misjudged anyone as much as it seemed I had misjudged you."

"I'm glad you came over," he said. "I have never been so happily misjudged."

She looked around, as if relieved. "This is a really nice apartment."

"It must be the same layout as yours, just in mirror image."

"I think so. But my great-aunt doesn't have the same sense of style. She just has a jumble of furniture inherited from the family. This looks like it was put together with, you know, an idea behind it, taste."

"You're living with your aunt?"

"My great-aunt. My grandmother's sister. For the summer. She's away right now. I'm going to graduate school in the fall and I lost my job last month anyway, so I'm just staying here until school starts, saving money and trying to find a job so I can pay for graduate school."

The kettle began to screech so he went to the kitchen and poured the boiling water into the pot, put a strainer and a cup and saucer on a tray, and brought them back to her.

"I feel like I'm in Downton Abbey," she said, as he set the tray in front of her.

He laughed. "Except I get to play the butler, the cook, and the head of the house. Upstairs and downstairs at the same time. Or maybe just spending my life on the landing." He regretted this compulsion to follow his thoughts to exhaustion, instead of shooting them down at their zenith.

"Well, I guess we're modern people."

"What are you going to study?"

"I'm a librarian. Library sciences."

"A noble science. Not a dismal one."

"Are those your parents with Bill Clinton?" she asked, pointing to the photo on the table beside the armchair she sat in.

"Yes. My father was the acting ambassador in Ghana then. Clinton refueled on one of his Africa trips. According to protocol, my father had to go to the airport to receive him. My mother had insisted on going along. She was desperate to meet him." Owen could not avoid letting slip into his tone his disapproval of his mother's eagerness.

"Your father is a diplomat?"

"He was."

"He retired?"

"He died quite a few years ago."

"I'm sorry."

"After all these years, I still find it hard to tell people that he died, and I still feel comforted when they say they're sorry, even if they never knew him—or in your case probably weren't even born when he died." All that he had just said was true. He had felt a genuine sense of surprise as he heard the words coming from his lips. He had never said them to anyone before. He took a sip of whiskey again, to hide his face or buy some time to compose himself. And then he reminded himself to drink more slowly.

"I love Bill Clinton," she said. "I wasn't really aware of politics when he was president. But he's done so many good things since then, and I think he was a great president anyway."

Owen nodded automatically, deciding not at this moment to redirect her. He did not remember very well all the reasons he himself had disliked Clinton. It was not a topic for now. She was prettier in the soft hues of his mother's lamps than he had ever dared to imagine her from his perch on the fire escape.

He lifted his glass from the dampened coaster. The journal was open beside it. "Were you writing?" she asked, glancing at the journal.

"Reading," he said. "This is a journal from a long time ago, when I did some traveling."

"Aren't you old-fashioned." She laughed. "Tea in a pot, notebooks, classical music. A nightcap."

"Being in this apartment makes me behave. Except, I guess, for the drinking."

"And the smoking."

"That too. Don't tell my mother if you ever meet her, by the way. She thinks I've quit."

"Well, you shouldn't do it anyway. It's not good for you."

She was pouring more tea and he watched the swell of her breasts beneath her blouse as she bent over the pot. She was half smiling, as if both embarrassed and pleased at her decision to rebuke him, as if realizing that it was an odd intimacy, but saved by the fact that the demands of public health excused all indiscretions in modern America.

He smiled back. "You're absolutely right," he said, and more than anything felt like having a cigarette, now that she had reminded him of it.

"Well, even with the smoking I have a much different—*nicer*—image of you than I did the other night."

He thought there was little about her of what one imagined—or read—of young women these days: their vulgarity, or lack of courtesy, or want of grace. She had not, for example, once used "like" as a spoken comma. She knew her teas and how to use a strainer.

"I don't think I realized that night how frightening I must have looked. I had forgotten my umbrella, you see, and I was rather tired."

"Let's forget all that," she said with charming finality. "Where did your travels take you?"

He realized then that his glass was empty. "Do you mind," he asked, "if I have another?"

"If you behave," she said coyly. "Anyway, I'm the one interrupting you. And I still have a whole pot of tea. It's delicious. What is it?"

"It's a ginger tisane. My mother brought it from Turkey, I think. On one of her trips. She goes abroad every season. If it's summer she's in Europe. Like now."

"She has such good taste. I'd love to meet her."

"She'll be back in a few weeks, if you're still around."

He got up and went to fill his glass again. There was a little more left in the bottle than could fit in the glass, but he put in two ice cubes instead of three and was able to nearly empty the bottle except for a few frustrating milliliters left behind. He took a deep sip in the kitchen to make sure that the glass wouldn't spill on his way back. Then he carried it back and set it down gently on the coaster.

"After my grandfather died," he said, "since he had left me some money, I decided to take a year to see the world. I had grown up abroad, a diplomat's son, so I had friends here and there. In those days I wanted to be a novelist, and of course I was a big fan of Hemingway, having no taste of my own. I remember a line Hemingway had written about war. He said it was the ultimate topic for a writer, and it was looked down on by those writers who hadn't experienced it, but that it was the essential experience and the ones who looked down on it only did so because they were jealous. So I went to Africa, to Afghanistan, to Burma. I wrote a few articles but mostly tried to understand what war was so that I could write about it. And I also had friends in decent places, like Normandy and Buenos Aires, so I went to those places too to try to write a novel. I think I'm becoming boring."

"Not at all. What happened to the novel?"

"Novels. Quite a few of them. I wrote them but publishers turned them down."

"Weren't they good? I'm sure they were good!"

"I used to think about that for a long time. I thought they were good, of course. But now I've given up on it and don't care. I published a few short stories in very obscure literary journals, and some poetry, but no novels. It was in the end not my calling, I guess." As he spoke he decided not to mention the non-fiction book he *had* published. Something, at least, told him not to mention it. It might

69

have been the grinning maw of Clinton, the ex-president she loved, beaming at him from the photo. "I think that for all my interest in war, I was never good at establishing conflict in my fiction."

"What writers do you like—besides Hemingway? I'm a librarian, after all."

He had already forgotten that. But it felt like heaven to talk novels with such a young pretty face. Her chin was resting on her clasped hands, her slim fingers interlocked, her eyes fixed on him. "I don't read many modern writers. After the great triumvirate of the pre-war period—Hemingway, Faulkner, and Fitzgerald—I find myself going back in time and away from America. Dostoyevsky, Tolstoy, Flaubert, even Cervantes. Among more recent writers the only one to me who has something to say and is authentic is Kundera. What do you read?"

"I love Jonathan Franzen and Barbara Kingsolver."

"I've never read Franzen. I read *The Lacuna*, though. That period of American history interests me."

"McCarthyism?" she asked.

"Have you read *Witness*?" he asked. "Whittaker Chambers. A great deal of it involves Baltimore. Druid hill. Like *Lacuna* it involves transcripts of hearings in the fifties. Alger Hiss, all that. A famous case." He waited attentively for her answer, perched forward.

"They made a movie out of that," she said.

"No," he said, deflated. "That was different." His tone, he realized, had been close to condescending. She did not answer him. She stared at her tea. In the silence that followed, he was so afraid that she would leave on that sourest of notes. And, as he thought furiously of something to say to get them back to the more pleasant place where they'd been, the Chopin CD suddenly ended as well. A conversation was like a fire that needed fresh, dry wood. He could not find any wood. He could burn the harpsichord for her! He had never been good at small talk. His big ideas about travel and literature had been exhausted. He had successfully avoided talking about politics. He searched for a question about her that would not sound inane or too intimate, staring into his glass and not finding it, suddenly tired.

"Well," she said. "I feel like I invaded your evening."

"The anthropologists may protest, but not all invasions are unwelcome." Now that, he thought, was obscure and unromantic.

She smiled and stood, her slim, lithe body inches from him, the odor of Amarige radiating from her still, and he realized she must have put it on for him, just before coming over. He stood as well, slowly but straight, his head ending up slightly above hers. She was almost as tall as he, but with that carelessly sensual carriage of youth. He suddenly wanted to take her hand and lead her to the bedroom, and felt his body actually listing in that direction. Or perhaps it was the drink. He rebalanced himself, he hoped imperceptibly. She was so impossibly young. "Why don't you come by for dinner one of these nights? I'm not a great cook but I have a few trustworthy recipes. We're two people living in other people's apartments. We have that in common. And books. I promise to be a better conversationalist. Today has been a long day."

"We could do that," she said. "Send me an invitation. My apartment is 5B, in the other wing, opposite yours."

"It was a pleasure," he said. He shook her hand awkwardly and she took the stairs, not bothering to call the elevator.

She had left and he could not help himself afterwards. He smoked another cigarette on the stoop and as he lifted the cigarette to his mouth, the smell of her perfume on the hand he had just shaken when she left mixed with the heady smell of tobacco and the dying taste of whiskey. It had been like that with Lisa many, many nights.

CHAPTER 8

Millstones

It hurt in the morning, as it always did. It hurt more and more as he approached his forties. He had forgotten to close the curtains in his mother's spare bedroom the night before, and the sun shone in directly on his face, waking him before his alarm, depriving him of an extra half hour of sleep he could have used. He turned over and buried his face in the pillow, but he knew he would not go back to sleep again.

The routine began: to the kitchen for a glass of water and to put the coffee on, to the guest bathroom for a shower, to the closet for a suit. These movements often occurred with surreptitious stumbles and indignant self-righting. But he was metronomic about it. It was the first cup of coffee and the first smell of cologne that began to wake him up. It looked like it would be a hot day—the sun seemed intent—but the hand that he waved out of the window reported that the morning at least was still cool for summer.

He drank his coffee on the fire escape with the day's first cigarette and still feeling rotten. He couldn't really remember how it had begun. He had learned as an adolescent to drink responsibly, with meals, with his parents, listening to his father's instruction on pairing wines with foods, on how a judicious amount of alcohol "opens up" the flavors of food.

His father would often have a cognac after a meal, which Owen was not allowed to have until he was eighteen. Then his father would often retire to his study and "work," not to be disturbed until he emerged from behind the locked door. He did not realize that his father was a drunk until he himself had become one and began to learn the art of subterfuge.

His grandfather on his mother's side, the great Silas Stone, had been a proper alcoholic, of the old school: martinis at lunch and cocktails before dinner, then wine at dinner and a cordial to digest. More than that, there was an ethos to it; alcohol formed a community that was the opposite of religion. If in religion everyone celebrated each other's virtue whatever their faults might be, the community of drunks celebrated their great fault, and its consequences, whatever their other virtues might be. Owen had thought, and then thought better of, writing an essay on the community of drunks while at Columbia.

Yet he always remembered his grandfather's imitation of Faulkner's reply to an interviewer about whether he preferred scotch to bourbon. His grandfather had been for some reason magnificently and happily drunk that evening, and had aped Faulkner's drunk and drawled reply: "Between scotch and bourbon I'll take bourbon. But between scotch and nothing I'll take scotch." His grandfather, who had worked with Faulkner in Hollywood, then imitated the great novelist drunkenly reciting his Nobel Prize banquet speech. "He writes not of love but of lust, of defeats in which nobody loses anything of value, of victories without hope and, worst of all, without pity or compassion." His grandfather knew the short speech by heart. "His griefs grieve on no universal bones, leaving no scars. He writes not of the heart but of the glands."

He was already old then, his grandfather, and rich from years of royalties, with a youngish Italian mistress, Valeria, to take care of him, a mistress who in fact did not much care what he did, as he did not much care what she did in the afternoons, when he was peacefully drunk, sitting in his study and pretending to work, or snoozing on the terrace above the lake, an expensive and blank notebook closed on his lap, and in its crease an uncapped pen whose nib dried in the air.

He was a good drunk, his grandfather; he would often merely fall asleep after a bit of slurred conversation, then wake up, have another drink, and write his screeds late into the night, most of which he fortunately didn't publish, except *that* one. Owen, who during that last summer had once dared to read the onion-skin pages typed on the old Remington, was horrified by some of the thoughts his grandfather had put to paper. He dismissed them as the results of drink and isolation and bitterness, or experiments—first drafts that would be toned down; or as the still-suppurating old wound that had never healed.

There was some justification for his hate. Some days his grandfather gave up on writing and painted watercolors instead—a strange, light, fluid medium for such a lover of Caravaggio, but he was not unskilled in it. He told Owen to be aware, if he ever painted watercolors himself, that the colors dried darker than they were painted, and one should always use more water than you thought you should. Because the old man himself, when he sat in his favorite rattan chair overlooking the lake, and smoked his cigar, and told Owen the stories of his life, was curiously gentle. Owen remembered once when they had taken a detour to Bergamo on their way back from Milan, his grandfather had insisted on buying Owen a decent suit and even a Borsalino hat from a little shop in the Galleria. They had taken the funicular up to the Citta Alta and walked around the medieval city, then had had a hot chocolate thickened with maizena at the cafe there. They looked down over the low city and plain of the Po Valley, which was flat and wide as far as the eye could see, cut here and there with lines of poplars like embroidery on a wide tapestry. Owen had watched his grandfather, imagining him imagining a watercolor that might come out of it—the mists that afternoon almost demanded a watercolor. Instead, his grandfather said with the gentlest of voices, pointing to the plain: "No wonder the barbarians had such an easy time of it once they had gotten over the Alps."

His grandfather had not shied away from the mistakes he had made, almost seeking out Owen that last summer as a sort of proxy for his daughter, whom he had mostly ignored, as if trying to be, for a summer at least, the father he knew he had never been. Owen did not care, or did not realize then, what his grandfather had sought; he merely enjoyed the attention of a man who had once been world-famous and whose own blood was in him. And he enjoyed the stories of the old days. Not all novelists, he thought, were born raconteurs, but his grandfather was, and had lived the stories he told. And the man who told the stories seemed so different from the man who retired in the evening with his bottle of bourbon to write his embarrassing screeds, only one of which ever escaped his study, and ultimately—Owen was sure—killed him in the end.

He, Owen, took after his grandfather in being a happy drunk. His father, on the other hand, had been a drunk but a cautious one, gentle but afraid of whom he might let down by the inevitable carelessness of drunkenness. He liked to leave parties early, often leaving his mother behind, and continue drinking alone—"working"—in the various studies in the various diplomatic residences he had occupied during his underwhelming career. Owen could remember finding his father in the morning: still wearing his suit from the previous day, now badly wrinkled, as he slept in his chair, with jowls pressed against his chest, and some book in a foreign language open in front of him, next to a glass on the desk, the liquid tinted by melted ice. Then his mother would pull him away, explaining that his father had worked very late again and she would take care of him now.

Owen did not know how it had happened in his case. At some point the drink on Friday to celebrate reaching the end of the week became normal. Then it seemed civilized to have a little drink on Thursday once in a while. Gradually, one became so grateful to reach the end of the day, especially difficult days—and as one got on in life it seemed the days became more difficult—that one needed a drink to unwind each day.

For Owen, this phase had begun during the writing of his dissertation. He had been able to sustain long periods of reading and writing. He had sat and worked at his grandfather's vast desk in the New York apartment. When his mind began to go blank, he would look up and see the four first editions of Gene Powell Davis's novels, prominently placed by his grandfather on the desk itself between two bookends that formed two halves of a globe, as if the world encompassed the oeuvre of Gene Powell Davis. He had disciplined himself to sit at the desk until 6 p.m., even if his mind remained blank for hours, staring at the opus.

Owen had then been living a relatively healthy life for an obsessed academic, exercising in the morning, eating well, then writing through the day. For most of those years he had given up smoking. At six, however, it seemed proper to shake a martini, fry a steak, and have a glass or two of wine while eating and waiting for his wife to come home. She was in her first years at Skadden Arps, years in which she had to prove herself by working long hours. That would lead to another

77

bout of reading and note-taking (he did not like to actually write while drinking). Nine or ten glasses of whiskey did not seem to do any harm. He was young and healthy, and slept well, and woke up the next day with the same pattern. He had not yet reached the phase of his grandfather, of beginning to drink at noon. But it had come to what it was now. His lifestyle now was not as healthy, his exercise less frequent. He was smoking again. Now the three or four glasses of whiskey at night hurt the next morning, but he still needed them at night.

Several nights after the surprise visit of Audrey, he was having his end-of-day drink again, having come home from the institute on the 5:23 and having worked on the speech for an hour and a half. He was sitting on the fire escape and had lit a cigarette when the emotional sag that always followed intense concentration hit him. It hit him with the first drag and the first taste of the not-yet-cooled scotch. It hit him as the realization of the essential meaninglessness of his life: the emptiness of days whose completion still seemed to merit such whiskey celebration. He realized now it was merely the fact of having endured that he celebrated. It hit him with an almost physical force that he was the end of the line of what his ancestors had worked and sacrificed for; unable to have children; unable to continue the line; unable to make the sacrifices they had made for the future; the recipient of that huge and valuable apartment, a generous trust fund; the comfortable, useless, unproductive, unreproductive end of the line—terminus. He felt his shoulders sag; he felt very old. He felt the castigation of generations before. He imagined them staring down on him from the heavens, the teetotaling Norwegians and the God-fearing Huguenots. Even his father he imagined to be slightly ashamed. Only his grandfather he imagined to be sympathetic.

His forebears on his father's side had been energetic enough even after a full day's work on the farm to spend their nights lying beside the Minnesota backroads with a detective camera waiting for bootleggers to drive by. For them time had been filled by work, duty, family, the building of a future, investment in capital and sweat, forbearance of things in the present to give to the future. He drank, really, to pass the time and to dull the hours of this, our exile. He drank because he lacked the discipline of compassion—this was something he used to confess when he was still a good Catholic, and once a stern priest had told him to find a soup kitchen or become a Big Brother to an underprivileged kid. He had tried; it had not lasted. Unlucky people frightened him. Otherwise this deepest sin, this drinking from despair, was generally expiated by ten Hail Marys, a moment of reflection and prayer kneeling before a statue of Saint Francis, and a firm resolve to not offend God again. God, he asked, kneeling before Saint Francis, why did you create me without any firm resolve?

On the fire escape, head bent over his end-of-day whiskey, he recoiled from the sanction of those sturdy Norwegians whose blood he bore, who had, stone by stone, laid a dam across the river in their land of Minnesota; cutting first upstream into the stony ground to create the diversion, then hauling the stones and placing them in neat earth-packed rows to stanch the water; building the mill foundation, tree by tree hewing the planks for the mill wall, nailing together with perfect precision the massive wheel, building the bins and setting the framing; team by team hauling the millstones and placing them at once precisely on the mill wheel's swivel; watching with satisfaction as the dam held and the channeled water turned the wooden wheel that powered the heavy millstones; and, on Sundays, heads bowed in prayer, gnarled knuckles curled around the family hymnal, children beside and fidgety, understanding how the stones were cemented to heavy stones to build something that would stand forever. And then there was him: the last of the dissipated, producing nothing, adding nothing, using everything that was left, and afterwards, because of him, there would be no more.

The summer before going to college, his father had taken him to Minnesota to see the old family house, near the mill his ancestors had built, though the river had been diverted long ago and the millhouse had since become a bed-and-breakfast long since passed from family hands. He had felt lost in the middle of America, hankering instead for the cities he had grown up in as a child, European cities, Asian cities, Latin American cities, even Washington. The rolling vastness of the heartland exhausted or confused him; the silence bored him. He had not known how to react to his father's almost nerdy nostalgia for the site of his own youthful summers on the farm. Owen just wanted to get to college, to his future. Four years later, when his father died, the first thing he thought of, uncontrollably, was the vastness of Minnesota, the hot quietude of its summer, the old family house, and his father who he thought had almost been crying when they had gone there together only that one time.

CHAPTER 9

My Fellow Americans

He napped on the MARC and avoided the liquor store on his walk up Charles Street on Friday. At home he put on a kettle to make a pot of strong tea and smoked a cigarette on the fire escape while it boiled. He glanced over at Audrey's great-aunt's apartment. He thought of calling her but the lights were out. Since the evening she had come over, a week before, they had had dinner once at her place and had met for a drink and a movie, hands gripping each other eventually in the dark of the theater.

Once the tea was made, he took the pot into the study. It was, like everything, tasteful, dominated by the imitation Louis XIV desk that his father had insisted on buying years ago when posted in France—the only piece of furniture apart from the harpsichord that he had truly wanted. It was, for being a copy of an antique, quite expensive when they had bought it. He switched on the desk lamp and pulled out some ruled paper, uncapped his fountain pen, and began writing. This, if only he could have a cigarette beside him, was perfection itself, as long as the ideas came—and the ideas were coming! He wrote, and crossed out, and wrote, and read his lines out loud to a mirror, as if he were the candidate seducing the nation with his rhetoric. "My fellow Americans..."

Until Stiles had set this challenge before him, he had never imagined what it meant to write for a people as diverse as the Americans, to try to say something the majority would agree to, facts they wouldn't quibble with, innocent statements that wouldn't accidentally offend them. He somehow felt called to the challenge, up to it.

He woke up earlier than usual on Saturday morning, not having got drunk the night before, and put on his shorts and a T-shirt and went for a run. It felt surprisingly good to run in the morning, with the air still cool and fresh, and the streets mostly empty except for the bums and the early-morning drunkards, and he even felt lighter of foot for having slept early and well. He did not much enjoy running; he was not a natural runner, and the best way to pass the time and ignore the discomfort was to fantasize. So he imagined a Romney victory. He imagined a position for himself in the West Wing writing more speeches for the president. He imagined giving Audrey a tour of the West Wing, the cramped offices, perhaps a chance encounter with the president, where he would introduce her to him and he, the president, would say how valuable a member of the team Owen was and how he wouldn't have won the election without him and his brilliant foreign policy speech that even the *New York Times* had had to admit, in its otherwise scathing editorial, nonetheless contained "elements of coherence." These musings, scenarios in his mind, acted and re-enacted, covered miles and he felt almost as energetic at the end of his run as he had when he started it. He had not fantasized for a long time, not since, much younger, he had dreamed of becoming a famous American novelist.

Back at the apartment, he showered, and changed into a pair of jeans and a fresh T-shirt. In the kitchen he blended a smoothie. It felt, he thought, incredibly easy to be healthy. It was nearly noon and he didn't even feel like having a drink. He would brew some coffee and then use the rest of the day to work on the speech.

She called him later, early in the afternoon, and said, Why don't you come over for a drink? He had reached the point where he knew he had to take a break from the speech and was about to have a drink on his own anyway. He put on a fresh button-down shirt and decided not to smoke a cigarette, putting on a bit of cologne instead. Not sure she had whiskey at her place, he put his own half-full bottle into a dark plastic bag, walked down the five flights, crossed the foyer, nodded to the concierge, and walked up the five flights on the other side.

Opening the door, she was wearing a dress and it looked like she had put on some light makeup for him— quite unnecessary at her own home on a Saturday. She was beautiful enough without it. But he appreciated the gesture and the generosity behind it. And she sensed he noticed and smiled at him.

She saw the bag. "What do you have there?" she asked.

"I wasn't sure if you had whiskey, so I brought my own." She turned quickly. He could not read her expression. He followed her into the apartment. It was the same layout as his mother's, but very differently done. Her great-aunt was the widow of a real estate lawyer, and his tastes in furniture had tended towards, it seemed, whatever he had inherited from previous generations, and thick-framed photographs of family hung from the walls, along with a few cheap paintings that, Owen surmised, the great-aunt had picked up to add a touch of class. They went to the salon, which in this place was furnished like a man's den, with a leather settee and armchair arranged around a glass-topped coffee table, with a large-screen television and a liquor cabinet, too, all resting on a shag rug. It did not correspond at all with the adjacent feminine and frilly living room.

"Normally people bring things for other people," she said. "At least that's what I was taught."

"I'm sorry," he said. "I wasn't thinking. You called just when I was about to have a whiskey, I thought you might not have any, and I thought I'd bring a bottle." He paused. "I can go to the store. What would you like? I can get some dessert."

"Sit down," she said. "I'll get you some ice and a glass. I just thought I wanted some company." She brought him a glass with ice cubes. He noted with dismay that the cubes were small and would melt soon. He was particular about large ice, but he poured his whiskey into it anyway. She had poured for herself a glass of white wine that he knew was cold because of the sweat beads on the glass. Mentally, he felt, he was still panting from working on the speech. The ideas still spun in his mind and he tried to get them to settle so he could talk to her without making any more mistakes. Her anger at his lack of courtesy worked on him as well. How could he have been so thoughtless? The first sip was sharp, as always. The small ice would melt it soon into something flavorless and he was melancholy about it already.

She sat opposite him on the masculine leather armchair, one shapely leg hooked over the other. She placed an elbow on her knee, the elbow of the arm that held her white-wine glass, and stared at him for a moment.

"I'm sorry I snapped," she said. "I'm frustrated. My job search hasn't worked out, so I'm probably going to have to take out more loans than I expected for graduate school."

"It's a terrible economy," he said. "Especially hard for your generation."

"This is the Bush economy still," she said. "He ruined so many things. I voted for Obama and I hope he wins again this year."

He stiffened, but she was so beautiful and now she was trying to be nice again. So he tried to be nice as well. "Are you afraid he won't?"

"There's so much negativity. He hasn't really had a chance to implement his agenda, with the Republicans blocking everything."

"But doesn't he have to meet them halfway? Or at least part of the way?"

"Why?" she said. "He won, didn't he?" She was angry again.

"Let's not talk about politics," Owen said.

"Everybody's talking about politics these days. Why shouldn't we?"

"I'm a foreign relations guy. I grew up abroad, in diplomatic postings, two years here, two years there. I gnawed my teeth on State Department-issued furniture. I just find American politics hard to understand. From abroad, both parties are despised for different reasons." Yet he wondered how she would react if he threw the bomb: By the way, I spent all day writing a speech for Romney.

She shrugged, she leaned back on her elbows, her breasts thrust upwards, a squall of sudden petulance across her face. "I've been wondering," she said. "Don't you find me attractive?"

He had not expected this; his surprise must have showed; her eyes narrowed on his as if searching for the lie. How long had it been since he had last had sex? Lisa had left him feeling unlovable and dry. A long time. "No, you are very wrong," he said. "I find you extremely attractive. More than you could know. More maybe than is allowed." He allowed himself to smile but it felt wrong, like a grimace, unnatural, insincere.

"We've been alone a few times now, but you've never done anything. Most men do. All you did was hold my hand in the movie. Most men would have tried by now. What's wrong with me—or with you?"

"I am considerably older than you. And I didn't want you to think that ..." He did not know how to conclude the thought, so he let it trail, while trying to think of the best way to complete it, or recover from it. She didn't let him.

"You never thought of having sex with me?"

He smiled again now with greater discomfort, and he turned the question over in his mind; he had certainly turned her over several times in his mind. Was this the way this generation spoke about sex? Or was it a trap? He found himself responding to her posture, her expression half open—mouth half open, eyes half open, bangs half open. He wondered if an admission of lust would lead to the desired inevitable, or instead a scandal, accusations, the warping of his universe, accusations of rape long after the act, in which he would be presumed guilty. But still, hung between desire and damnation, he could find no words, and he reached for his drink for inspiration.

"I've thought about doing it with you," she said softly. "But what do you think about when you smoke your cigarettes on the fire escape, and I'm just across the way, and I see you sometimes looking towards my window? What do you think about? Do you ever think about me? About me naked? Do you wonder what I look like? My scars or my tattoos?"

Tattoos, he thought, hoping that she hadn't. "I've wondered every night what it would be like to sleep with you," he said. He was searching his way through this conversation, fighting for time, but fighting like a deep-sea diver on an

86

oxygen tank, where his panic at losing oxygen made him breathe heavier, taking more oxygen, knowing his breaths were defeating him.

"But you haven't acted on it."

He bent over her and kissed her and her mouth opened. He found her tongue and tasted it and then pulled her towards him. Suddenly she pushed him away. "Not like that," she said.

"Like what?"

"Like you're doing it to please me."

"And also to please me."

"Like you're just being polite. Like you wouldn't have done it if I hadn't talked you into it."

"Audrey," he said. "Can we just accept that I would at any moment of the day or night love to strip your clothes off and have my way with you? But I have enjoyed just being with you, too. I suppose I was afraid that I would lose the one if I moved too fast on the other. I don't know how you kids do it anymore, the codes you send each other to let each other know that you're available. I've been out of the game a long time."

"'You kids.' 'Anymore.' 'Out of the game a long time.' Why do you always bring up the age thing? And if you're not saying it, I know you're thinking it."

"It's a reality, isn't it?"

"I don't like you when you're like this. 'Have my way with you.' 'It's a reality.' What's that? You sound like you're just trying to make me happy, not being yourself. I liked you when you were yourself. A gentleman. Are you sleeping with someone else right now? Is that why you seem so indifferent?"

He stood up. As he did so he did not know if he felt more like a lover being rejected, a father about to admonish, a friend being insulted, or a wooer being invited. She had tied him up, this girl, and made it impossible to act, natural or otherwise. He recognized defeat because he had seen so much of it. He felt like a hypocrite or a coward, and he didn't know which one he was or which one was worse. Yet neither was what she wanted. So he stood there, helpless, wanting more than anything to do the thing that would convince her, and yet not able to figure out what that thing was. So he stood there, arms limber by his sides, longing to reach out to her, his mind racing furiously, going through the options, a diver drawing breaths. "You've made it so..." he said. He paused and tried again. "I'm sorry that there's no plausible ending right now that would be honest for either of us."

"Are you?" she said, now suddenly on the verge of tears. "Are you really sorry?"

"Don't you know that I can't sleep with you like this? Not just now," he said, some impolitic honesty breaking to the surface and resolving the situation in the worst way possible. "For the first time between us—like this? Make-up sex before first-time sex?" He was standing now above her, arms tense as if about to seize a crowbar to loosen a recalcitrant stone, while she sat, but less than sitting, sagging, her body bowed in her chair, not looking at him.

"The problem is," she said, looking up at him finally with a wounded intelligence. "I don't know if you're being too good or if you're just the most awful man I've ever met. You have too many barriers." Tears formed at the corners of her eyes. "Too many secrets. I can't figure you out. I want to trust you and I don't know if I can. I want to sleep with you but I'm afraid you'll reject me. You're always there but you don't make a move. You're too old to make love to me but not mature enough to act like a man. So I'm confused. That's all. And I'm lonely, terribly lonely. And you're there and not there at the same time. And I have feelings."

"Let's leave it for tonight, then," he said. Something in her soliloquy had struck some deep and terrible truths. He would not shoot the messenger but neither did he feel like consoling her.

He left her and went downstairs and across the lobby, past the night concierge, the one who had rescued them the night they met, saying he did not need the elevator, and walked up the five flights again and into his mother's kitchen, where he realized that he had forgotten his whiskey. There was some wine; he poured a glass. He drank it and then poured another. He put a Chopin CD into his mother's player in the kitchen, and as he drank he listened to the thirteen minutes of the Polonaise-Fantaisie and listened to it again and perhaps drank again. He returned to his journals at some point and read what he had written about Lisa—Lisa in those early days when they had met and he had traveled; Lisa in those later days when they had married and they were briefly happy. Lisa whom he had also disappointed. Lisa who might have given much the same speech that Audrey just did had she been talking to him at the end of it.

Later, across the courtyard, Audrey told herself, "Fuck it," and took the same passage past the lobby and night concierge and up his flight of stairs. She knocked gently on his door and knocked again. He had hardly heard it the first time, not believing it, still reading his journals, lying on the couch in the salon, but the second time it was real. He opened the door, and when she saw him she almost melted. He had been awake; not alone, she thought, but with his mistress, his liquid mistress. And when she saw the look in his eyes she simply entered the apartment. It was the sorrow of solitude in his eyes, it was the wide-open door, it was the low light casting yellow shadows, it was the echoing music again. He welcomed her in.

"You forgot your bottle," she said, handing the black plastic bag to him. The piano music was on, the lights softly glowing, as it had been that first night. And his notebook was open, where he had been reading, as he had been doing that first night she had come over. It was as if her presence in his life had made no mark and now she was determined that it would. She took his hand and kissed him on the lips and he kissed her hungrily back, closing the door of the apartment with the hand that was caressing her ivory back. She led him silently, understandingly, down the hall to the bedroom. It was to her strange to make love to a drunk man such as him. She had made love before to men who were drunk, but not while they tried to disrobe while trying to disrobe her while walking down a long corridor, half bouncing against the walls.

By the time they got to his room and his bed—a twin bed in the guest room of his mother's apartment—it was adolescently sweet. It made her remember her first time, with an eager, thrusting, too-quick boyfriend in his suburban bedroom. This old, drunk man was a kind lover in his fumbling way, if not quite the gentlest or most virile one at that point, but there remained traces of a man who was aware of the regret that might follow, and was determined to make it less regretful by his own sincerity and by his desire to give pleasure as well as take it. Kindness, even drunk kindness, was kind of nice to her, who had wanted only to apologize and had been ready to do it by any means necessary, but had simply fallen for him as soon as he'd opened the door, fallen for him.

She found it strange to find it so sweet, his wine-sweet tongue between her legs, his hands grabbing her buttocks like the edges of a chalice. She found it strange, afterwards, to enjoy the heat of this odd man lying next to her, naked, now asleep, a light arm slung over her, his breathing heavy and cigarette-roughed but not quite a snore. His arms were delicately muscled; his wrists tapered to almost a feminine width, and they cast across her flat, young belly a muddy yellow shadow in the light that came through the uncurtained window. It was a hot evening with the thick air from outside pushing in through the open window. She watched that arm and that shadow for a while, feeling the heat, unable to sleep but not wanting to move. His wine-smoke breath was stale and warm where it blew rhythmically across her naked shoulder.

All *that* she could have borne. Eventually it wasn't *that*, though, it was that she wasn't tired. And not being tired, as much as she wanted to lie with him in that tight twin bed, she loosened herself from the cage of his light bones and walked back down the corridor to the salon where he had left his empty glass of wine, where she had placed the whiskey bottle he hadn't had time to drink, and where lay the journal he had been reading when she had interrupted him. She took the whiskey into the kitchen, filled the glass with ice and poured a bit of fresh whiskey. Then she went back to the salon and, after a moment of hesitation, picked up the journal and began reading, at first curious if she could even decipher the back-slanted handwriting, and then she was pulled into it.

CHAPTER 10

Lisa

They had met in New York, of all places. They were both Washington people at that time but happened to be in New York for different reasons. It was a few months after his grandfather had died and after Owen had quit his job with Senator Douglas. The estate had been settled and Owen was the owner of a grand apartment on Central Park West, staying there, learning its nooks and crannies, and consulting its 1950 atlas as he planned his around-the-world trip. The world was a different place in 1953, when his grandfather had last been in the apartment, and (partly, she learned later, thanks to his grandfather's efforts) there was no longer a Soviet Union or a Yugoslavia to visit anymore. The coastlines were the same though, and the mountains and rivers had not much changed.

The inheritance had been wholly unexpected. In the back of his mind he had always wondered what his grandfather would do with his property, but he had always assumed it would be something imaginative rather than hereditary. Several times over the previous few years he had written to his grandfather suggesting that he might visit him in Como. Valeria had written back saying his grandfather was tired and now might not be the best time. And the senator's schedule had been hectic, while Owen had enjoyed being a young up-and-comer on Capitol Hill and didn't want to miss anything. So he was surprised, after the funeral, to learn that his grandfather had made him a wealthy man.

His mother immediately began to plot her contesting of the will. Although she resented that the apartment had been left to her son, that was manageable. But she could not get over the Como villa's being left to Valeria. Owen had not realized how much she longed to retire there, how much she felt stifled in the grand Baltimore apartment his father had bought. He could only imagine the summers she had planned, inviting her friends to Como, living the life of a duchess that she had always believed she deserved. Now that destiny was thwarted first by a father who ignored her, second by a husband who disappointed her, and third by a son who replaced her. "Being of sound mind and sound body," she had said. "Your grandfather was the same old son of a bitch when he died that he was when he was alive." This was during one of the few conversations they had had after the old man's funeral. He was buried, of course, in Italy; he never came home. Owen had put his mother's catty comment down to a mixture of grief and the anti-depressants she was taking. When she began contesting the will, it became clear that she, too, was of sound mind, rational calculation, and determined vindictiveness, and would plow through whatever was in her way.

He had taken a leave of absence from the senator's staff to deal with the complicated legal issues and had found himself when everything was resolved wondering what he really wanted to do with his life. He had long thought of getting a PhD and of writing books. His visit to Italy for the funeral had reminded him that he had been too long in the U.S., and that he was more at home in the world. The idea of taking some of his new money and taking a grand tour became more and more appealing. He had a Protestant conscience (from his father's side) and considered that what his grandfather had left him was not really his, that it was for some other purpose, but that this small indulgence of a year's travel would have been understood, and might be necessary to reveal the larger purpose of his inheritance. He sensed two things about his grandfather's wishes for him: that he would not sell the apartment but keep it as it was, and that he would not dissipate his fortune on idiotic and futile activities. He set aside ten thousand dollars for his trip and reasoned that the same amount would be more than made up while he was gone by the return on the investments in the significant endowment his grandfather had left him.

Everything in New York was there to be left behind. Everything ahead was to be leapt at and grasped for. The city was as disposable as a paper coffee cup. Staring over Central Park one night, the apartment dark behind him, the sun setting on the city, refracting across the buildings, daubing contour in pastels, making the city magic—he, the lonely baron of an unknown fief, felt oddly full of possibility even in his lonely grief. He could not know, at that moment, somewhere below him, that his Lisa was wending her way through the city, herself not realizing that she was wending towards him.

The day he found her he had gone downtown to the federal office building to pick up his passport. He had taken advantage of being in the general area of the Strand to purchase a traveling library for his upcoming journey. He wanted dense, long, complicated books, so that each one would last him a while. He had picked up *War and Peace*, of course, and several volumes by Henry James, as well as Rushdie's *Midnight's Children*, and, though it did not quite meet his criteria, he had also chosen *Confederacy of Dunces*, because his grandfather had always recommended it. It was a late summer day but milder than it had been the previous week. It was enjoyable to zigzag on foot through southern Manhattan, across Washington Square, to the passport office on Hudson Street, where he waited for his number to be called. He managed to get about twenty pages into *Confederacy* when they called him to pick up his passport at the desk.

Then he was riding uptown on the local 1 train, having got on at Houston Street. It was a long ride to Seventy-Second Street, and the air conditioning and the late-morning emptiness of the subway car were soothing. Farther down the bench an aging Latina woman with a load of grocery bags and wearing domestic servant shoes sat staring at the public service ad for condoms; across from her a businessman or diplomat who looked as if he had had a hard night gripped the pole. A few other souls populated the car as it heaved through the underground darkness between Houston and Christopher Streets. He pulled out *Confederacy* again.

It was hard not to laugh out loud at the early predicaments and acid observations of Ignatius Reilly, and therefore Owen did not immediately notice the young woman who had sat down on the bench opposite from him at Christopher Street. He looked up at her, and she was staring at him and smiling. He had never mastered the natural smile and felt himself grimacing and raising his eyebrows back at her. She was very pretty, with brown hair, and wearing a miniskirt and high heels. He wondered why she had smiled, put his head down, and grimaced at his pages in a delayed effort to return her smile. She was casually dressed, but not carelessly so. It was too early for lunch and too late to be going to work (except for the hungover diplomat, who now was dozing, his head against his hand that gripped the pole). Who was she? Where was she going? What about Owen did she find so amusing? He looked self-consciously at his shirtfront for a stain, and then at his lap to see if his fly was open. When he looked up she was still looking at him and smiling. Slowly she pulled out a copy of *Confederacy of Dunces*, in exactly the same edition he was reading. "What page are you on?" she asked, a faint Southern accent dusting a voice that rang nevertheless bell-clear through the clang and rush of the train through the tunnel.

He looked down at his open book. "Twenty-nine," he answered. His voice, louder than hers, startled the sleeping diplomat and jerked the Latina maid from the scriptural tract she was reading. He did not like to make himself conspicuous in public; he could not resist Lisa's smile either.

"I'm nearly done," she said. "Do you find it funny? I think it's hilarious."

"I laughed out loud at the lute string, which is on the second page. I loved this line, when the cop is harassing him about whether he has a job..." Owen flipped back a few pages, though clearly looking for something and knowing it was there. "'I dust a bit. In addition, I am at the moment writing a lengthy indictment against our century. When my brain begins to reel from my literary labors, I make an occasional cheese dip.' Why a cheese dip? I think you have to be a certain kind of person to find that funny. I read my favorite bits to my roommates."

Fourteenth Street came and went.

"I would also like to write an indictment against our century," Owen said.

She was now leaning forward, as if actually interested in what he was saying. He found it unusual. She was even prettier

96

when she was closer. He found himself leaning towards her as well.

"What are the charges, then?" she asked, more Southern than before, but Northern-Southern.

"Confusing the internet for reality, perhaps. And Tamagotchis for live things. Or something like that. I haven't quite formulated the theory of my case. But in the meantime I am looking forward to making a cheese dip."

She smiled and leaned back. "Well, it looks like you did well at the Strand." A few more people got on at Eighteenth Street. Impulsively, but because he thought it was absolutely necessary to his existence, he got up, crossed the car, and sat next to her.

"That's a little forward," she said, leaning away from him.

"I'm sorry," he explained. "It's just that at Times Square a lot of people are going to get on. It would be hard to finish this conversation. But I think that the ghost of O'Toole would want it."

"Appealing to ghosts! But I'm getting off at Times Square."

"Do you have time for a cup of coffee?"

"This is New York. Don't you have anything real to do?"

"It's a long story, but I don't."

"*Midnight's Children*," she said, looking into his bag. "I never could finish that one."

"Did you try? Were you a literature major?"

"Why do you ask? Because I'm a woman?" He flinched. He had not expected that Northern attitude towards gender.

"No, because you've read so many books," he answered.

"I was pre-law. Next year I'm going to be law."

The train had come out of the tunnel and rushed along the platform at Times Square. She stood up, presenting a slim figure, long legs in hose and corporate high heels, brown hair down to the middle of her back, and a head full of books and an accent that made her seem like the least pretentious pretty girl he had ever met, except for that one Northern comment.

"Well," she said, tossing her head back and looking down at him from over her shoulder. "Are you coming?"

They were both in their final week in New York. She had finished her paralegal summer and was getting ready to pack up and start at Georgetown. Her father had just been in town to visit and had forgotten his Filofax at the Sheraton near Times Square. She had promised to pick it up for him. Owen went with her to the hotel and they had coffee in the lobby, and then had so much to say to each other that they turned it into lunch as well. He insisted on paying, justifying the expense with the thought that his grandfather would have liked this girl.

"You're a funny guy," she said while they were waiting to share a cheesecake for dessert.

"What do you mean? Like Charlie Chaplin funny?"

"Not like Charlie Chaplin. Odd funny. Like a character in a Whit Stillman movie. A little bit lost, not really minding it, but somewhat interested in looking for a way back in. Not as clueless as Ignatius, but not quite right in the world either. And totally unconvincing as a maker of cheese dip."

"Whit Stillman? You might not realize it, but you're flattering me."

"Have you heard of Whit Stillman?"

"*Barcelona* is my favorite movie—after *Casablanca*."

"Do you only like movies named after cities?"

"I thought *Manhattan* was pretentious."

Owen paused while the cheesecake was delivered with two forks. Then he said: "I'm leaving town soon for what I plan to be a yearlong trip around the world." He paused, then heard himself saying what he was thinking. "I think you're beautiful and I haven't met many Whit Stillman fans. I feel almost like I should cancel my trip and try to court you."

"Don't cancel your trip," she said. "Not for me. Not yet. Not for beauty. You'll find a world of beautiful women."

"But probably few who are Whit Stillman fans."

She laughed because he had said it so earnestly. She was not even sure, as she laughed, whether he was being ironic. "Why don't we say we meet each other here, in this hotel coffee shop, a year from now, and see how we feel?"

"Maybe, to be on the safe side, we should exchange addresses. I've seen how badly this movie could end."

"Badly?"

"The point is that life isn't easy. Neither is what they call love."

She gave him her address and he promised to write her during his travels.

He walked her to the subway and when they reached the steps he kissed her on the lips and she kissed him back and for him it was like the creation of the world. He felt her wiry warmth and smelled for the first time her perfume that he would never forget. Then she told him they should save the rest for when he returned but she laid a careless finger on his cheek that almost burned. He nodded, holding her other hand, then she pulled away and descended the dark subway stairway but she looked back at him and smiled. He had never stopped staring at her and he knew she knew it.

He would remember forever how she looked as she pulled away from their kiss. He would remember it because he knew that however far he traveled, he would always be trying to find that look again, on that very face, that only face. He walked dozens of blocks to the apartment, like a troubadour, writing songs to her in his mind.

So he traveled around the world, leaving that fall as she began her first semester of law school. Except for the books, he had packed light, infused with the idea of going as far as possible with as little as possible, yet unavoidably heavy with thoughts of her. He visited a college friend in London and then went across the channel and saw a high school friend in Paris. It was chilly and raining there, and from a *bar-tabac* around the corner from his friend's apartment he looked away from the wet streets he had been contemplating, pushed aside the brandy he had ordered, made room for a piece of paper, and then applied his fountain pen to his first letter to her. After a while he set it aside, ordered another coffee and another brandy, and began writing his first novel to her. When he began to flag, several pages in, he folded up the paper and stared out the frosted window at the wet and gray Paris scene. Thinking of those writers in the thirties (he told himself), not all of us can order *fine à l'eau* and count on dreams of literary fame, those who sit and scratch desperately at their pads of paper, writing so thickly and sharply that their nibs tear the paper, leaving shreds of their ambitions. Or do they even realize it? Is the sequence of moments before deciding to take the boat back that dramatic? Or is it just a sign of resignation and a visit to the Cunard office? Because between Hemingway and Henry Miller, there must have been many who resigned and booked a berth home.

At the Louvre and later at the Musée d'Orsay he imagined himself with her in Paris, taking her to his favorite places, where he spoke the language and felt at home and knew the good out-of-the-way restaurants and could tell the good inexpensive wines from the bad, and afterwards they would make love in one of those tiny, cheap Parisian hotel rooms because they were in love and young and didn't need mansions.

Then he took the fast train to Geneva, where he stopped only long enough to buy some chocolate, a six-pack of beer, and a lighter to replace the one he had lost in Paris and then caught a train to Zurich, finding an empty banquette in a smoking car. He opened a beer and smoked a cigarette and watched the lake that hugged the tracks on his right, edging along its grand northern curve, past the city where the road ran up to where his mother had spent her adolescence in boarding school, and then up to Zurich. There he changed to the Como train, followed Lake Lucerne southward, and then climbed, emerging from the Saint Gothard tunnel into Italy and descending again.

At Como he got off and took a taxi to the old villa. He had alerted Valeria that he would be arriving and she was waiting for him, a bit shyly. Now that his grandfather was dead, knowing that his mother had tried to contest her inheritance of the villa, Valeria had perhaps wondered what side Owen had really been on. The weather in Italy was better than it had been in France—clear skies, a Mediterranean sun hitting the side of the mountains during the day, clear but too chilly to eat outside at night.

That evening, sitting in the grand room upstairs, he wrote another letter to Lisa, fifteen pages long. It was the letter in which he told her who his grandfather was and tried to explain him to her. He tried to explain, also, the curious way he kept thinking about her, not in a nagging way and not in an unpleasant way, just that thoughts of her were following him around Europe and images of her were appearing like apparitions of the Virgin Queen in the most unexpected of places. The girl who served him a macchiato at Gare Cornavin in Geneva wore her perfume. A passenger on the train from Zurich had nearly the same handbag. He mailed the letter from the post office in town the next day, using his grandfather's old but hardly driven Alfa Romeo to get there. He mailed it hoping she would understand that he was trying to say he had somehow fallen in love with her, but knew it was too soon for him to declare it or for her perhaps to believe it. Driving back to the villa, he yearned for troubadours while considering the perversities of modern love: One had to be very careful about not rushing into declaring it; such declarations normally happened long after the first copulation. But they had only kissed briefly. And to say anything as foolish as that he loved her would be read by her, he imagined, as a sign of instability.

He spent a night in Florence and visited the Uffizi. He would never forget when, one of those summers his parents had left him with his grandfather, they had taken the train to Florence. Owen must have been around twelve or thirteen. His grandfather hated to drive, mostly because he liked to drink in the afternoon and was a distracted driver even when sober. In Florence they had taken a taxi to the Hotel Davanzati, his grandfather not only fluent in Italian but arrogant in it. They shared a suite and Owen, still jet-lagged, had fallen asleep early. He had woken up early the next morning with his grandfather still asleep and snoring, a half-empty bottle of cognac in the living room of the suite. One of Owen's school assignments that summer was to write a short story. He left a note next to his grandfather saying that he had gone down to breakfast. In the breakfast room he ordered coffee and rolls and began to write. The waiters seemed to treat him like a little man, and he spoke then a bit of Italian, enough to order. He had been writing when his grandfather finally came down. When he looked up from his notebook his grandfather was standing over him, a wonderful smile on his face.

"What are you writing?" he asked.

"A short story. For school."

"Will you show it to me when it's done?" Owen said he would.

"I have planned that we will go to see the Uffizi today," his grandfather said over his first coffee. "I can't think of a greater gift to you, but you are young. Remember this later because you won't understand today."

Owen had said nothing. He had momentarily resented that his grandfather thought there were things he couldn't understand, so he resolved to understand, and he entered the museum with eyes open to secrets that would be revealed.

Of that day, Owen still remembered two things with an indelible clarity, a clarity comparable only to the memory of when he had learned of his father's death. First was stumbling into the vast hall where Michelangelo's "David" stood majestic and radiant under a skylit dome. He had seen pictures of the statue the day before, in the train station when they had arrived, and as six-inch models, but to see the thing itself had been paralyzing. The second thing he remembered was standing before Caravaggio's "Isaac." He remembered it not because the painting struck him—it had not, at least not with the majesty of the "David"—but because his grandfather had stood before it for a long time, undisturbable, saying nothing. Owen, after a while, had gone to sit on a bench on the other side of the corridor, under a lead-lined window, thinking of the "David." He longed to see the "David" again, though even at that age he realized that nothing would replace the shuddering awe of stumbling on it for the first time. This time, alone in the Uffizi with his grandfather dead, the "David" did little for him but what one would expect. He made a point of seeking out the Caravaggio but could not find it. When he finally asked a museum official, she said it had been removed for restoration.

He continued to wander through the world, next through the Balkans. Another high school friend was working for the UN in Kosovo. He thought about Hemingway's comment on war and the writer. In this case, the war was conveniently located but basically over, though you could still see its traces in the scarred buildings and ruined roads and tired faces. He went overland through Turkey and even managed to obtain a visa to travel through Iran to Pakistan. He visited Peshawar, where there was gunfire, but it was only a fusillade into the night sky to celebrate a wedding. He wondered what happened to the bullets when they fell, and the next day managed to make his way to the lip of the Khyber Pass and peer over into Afghanistan, where there was another war going on, and where foreigners were generally not allowed to travel. He met the homosexual Persian professor, traveled to Mastuj, drank his liquor, and fended off a tentative, drunken advance.

He continued to write to Lisa at stops along the way; she had continued to follow him around, as he found himself at those places of impossible beauty or solitude, like Petra or Angkor Wat or riding along the Karakoram Highway, thinking that the only thing these places lacked was her presence. She had written him back now and then, their friendship, as she called it, nurtured by *poste restante*. Yet he found her letters, like the climate he was traveling through, growing warmer, blooming into a more tropical mood, a little looser, a little freer, a little more skin showing. She was, he knew, like many Americans, easily seduced by adventures of travel, and he tried not to overdo it in what he wrote. He did not want her to love him as a traveler. He needed her to love him as the man who would always be beside her. And along the way, in notebooks bought in Third World stationery shops, he had continued writing his novel to her, batting flies away at youth hostels, watching the sun set on Thai beaches, drinking local brews for inspiration, smoking to keep the mosquitoes away, and yes, despite the yearning for her, not declining little traveling affairs. Big Dutch girls, a slim, large-breasted girl from Bangalore who had grown up in Boston and was forward-thinking and had a tongue that for once actually felt like it was a muscle, and others lost in the mists of his well-tempered alcoholic fugues all had offered themselves to him. He reasoned that he had already decided to marry her, Lisa, and these flings were the last flings. She was the queen of his troubadour wanderings.

Where were his letters to her now? he wondered. They were hers and they had disappeared in the division of spoils after the divorce, a division that he had tried to make as frictionless as possible by giving her everything that was his to give. It had not, in the end, been very much. He had, still, in his packed-away affairs, the novel that he had typed up after returning, which he had tried to publish with the idea of being famous for her. It had been difficult, the last time he read bits of it, years ago, to remember what was fact and what was fiction. The facts were in the letters and they had always been hers; he imagined she had burned them by now.

She was available when he returned to New York late the next spring at the same hotel coffee shop, as they had agreed. She told him how much she had enjoyed following his travels through his letters. Then they made love finally and afterwards he told her he loved her. They were married in Dahlgren Chapel at Georgetown University. It was a sunny summer day and his mother, while still drinking heavily then, nonetheless behaved despite despising the politics of the family he was marrying into (Lisa's father was a Republican lobbyist) and still resenting Owen for inheriting the apartment and abandoning the lake villa without a fight. *That* wound had not healed. She smiled at everyone and tried to not make a scene. Only later, at the end of the evening, as he walked her to her hotel room in the Hay Adams after the reception in the basement bar there, did she peck him on the cheek and say, "Thank God your father didn't live to see the day you married a Republican. He *marched*, you know. Against Vietnam. For civil rights. I marched, too. With you in my womb." He went back to the reception at the oak-paneled bar below and drank more than he should have on his wedding night. As the night wore on he found himself briefly alone. Someone was dancing with his wife to the low Sinatra song that was on, and her friends were talking to each other. He wished so much his father had been there to see him get married that a tear formed in his eye. He wiped it away. Lisa was beside him, her arm around his shoulder. She had seen it in the mirror. He had not noticed that the song had ended. "What's wrong?" she asked. "Do you already regret marrying me?" she teased.

"Of course not," he said, and he kissed her but never explained the tear.

They honeymooned in Mexico and when they returned he enrolled at Columbia for his PhD while she started at Skadden Arps. He wondered later if it had ended for her as quickly as it had begun for him: that one day she had simply decided he was not the one. It had to have been more—he wanted to believe—than their inability to conceive and his unwillingness to play dice with God. Shattered love leaves ruins, too, like an archaeological site. For many months afterwards, during the loneliness of the final years of his dissertation-writing, when the apartment still seemed draped with her memory, haunted by the lingering smell of her, the closet empty of her, when he still found little things in the cupboard that he would never have bought for himself— the strawberry tisane, for example—he sifted through the ruins for clues of how the city had been destroyed. Then he began not to care. It was only the freshness of Audrey that made him, if not actually care about the destruction of Lisa, question again whether he was the sort of man who could raise a city from its ruins.

* * *

It was late when Audrey put down the journal, almost early morning. The man who had written it slept soundly, drunk, satiated, a few yards away, and here were his writings. Though the two men were the same, she was uncertain how they were connected. What she felt for the first time was that she loved him. It could have been the late hour, her tiredness, some up-to-then-unfelt susceptibility to romanticism, but she suddenly wanted to return to the twin bed where they had made love and hold him.

"I might have done an unforgivable thing last night," she said a few hours later, when he had woken up. She was looking at him with contrite eyes while he made coffee, as sunlight slanted into the kitchen. "Even if you hated me for it, I think I would do it again. But I don't want you to hate me. But I feel I have to be honest with you."

"What have you done that is so monumentally wrong?" he asked her, finding her more beautiful than usual in the morning sun, wearing one of his shirts, her unexpected contrition softening her.

"I drank some of your whiskey," she began.

"That's unusual for you, but certainly forgivable by me."

"I drank some of your whiskey because I was reading your journal. You left it out there. I just opened it and read a few pages and then I got a little bit hooked. I just fell in."

He tried to remember which journal he had been reading. It was the first one, about meeting Lisa and traveling the world. He knew that he should be angry with her, that she expected him to be angry. But he was somehow flattered; he had written these journals to be read one day, to be published posthumously for students of his fiction generations later to better understand his creative process. Lisa had never been interested in reading them; Audrey was the only person in the world besides himself to have read them. He loved that she loved them. "I see," he said, pretending to be conflicted but in fact eager to know what she had thought of them.

"What about the novel you were writing?" she asked. "About that girl. What happened to her?" Now, he realized, there was something that bothered her. Who did she think she was falling in love with? he wondered. The young, artistic cosmopolitan who had fallen in love for the first time? How much of that young man did she see in him now? How little she understood of how he had changed. What *had* happened to his literary ambition, to the novels that he had once written. And since he had, up to now, concealed from her a few non-trivial matters about his current political beliefs, he suspected she was mapping what she thought was a young artistic liberal onto what she now considered an older, more experienced liberal. Everyone knew that conservatives couldn't be artists. On this matter of his conservatism, he told himself, he would eventually have to set her straight, but not now—on this pleasant morning, coffee à deux, about to go together down to the Peabody to see the exhibit on writing instruments "From Paris to Persia," and hold hands like a couple in love. Not when the wounds from yesterday afternoon's fight could still break open.

"That novel, along with about three others that I wrote in those years, is in a box in my mother's storage in the basement, unread for some time, perhaps yellowing and disappearing."

"I would love to read it," she said.

"It was not very good, which is why it didn't get published. My travel musings were insufficiently universal."

"I don't care about that. I just want to see how you wrote in those days. Maybe it was always meant to be a novel written for me alone."

"That had never occurred to me," he said. He enjoyed the thought and almost loved her for it: that somehow while young and desperate to get published, and writing a book to woo the woman that he loved—whom he would eventually marry and divorce—he was in fact writing for someone who had barely been born, with whom he had just shared a bed, with whom he wondered if he were falling in love, whatever *that* could mean after Lisa.

CHAPTER 11

War Makes The State

Twelve young faces sat around the conference table in the room with peeling pale paint and a churning air conditioner. This had once been the master bedroom, then the ambassador's office, and now it was a classroom. Most students had laptops open, some had PDF printouts of the readings, with bits highlighted the old-fashioned way. He would soon find out if they had highlighted correctly. These kids were generally conservative—that was the purpose of the institute, after all—and they dressed more conservatively than the undergraduates he had taught at Columbia.

"'Take away justice,'" he recited, "'and what are kingdoms but great robber bands, and what are robber bands but small kingdoms?'" He paused and looked around the table. "Who wrote that?" No answer, yet it had been in their readings. When he first read it, years ago in an undergraduate political science course, it had jumped out at him. "Nobody has it highlighted?" he asked. There was no response. "Then why doesn't somebody Google it."

"Right now?" a cutish girl asked. She had dark hair and an olive complexion. The rest of the students were very white.

"You all have your computers open, why not? Let's see who gets it first."

The majority who had laptops or iPads set themselves to Googling. The others flipped through their printouts helplessly. He watched them bent over their screens, catching from the corner of his eye the sway of a leafy tree out the window on the other end of the room, and the patch of blue summer sky. "Augustine!" one said triumphantly.

"Correct," he said. "What century?"

Quick glances back to Wikipedia. "354 to 430," another face announced, and it sounded like a class schedule.

"In what century is the year 430?" he asked.

"Fifth," said another student, not having to consult the internet.

"OK. Good. Now here's another quote. Tell me who said it. 'The function of the state is to suppress all such injustices that it does not itself commit.'" He let the seconds pass while fingers rapidly typed the quote into the search engines.

"Ibn Khaldun?" said a timid voice immediately, rising above the clattering of keyboards, faster than the others could even Google. It was the cutish girl who had asked "right now?" Her name, he remembered, was Maria.

"Exactly," he said, smiling. "And all the better for not having come from the internet. Maria," he asked, "why did you know the answer?"

"I thought it was interesting when I read it. The idea that the state is just a monopolist of injustice. I highlighted it."

"That's a great phrase," he said. "A monopolist of injustice. Who was Ibn Khaldun?"

"He was an Arab historian of the 15th century."

"Excellent." The rest of the class watched this dialogue uneasily. "Augustine was Catholic; Ibn Khaldun was Muslim. They lived a millennium apart, though in fact not very far from each other, in North Africa. And they have this similar idea of the state. You could say that Augustine saw the state as a monopolist of justice, to emend Maria's term, and Khaldun as a monopolist of injustice, but the provision of justice, whether positively or negatively, is at the heart of these two statements. Now, who can tell me what the central thesis of Charles Tilly's piece was?"

"That war makes the state?" said George, a tall, handsome young man whose father had once been a congressman from the Southwest.

"That wasn't too hard, since that was essentially the title," Owen said. The class laughed. "Tell me how war makes the state, then, according to Tilly."

George went through a decent summation of the argument. He had read the text at least. Owen felt the class warming up. He said, "There is a line in Tilly that ought to have made you think of Augustine and Khaldun. What is it?" The young heads bent over their texts again, electronic and not, seeking the answer. He watched them for a few seconds, but only to rest his own somewhat tired mind, hungover again. There was no way that anyone would find the phrase skimming the article like that, not quickly at least. "It's this," he said, ending the ritual: "'If protection rackets represent organized crime at its smoothest, then war-risking and state-making—quintessential protection rackets with the advantage of legitimacy—qualify as our largest examples of organized crime.' Now, Sam Huntington, who we will read later, wrote that 'the capacity to create political institutions is the capacity to create public interests.' We are back to the *Oresteia*, which we discussed a few days ago: that key moment of political transition when public interests were elevated over private ones, when rule of law superseded the law of blood, when, in Weber's terms, the 'legal-rational' took over the 'traditional.' Who can tell me what the Latin origin of our word 'republic' is?" Another long pause. The air conditioner continued its persistent grumbling. "It was in your readings," Owen informed the silent faces, now nervous again, staring at him in the expectation and hope that one of them would supply the answer, but none did. Owen allowed the uncomfortable silence to hang, to let the discomfort build. He, after all, knew the answer. He, in the end, did not mind the silence. There was a great power to this silence that only he and the grumbling air conditioner seemed to understand. He quite enjoyed the discomfort on the young faces as his eyes met their frightened eyes around the table. "Maria?" he asked. She was flipping through her papers, hoping she had highlighted it. "I think..." she said.

"Can we at least try to recognize one English word within the word 'republic'?"

"'Public'?" a student ventured.

"Exactly," he said, sighing. "Has nobody ever wondered why the word 'republic' contains the word 'public'? For example, I'm a Republican," he said. He could admit that here; most of them were Republicans too. He would never have dared to say it at Columbia. "Republicans are seen as elitist and hard-hearted and closed to the concerns of the poor and the masses, but the word 'republican' contains the word 'public'."

"*Res publica*," Maria said. She had found it on her printout. Owen was secretly glad that she, with her papers and pens, had found it faster than the Googlers.

"OK. What does '*res publica*' mean?"

"'The public thing,'" she read from her page. Despite the fact that she was merely reading from the text, he still liked her. She had picked out the Khaldun thing, after all, from the text.

"Exactly," he said, in a way he thought was encouraging. "It means those things that are shared. Remember what I just said about Huntington: Political institutions don't exist unless there are political interests, public things, things in common. Things that are shared. Things that need to be decided together. That is where politics begins. Now let's approach the problem from a different direction: What is the opposite of *res publica*?"

"*Res* private?" a wag suggested. Tittering laughter. It was all right, Owen thought. At least it had come from a brain, not a website.

"Funny," he said. "But cheap too. Think of *The Godfather*—the movies."

"The Mafia?" George asked.

"Good. Getting closer. What's another phrase, one that the Mafia uses to describe itself? I'll give you a hint: It's not in English. But it's not in Latin either."

He looked around the table again, let the stifling silence fall across it again, sensed the discomfort again and let it fester again. Since he was looking intently around the table, face by face, no one dared touch their screens to Google. "Does anybody speak Italian?" he asked.

"Tutti-frutti?" the wag said, and the tension was released in laughter. This was going to be harder than he imagined, Owen thought, then decided to end this attempt at the Socratic method that suddenly seemed cruel. "*La cosa nostra*," he said. "Has anybody heard of that?"

Heads began to shake, some looking down at their screens, as if the answer had been there all along or an explanation would magically appear. "It means," he explained with a sad patience, "*Our thing*. The thing that is ours. It's how Mafia members describe their business—a euphemism. It's exactly the opposite of the thing that is public. Huntington, remember, said that political institutions begin with public interests. But the point I was trying to get at was that the difference between *la cosa nostra* and the *res publica* is exactly the same thing that Augustine pointed out when he made the distinction between robber bands and kingdoms. We are taught to think of the state as virtuous and stable. But if we are free thinkers, and interested in the origins of this particular species of the state, we should not hesitate to remind ourselves that the DNA of a state shares 95 percent of the DNA of a criminal organization. For the next class, please do your readings. Read for meaning, read with a pen, read like it's a treasure hunt. I promise you there are gems in everything I assign. Find them and cast them in front of me in class. Don't make me show them to you all the time. We'll get very bored very quickly if you do, and you will all get mediocre grades. My job is to give you the secret maps. Your job is to learn how to find the treasure chests."

That afternoon, alone in his office, he put what he decided were the finishing touches on the Romney speech. The white paper was covered with the blue-black ink of his fountain pen, his tight, almost unreadable scrawl slanting across the page, hardly straight lines with arrows repositioning text, slanted thin lines cutting across the text to indicate entire sections to cut, asterisks denoting lines he thought were particularly great, lines he'd have to reconsider, or darlings, maybe, that he'd have to kill. Then he typed it up, printed it out on his mother's old printer, corrected the proofs, read it out loud—essential for speechwriting—then corrected it again. He worked under a painful sobriety filled with dreams of when he would have a drink. But he had stuck to his discipline for the last three nights, having not more than one bottle of wine across three days. Then he sent it to Stiles.

* * *

The next weekend, on a whim, because the weather was particularly nice, he said to Audrey, "Do you like sailing? Let's go to Annapolis." It was his last weekend in Baltimore. His apartment in Washington would be ready the following Monday.

"I haven't really sailed," she said.

"I have the keys to my mother's car. Let's go next weekend. We can rent a boat. If you haven't done it, it's the most wonderful thing in the world." And so they went.

She found his ability to harness the wind and drive them through the water almost thrilling. He was a different man on a boat: confident, defiant, the master of a floating universe whose only other inhabitant was her. She could not help but smile as she followed his instructions to raise the jib and to duck as the boom of the mainsail swept across the boat. They tacked out of the Chesapeake towards Kent Island. Then they came around and sailed downwind for a while; the boat that had been slashing across the waves, tilted by the wind, was suddenly calm and stable. He pulled some beers from the cooler and lit a cigarette in the lee. This to him as much as anything was America, the seaways and the coast, the freedom and the mastery of nature, the risks and the exhilaration of defying the risks.

For a moment he remembered the happy days when they used to sail—his mother, his father, and himself, when he was younger. Whenever they returned to the U.S. in the summers from whatever postings they were in, his father would arrange a week of sailing. And in the years when he was stationed in Washington, most summer weekends involved a trip to Annapolis to go sailing, where he had got his certification. He looked at Audrey, face turned to the sun, eyes closed and smiling, and thought this would be a tradition worth reviving.

In the evening they drove back to Baltimore, tired from the sun and the waves, but it was a pleasing fatigue. Audrey found a radio station she liked. There was a ballad on and she awoke briefly from her beautiful sleep. "I love this song," she said. He had never heard it before but now he loved it, too. They stopped in Pasadena, at the McDonalds, because they were suddenly ravenous. As she ate her burger beside him listening to the ballads on the radio, he sneaked glances at her tanned legs in her white shorts, desiring her in a way that made him feel much younger. Dusk was settling as they headed northwest, casting its pink light in his eyes. "I wish I could drive forever," he said suddenly, not thinking or caring. "I love this: the road and you beside me, the music."

"It's at the funniest moments," she said, "that you suddenly burst out with these almost romantic statements and I'm totally unprepared."

"What do you mean?"

"With my mouth full of fries. You're crazy and I want to kiss you, but you're driving and I'm eating."

He smiled. She placed her hand on his thigh and he took one hand from the steering wheel and held hers. Later, when they arrived in Baltimore, they went immediately to his mother's guest room and made love on the small bed, fervent with the honesty of reconciliation, with the last energies of a day that had exhausted them. He was so tired he did not even have a drink. They slept together afterwards in the twin bed, holding each other, breath on skin as if adrift on the calmest of seas. It had never—Owen thought once just before falling asleep—seemed this easy with Lisa.

CHAPTER 12

A Studio

He had determined to live within his means, though his salary at the institute was meager. He had rented the cheapest apartment he could find. It was in Foggy Bottom, in a building mostly inhabited by George Washington University students and a few retirees. He could walk to the institute in about twenty-five minutes. It was not close, but close enough, and it would save him Metro fare. The apartment was a room large enough to hold a bed, a table, a futon, and an armchair. It had a small separate kitchen and a closet adjacent to the bathroom. It was cheap, he thought, because it was on the ground floor. The windows had bars, and the view through the bars was of a small grassy bluff and a wooden fence that hid the parking lot of the neighboring apartment building. If he was not extravagant—and Cutty Sark was one of the cheaper blends—he could afford the rent and live on what was left of his small salary.

There is, he thought, however modest your accommodation, a feeling of luxury when you move in. The space is new, and because it is new, and empty, however cramped it is, it feels momentarily vast. Even old furniture—and he had brought in from his mother's basement storage a few basics that belonged to him from a long time ago—seemed fresh. The building was well-managed. They had repainted the walls after the last tenant had moved out, and the parquet floor gleamed. Owen had seen the last tenant when he had been shown the apartment the first time: A young slob of a man, a recent GW graduate, had been watching a movie on his laptop when the manager had opened the door. He had been sitting in a canvas camp chair, a hole in the arm for a Red Bull, with his computer perched on a five-dollar foldable TV tray, and clothes and other junk strewn around him. "We'll clean it all up and repaint," the manager said within earshot of the young slob. "You won't recognize it." But Owen had already decided to take it. He wondered where the bearded youngster was now. Back at home perhaps, Mac hooked to his parents' Wi-Fi, still watching movies and resigned to his life going nowhere in the Obama economy. This was the sort of fellow, Owen had thought, who ought to vote Republican but probably would not because common sense had been drilled out of him by his undergraduate education.

The movers brought in a bit of furniture from Baltimore. He would have to buy a bed and a box mattress, but in the meantime he had a sleeping bag. He had bought a bottle of whiskey and a bottle of Malbec at the liquor store on E Street and Virginia Avenue. There was the box he had brought from his mother's storage, with his old writings and a few mementos to decorate the place.

Walking down the long hallway from the street-level entrance way with his just-purchased bottle, he began to smell the most delicious cooking. The smell was most intense just as he was unlocking his door, and he realized it came from his immediate neighbor. He unlocked his door, put a frying pan on the stove and heated it, put a boneless chicken thigh in the pan, and poured a glass of wine while it cooked.

Had Audrey, he thought, seen instead the journal that began after his father's burial, when he was working for a newspaper in Northern Virginia as a cub reporter, before he got the job with the senator, she would have read the following:

My beat, they call it "cops and obits." "Cops" is for the Police Beat column, a summary of the previous day's arrests, each item about 20 words *condensed from the fax the police department sends us, with all the "allegedly's" carefully* inserted. "Obits" are obituaries. I do not like writing obituaries.

* * *

Today was not a bad day at the Journal. I'm getting the hang of it. I wrote my longest story today—maybe a whopping seven inches. Paul, the editor, not too prone to acknowledging my existence, said it was "solid." Then he said he'd like me to write a short story each day, as well as cops and obits. I think I've reached some sort of truce with Shepp at the copy desk. The other day we got into an Electronic Message war. He chastised me quite brutally for omitting the cause of death in an obituary. (Here you cannot have an obituary if you cannot state the specific cause of it.) I shot back, explaining that no one knew the cause; the deceased, at age 87, was said to have died of "old age." I outlined all the steps I'd taken to try to find out the cause. He sent back a much mellower response (for him at least, lord of the copy desk) but ended it by saying "without papal dispensation we should always have an accurate cause of death." I replied: "Sometimes it's easier to call the pope than to call these families."

He answered: "You're too young to be a smartass, buck," which I took as a compliment.

* * *

An interesting development today. There has been a spat among the College Republicans at George Mason University. It seems that a disagreement over whether to welcome or not Clinton's impeachment led to a fistfight, then death threats on a phone answering machine, and a split into two groups: the College Republicans and the New College Republicans. Paul asked me to go interview them and see if there's a story there. He said that I should appear sympathetic to them to get the information. But he loved the idea of an intra-Republican spat. He wants me to co-write the piece with Brian, who's the up-and-coming Columbia Journalism School grad who almost got an award for his coverage of the Oliver North Senate campaign a few years ago. Brian's politics are too well-known, so Paul doesn't want to send him to GMU for the interviews. That's my job. "Republicans turning against each other," Paul said. "A journalist's dream story. It might put us on the map." As if we were Woodward and Bernstein. As if he wanted anything to do with me being on his map.

* * *

I feel odd around these conservatives, who seem so alien to me. How did they get to be this way? And what has blinded them throughout their lives to the most evident verities accepted by everyone else: tolerance, inclusion, a sense of justice, free will, all that is modern and progressive, all that has been learned from the hard lessons of the past? Why do they want to live darkly in the past? Why do they want to stand athwart history yelling stop, as some conservative idiot apparently once said (I must find that reference). Never mind their clinging to religion and other (political) relics like this odd and pointless Borkian originalist interpretation of the Constitution. I simply don't understand how they can exist in our modern world; perhaps it's because I've traveled too much and they haven't had the benefit of seeing how other people live and understand the need to tolerate differences. I went to George Mason to do the interviews, as Paul requested, and pretended to be nice to them. I had to do a bit of research before, over the weekend. I went to the Politics and Prose bookstore and started going through some of the conservative magazines, to at least be able to talk to the GMU conservatives and pass as sympathetic. I can't believe some of the positions that they take—understandable in the seventeenth century maybe, but it seems odd to protest the federal income tax in the last decade of the twentieth century, as if government didn't need money to run, or as if taxes somehow undermined our entrenched freedoms. The GMU College Republicans themselves remind me a bit of Moonies, or some kind of cult people. They dress a little bit differently, but only a little. They pass but don't quite fit in. Their hair tends to be shorter and neater. I have to say their women are better-looking, or maybe just better groomed. But then they talk and say their anachronistic things and it's hard for me to just write them down without arguing with them.

* * *

I was surprised that the leader of the hardcore faction—pro-impeachment—is a young, articulate black guy from a poor background in Chicago (or maybe Detroit). How can a black guy be a Republican? He seemed to read my mind and asked me point-blank if I was incredulous that there should be a black Republican. He used the word "incredulous." I was afraid that my real sympathies would be revealed, and I needed his cooperation. It had taken me a week to convince him to talk to me, and he was absolutely crucial to the story. So I told him, of course not, and that I thought what happened to Clarence Thomas had been a disgrace. This was an easy line to take since I have always believed it. I don't care for his views, and would rather not have him on the Court, but to see the Senate of the United States of America devoting itself to porn titles and tales of pubic hair on Coke cans was sickening to any real democrat—or even a Democrat (capital D). And I felt some sympathy for the guy. One wonders how one can live a normal life and also go into politics. Normal lives are full of mistakes, and politics thrives on defining lives by their mistakes. That is a bipartisan observation. I said, more or less, all of this, and he, the black kid, said something like: being a black conservative is the last civil rights barrier that needs to come down, and he himself sometimes felt like Jackie Robinson.

* * *

Melvin Jackson, the black guy, is still reticent when he talks with me. I try to probe. I feel the care with which he picks his words. He feels that I feel it. "I pick my words carefully," he said in the middle of a thought, "because I know that you will twist them in the end."

"I won't," I said. "I'm out to get the objective story."

"But you will," he said. "I know how this works. You're nice now, inquisitive, polite, sympathetic, but it's all going to come down to me being an Uncle Tom and a House Nigger in your article. That's how it will end up; I'm just going to try to make it a little more difficult for you to twist it against me. It's never been easy for a black man to be free in this country. We were held in literal chains for centuries by the racist masters in the South, and now we're held in the ideological chains of a liberal elite that demands conformity, that pretends to be sympathetic, but that really lives on the petty exchange of lockstep votes for a pittance of welfare every month, bread without even a circus. I didn't join the

Republican party because they like people like me. They don't. I'm convenient to them because I make it seem like they're not racists. They are; they all are. But they want a small government, and I want a small government, too. I want a government that's so small that they can't use it to oppress me like I know they want to. That's why I'm a Republican."

I had never thought of it that way and I made a note to be sure to include that quote in the article. I thought it was the most interesting political argument I had heard in a long time.

* * *

I have actually become somewhat fascinated by this rift within the GMU Republicans, and even sympathetic to some of them, especially Melvin, who really is articulate. There is a story here, but it might not be the one Paul and Brian want. I have been doing a bit more reading to give conservatism some context in the article. (I've been giving my interview notes to Brian, along with my annotations, so he understands what the issues really are. He's been doing some of the writing of the main story, using my notes, but he hasn't shown me his draft yet. He says it's still in rough form. To me this is much more a human interest story than a political story. I hope that's how he's writing it.) I actually bought copies of the National Review and the American Spectator, as well as a few books that Melvin recommended. Actually, he was sort of surprised I hadn't read them, and he made me feel a bit uncultured. In The Road to Serfdom, he said, Hayek points out that the welfare state is not about charity, it's about redistribution of power. And everything I've seen of government pretending to be charitable, he said, is only government preventing you from reaching your true potential. I come from the projects and I've seen it, he said. I will, of course, have to make sure that I hide this literature the next time my mother comes to visit! Without really agreeing with these guys, I have a sort of sneaking admiration for the coherence of their thoughts. They begin with principles, rather than facts, and develop the principles—too rigidly mostly, and without due regard to more important principles, like injustice, like poverty, like inequality—that are very real and need to be corrected, and if history has taught us anything it is that only the state can really correct them. I also kind of enjoy the quirky but always lively writing in these publications. The articles that I do really like, and kind of agree with, are the American Spectator ones about Clinton. I have to say, I never really liked the Clintons' style. I was a Tsongas man in 1992. I find the Clintons a bit too much into the trappings of power, in a sort of nouveau riche way, and I could never take the fake folksiness of Bill. And these American Spectator guys, when they dip their pen in poison, they don't hold back. As a would-be writer, there's stuff to learn here, but learn how to do it from the left.

* * *

I had beers the other night with Melvin. We discussed Hayek and also The Closing of the American Mind. My father had bought a copy for me the year I went to college. He said it would help me understand my classmates (he understood better than I did the culture shock I'd have attending an American university after spending years in international schools). I tried to read it at the time but was put off by Bloom's fuddy-duddyness about modern culture like rock 'n' roll. But now I kind of see some of his points. He's not a conservative, or says he isn't, but as Melvin points out, Bloom ultimately laments the lack of conservative things: virtue, learning, etc. Melvin majored in political theory and is going to some fellowship in Claremont, California, next year on some conservative scholarship. I like Melvin more and more. And I've enjoyed the earnestness of these Republicans as they've debated their issues, although they'll never convince me. Melvin asked when the article was coming out and I told him it should be over the weekend.

* * *

I am really, really, really pissed-off with what Brian has done to the article. He's taken an interesting dispute among people who may be wrong-headed, but they are sincere, and turned them into caricatures. You don't have to accept their arguments to appreciate that they were real to those who made them. Aren't we supposed to be the objective media? The story is far less interesting if the central conflict is turned into a joke. I pleaded and pleaded with Brian to make some revisions. He refused, a bit arrogantly in fact. I went to Paul and made the same arguments, adding that my own credibility as a journalist with the GMU students would be completely shot if the article came out like Brian had rewritten it. It looked like I had misled them, tricked them, kind of used them. The way I was talking to them, and trying to understand what they were all about, they would never imagine an article like this. Paul said that's what I was supposed to do, what journalists do, and I had done it damn well. "Damn well," he had said.

"Damn him," I thought. I feel really very dirty right now, about myself and about this profession. After this, I don't know if I can be a journalist.

* * *

I feel like a true shit. The article came out a few days ago. I got a letter from Melvin, sent to the newsroom. He skewered me with great eloquence and learning. I really feel like a shit. He wrote: "Thanks for the low-tech lynching. Yours sincerely, Uncle Tom."

In the meantime Paul and Brian are prancing around the newsroom like Woodward and Bernstein, like they've unearthed some deep scandal that will ruin the GOP. It disgusts me. I don't think I can stay here much longer. They invited me out for beers to "celebrate" the article. Frankly, at this point I'd rather have a beer with Melvin, not that that will ever happen.

CHAPTER 13

Ghost Of Como

The last time Owen had seen his grandfather was between his junior and senior years at Princeton. His grandfather had written him at Princeton, inviting him to spend the summer in Como. He had told his parents he was going; his mother had said the hell he was; his father had said it would be good for him, and good for the old man too to spend some time with his only grandson. I don't give a damn what's good for my father, his mother had said. And what about your son? I don't think my father's a good influence on him at all. He's drunk half the time. He's living with a floozy who's probably stealing all of my inheritance, and anyway he's a fascist. His father for once had insisted that Owen should visit his grandfather and prevailed; Owen went and never regretted it and was always grateful to his father for standing up to his mother that one time.

In the end, to some degree his mother had been right. The floozy *had* inherited the villa and a substantial amount of his grandfather's money. In the several years after her father's death, years in which the will was litigated by Owen's mother, it was rare that she did not mention the great mistake she had made by not standing up to her husband. "It's not just that the floozy got everything," she said. "It's that he also obviously planted the seeds for your later turn to fascism."

The fact that he did not join his mother in her litigation for Valeria's part of the will had created a half-decade rupture between them. They did not talk to each other during those years. She had called him greedy, saying she did not want his share but did not believe the floozy should get her share. Owen had thought: Let the old man have his wishes respected. The floozy had taken good care of him. His mother wanted for nothing, had hardly worked a day in her life, and hadn't spoken to her father for decades. Had she been starving, Owen might have thought differently. But what other purpose is there to one's considered death except to propose one's own sense of justice?

He had mostly kept his promise to himself not to touch his grandfather's money, except what was necessary to maintain the New York apartment. There had been exceptions: the artificial inseminations, for example, where Lisa had worn him down; those had cost a lot of money because they were not covered by her insurance. What's the point of all that money if you don't use it? Lisa would ask. I don't feel like it's mine, he would say. I didn't really do anything to earn it. It's in trust. No. It's in your bank account, she would say; so it's yours. And this is important to me and I'm your wife. He knew his grandfather would not have approved of the procedure. But he had given in, up to a point.

What he later realized he admired in his grandfather, apart from his immense literary talent, was that he had never hidden who he was. If Owen found this stony hardness to be impressive it was because he realized he did not have any of it in himself. At Columbia he had felt like a dissident from the ruling ideology but had not risked anything; he had adopted more and more sophisticated subterfuges to avoid stating his real political beliefs, satisfying his conscience by not technically lying but never revealing what he really thought. These subterfuges had become second nature; it had become an effort to not deploy them. His grandfather, though, had not cared. Whatever the epoch and the issue, he had spoken his mind, even in that odious article that ensured the ruin of his reputation. More and more, Owen tried to cast his mind back to the conversations they had had on the terrace of the villa in Como that final summer, wondering if his grandfather had sensed in him the cowardice, the fear of the world, he now recognized in himself; wondering if his grandfather had been trying to give him clues to how to be courageous. Fuck the critics; they are stupider than you. Live for the everlasting truth, not the snipes of your era. But then you had to know the everlasting truth, and have no fear of your era. Owen, however, lived in constant dread of something he did not know.

One afternoon that summer he had returned from a day in town kissing his Italian girlfriend to find his grandfather asleep on the terrace—white-stubbled cheek, rough, and wearing only loose, old canvas pants held together by a fraying string, and an old V-neck Hanes undershirt that he had probably brought over with him in 1953. Owen had gone upstairs to his own room and on the way had seen the open door to his grandfather's study. He loved that large room with its books and its artifacts, with its view of the lake— sometimes misty, sometimes clear, always Alpine. He noticed that the file cabinet that was usually locked was open and that papers were strewn on the worn desk. He was not a snoop but he was his grandfather's grandson and was alive with the history of his family, so he went into the study. The study had a window that also looked over the lake, and over the terrace, and over his grandfather still dozing in the Alpine sun—half a glass of white wine losing its chill in the sun on the table beside him where a notebook lay open, a capped pen resting in the gulley between two blank pages, pages whose corners occasionally lifted with the light wind as if wishing to be turned. Owen sat behind his grandfather's vast wooden desk cluttered with the old tools of the writing trade, which his grandfather had never abandoned—a large magnifying glass, the OED in all its volumes, reams of blank unruled paper, an old brass paperweight in the shape of a bust of Marx, and several ancient Mont Blanc fountain pens.

There was a letter open on the desk, the desk that was normally so clean and hardly ever used. Owen did not dare touch anything, but he could not resist reading the letter pinned against the gentle breeze that came through the open window by a heavy, ivory-handled, dagger-like paper cutter.

"He would not do it," the page before him read. It was the end of the letter. "Not after all he had endured at their hands, not after what he had endured at your hands. Not when he was finally beginning to emerge from his particular nightmares of which you were the cause, and being productive again. Why would he do it then, at the end of his despair, when he was beginning to enjoy being a grandfather to my child? It is something I cannot believe; I can only believe that they did it to him...And you, we all know now, were part of *them*."

He heard his grandfather's steps, tripping tipsily on the stairs; he heard the hard old palm grasp the banister for balance, and Owen quickly left the study and went to his room.

"Owen," his grandfather called.

* * *

Owen had not expected the full vehemence of his mother when he told her he had found a job writing speeches for a *moderate* Republican senator after he left the suburban Virginia newspaper.

"A Republican? We're Democrats in this family. How could you?"

"It's not like I'm writing pornography. I'm working in the U.S. Senate. That should count for something."

"I would *rather* you were writing pornography. It would be less embarrassing to my friends. You should know better."

"That's a crazy thing to say. He's a moderate senator from New Hampshire. I happen to agree with a lot of his fiscal stands."

"I didn't drag you," she said through cold eyes, "from the Louvre to the Hermitage to the Prado, making sure you were fluent in three languages, for you to come back home and write jingoistic speeches for right-wing America. I never should have let you visit your grandfather that summer."

He had been first stunned then hurt by his mother's reaction. Of course they were Democrats but he had not felt that his new beliefs were evil, only that they were a different take on being an American. He stood there in silence, in her kitchen, expecting her to say something that would indicate a backing down. Instead she turned and took her glass of wine—those were still her heavy drinking days—and went into the study where the TV was and slammed the door. He packed his things and stood in the kitchen for a while and finally stuck his head in the door of the study and said: "I'm leaving."

She didn't answer. He left.

He walked up Charles Street carrying his weekend bag, towards the train station, thinking over the conversation, thinking how stupid it was. Like a delayed fuse, he now became furious. And *what of* the Louvre and the Hermitage? he thought. As if an appreciation for the exhausted faces on Géricault's raft demanded a subscription to the notion of the welfare state and federally funded abortion. Had not the communards wanted to burn down the Louvre in the name of fighting inequality? He remembered his dismay at seeing his Princeton classmates return from a semester abroad, bringing with them a superficial new distaste for America. They had not expanded their minds, he told himself, they had exchanged one set of prejudices for another. All this he thought, in the early-summer evening, walking towards the train station, his heart pumping faster, his mind twisting in knots, not only at the absurdity of his mother's remarks but also at the quick burn of her anger. So what if he had learned foreign languages, as if that automatically made one more open-minded and informed? Maybe it just allowed you to read *real* fascists in their original tongues. If an opening to culture did anything, it ought to make you more conservative; it ought to make you understand those faces on Géricault's raft, the tenebrism of Caravaggio; it ought to make you understand both the fall of man and the persistence of evil; it ought to make you appreciate the true, the good, and the beautiful—all the quaint standards that had been betrayed by the liberal sensibility.

His grandfather, he remembered, always went to mass, always sat in the back, never took Communion. Owen, not yet a Catholic, had asked his grandfather why he didn't confess. "I'm too weak a man to confess. I can't even tell God which side I'm on," he said. But he was not a weak man, and Owen suspected it was something else.

CHAPTER 14

The Smell Of Cooking

Several times Owen noticed, while walking down the long corridor to his studio apartment, the pleasant cooking smells from the neighboring apartment, seeping through the walls, melting his small space with their warmth. Sometimes it was the smell of baking, sometimes something deliciously spicy. Himself, he cooked in a basic manner in the small kitchen with his few utensils. He sometimes wanted to invite himself to dinner next door. On the second or third night, he heard for the first time the sounds of lovemaking from what he imagined was the same apartment as the cooking. They were the rhythmic cries of a woman, growing louder, more insistent, but the woman alone. There is nothing that makes a lonely man lonelier than the sound of a woman making love to another man. Each time it started he sat in his small space, surrounded by pencil shavings and tobacco ash, and became still and listened.

On his first weekend, he was awakened from his hangover by the sounds. He looked at his watch. It was not yet noon. She was in the throes of her own particular ecstasy. He sat back and listened, because it was impossible to concentrate on anything else. The cries grew closer together. Finally she said quite clearly through the walls: "I'm coming! I'm coming!

Come with me baby! Are you coming baby?" Owen did not know if he came with her; he was never heard from, the man, the silent producer of these ecstatic screams. Owen could not imagine their faces, only their intertwined bodies, and the stoic, working silence of the man; that silence the sound of some sort of fidelity.

Hurting from his hangover, he showered, dressed and then made coffee. While the coffee steeped in the mini-French press, he slathered butter on a piece of bread. After the first cup of coffee decided to go out to get a newspaper and sit on a sidewalk somewhere and drink more coffee. As he locked the door of his apartment, the corridor was already filled with the smell of baking muffins, as if she had leapt from her orgasm and gone straight to the kitchen. It was a sunny day, not yet too hot, and he found himself heading towards Georgetown, walking farther than he had intended, building up an appetite, finally sitting down at the Peacock Café with a *Washington Post*. The news was fairly promising about his candidate, if you could read between the biased lines of the *Post*. He wondered when he would hear back from Stiles about his speech.

After his late breakfast he went to the Georgetown University library, where he had borrowing privileges through an arrangement with the institute, and checked out several books he had been meaning to read for his Leviathan essay. He walked back home again, stopping at Georgetown Tobacco to pick up some cigars. He smoked one as he walked back down M Street and across the bridge, continuing on Pennsylvania Avenue until he was back at Foggy Bottom and then at home. Having earned a new hunger, he made a sandwich and more coffee in the French press. He cleared the table, now full of stacked library books and handwritten papers where he had made notes the night before. His notes, he thought, were precise and incisive; some could be transposed unedited into the manuscript, some hinted at chapters he had not foreseen. His argument, he felt, was coming together. This was a very good feeling: Being with Audrey and writing with purpose were really the only things that released him from that sense of dread. He washed the plate he had eaten his sandwich on and the whiskey glass from the night before in the tiny kitchen space and worked for a while longer.

The air conditioning in his studio was centrally controlled and was blasting, making his small space far too cold. He opened the stiff window slightly to let out the cold air and then sat down again at his desk. "Leviathan in Knots," then: His first book had been about the post-Cold War disintegration of the nation-state. This essay, which he hoped he could turn into a book, described the state's response to its gradual disintegration: a combination of incompetence and overbearing, misplaced righteousness. He examined the state of his own republic and found it disappearing. Between the stupid vote on the left that wanted government to give it stuff, and the paranoid vote on the right that required the sacrifice of civil liberties for security, the state would continue to blunder in the only direction that it knew: towards tyranny. There was no space left for the free man anymore. At the end of history the free man was an eternal refugee. The America that had opened the frontier in its inexorable march westwards had nowhere left to go; it folded the frontier back and began to do to its own citizens what it had done to those who had stood in its way. The essay would be, in the end, a eulogy for the free man.

When he was tired of writing, but too excited to stop thinking, he began to plan a weekend for Audrey in Washington. She had been hesitant recently about answering his texts; she had answered one in three, and that the day after he had sent it. He did not want to be oppressive, but neither could he stop thinking about her. There was an exhibition coming up at the National Gallery, pairing the works of Caravaggio and Rembrandt. Caravaggio's "Isaac," he noticed, was among the works that would be displayed. He wanted her to see it; he himself wanted to see it again. They would have drinks somewhere in Georgetown in the evening. He would make reservations at a good restaurant. He would use his savings for this weekend. Then they would come back to his small room and they would make love without complications and perhaps she would moan like Lisa never did, and like the neighbor did.

* * *

A short time after Owen moved to DC, Audrey found herself thinking of him frequently, cautiously, while not quite missing him. An old college friend, Laura, was staying the night with her in Baltimore while driving north to a new job at a hotel in Maine. Laura was a cook; they opened a bottle of Chardonnay she had brought from the last restaurant she had worked for. Laura had decided to create something out of the ingredients that were there while Audrey sat at her great-aunt's kitchen table and chatted, sipping her wine. It was not so hot that they needed the air conditioner, but it was hot enough in the kitchen that it made sense to open the door that led to the fire escape. Audrey sat near the door to take advantage of the fresh night air and realized that her gaze kept returning to the fire escape where she used to see Owen smoke his cigarettes and drink his scotch. She felt suddenly the same intense pang of sympathy that had brought her to his door that night. She began wishing he was there; she tried to understand her attraction to him, and why she still thought of him. Laura, her back to her, arms working the knife on the counter, was bantering about the shit restaurant that had canned her. For Audrey it was like trying to remember the words to one song while the melody of another one was playing, and the expert rhythm of Laura's knife against the cutting board went *clack, clack, clack.*

"I met an interesting guy," she told Laura, when Laura had paused to sweep bits of asparagus onto a plate. "I kind of like him."

"Aren't you still going out with Josh?"

"I broke up with him when I left North Carolina. It wasn't going to work."

"The distance thing?"

"The distance was the excuse. I didn't trust him was the real thing."

"He was cute, sexy—at least his pictures on Facebook were."

"He didn't seem to be going anywhere in life. Landscaping and surfing."

"It's hard for guys these days. I read something about how they're committing suicide left and right."

"Are they really?" She recalled the lonesome figure of Owen on his balcony, with his drinks and cigarettes— wasn't he, in his own way, committing a slow sort of suicide? Suddenly she felt afraid for him, almost responsible for him, then resented him for making her feel all that. She started biting a thin, paint-chipped nail.

"The article said that men are killing themselves four times more often than women." Lucky them, Audrey thought, to have at least four lives. Then she thought that was a comment Owen would like, or even make, and she smiled at his fire escape.

"So who's the new guy?" Laura asked. "You're so pretty you never have trouble finding them."

"He's old, first of all."

"Like, how old?"

"Probably nearly forty."

"Where did you meet?"

"Over there."

Laura looked up and looked at Audrey, then looked where Audrey was looking. "Where?"

"He lives in that apartment across the way. Or he was staying there. It's his mother's apartment. He works in DC. He was just staying here until he found a place to live."

"I hope you Googled him before you fucked him. These old guys can be weird."

"I did. There's not much about him on the web. Surprising, really. He's some kind of professor, some kind of writer. He wrote a book on international relations. He traveled a lot. His father was a diplomat so he grew up all over the place. His father died pretty young, and now his mother lives alone in that apartment. He doesn't like to talk about her."

"OK in bed?"

"Laura!"

"You used to give reviews. What, haven't you done it yet?"

"We have done it. He drinks a lot. Too much. And he smokes. But he's tender and I've never really had that before."

Audrey was still staring at the dark space where he used to sit, silhouetted against the kitchen's light. She found it strange that she wanted him to appear. She had wanted to tell Laura there was something mysterious about him that drew her in, like the first pages of a novel. It had not been like that with Josh—a cartoon—whose consistent late nights and regular weekend surfing trips just made her distrust him. These were different orders of mysteries. In the case of Owen, there were little secrets that made her want to follow the thin thread he had placed in her hand, follow it into the inviting murkiness of his being, where somewhere was the young man who had written so beautifully of his travels and his first love. Until now she had not realized how tantalizing he was to her. She bit her nail suddenly realizing it. Her eyes, she sensed, had enlarged as if she realized something for the first time. Then she let out a sharp and unexpected cry. Laura flinched and made a false move with the knife, and a bit of garlic arced to the floor. "Damn," Laura said. "What's wrong? You almost made me cut my finger off!"

"I just had a little scare." Just as she had been staring at the dark apartment across the way, half wishing Owen would come back, the light in the kitchen had gone on. She was about to call him and invite him over, but then she saw the silhouette inside; it was a woman. She realized it must be his mother, back from her trip to Europe.

"You should tell him," Laura said, "that he has to stop smoking if he wants to kiss you. That's a good incentive. Besides, kissing a smoker is like kissing an ashtray."

"Have you ever kissed a smoker?"

"Not really."

"Or an ashtray?"

"No. But I've seen plenty. My father used to smoke."

"I guess I never noticed. Kissing him was nice. He tasted of whiskey."

The light had gone out in the kitchen of the other apartment, but other lights were on. Audrey wondered what the lady was like and what she was doing puttering around her apartment—the apartment that by now almost felt like home to Audrey.

CHAPTER 15

American Exceptionalism

Chilton Stiles, having received Owen's speech draft, invited him to his office across the river in Crystal City to discuss it. Stiles's office was in a modern, anonymous glass building that had risen amid several others, less anonymous, that proudly announced they were international purveyors of arms. Entering the glass-and-marble lobby of Stiles's building, Owen saw among the list of firms there the names of several former Republican Cabinet members. A Hispanic doorman made him sign in and wait while he phoned upstairs. Upstairs, on the top floor, he waited on a plush leather sofa in a clear, comfortable lounge area, where a pretty, young Asian receptionist with high heels and pencil legs had directed him to wait. Stiles's own office, Owen noticed when he was shown in, seemed to belong in a different building. His desk was mahogany, the carpeting was Oval Office blue but with a large Oriental rug laid over it, barrister's glass-fronted shelves held books and knickknacks, and opposite was the obligatory Washington wall of fame—photos of a younger and slimmer Chilton Stiles, not only with presidents and foreign ministers (photos of a far higher rank than Dean Cernic's), but also in native garb standing on a tank with a robed and turbaned Afghan mujahidin, holding a Kalashnikov with rebels in Angola, testifying defiantly to Congress. Surrounding a polished coffee table were a large globe cradled in an oak frame, resting next to the arm of a leather settee, two leather armchairs, and a wooden university chair with the black-and-orange Princeton crest inlaid on the back. Above the bookshelves hung a gilded Kalashnikov. The large window behind the desk overlooked the Potomac and Washington, DC, as if the message were that Stiles had a full view of what he could nonetheless turn his back upon.

Stiles waved a liver-spotted hand towards the settee while Owen, gripping a hard copy of the speech, sat in the cushionless Princeton chair. Stiles was dressed in an expensive dark gray suit, a navy-blue-and-white striped shirt, no tie, and black tasseled loafers. Everything was perfectly tailored, though Stiles was heavy and actually seemed to be taller on one side of his body than the other. Owen noticed a hat rack from which hung a blue-and-red striped regimental tie.

"My fellow Americans," read Chilton theatrically from the printed pages of Owen's text. "A perfect start." Then he put it down for a moment. "Listen, overall you've done a good job with this," he said. "There are some really good lines in here." He held out the first page where less than a line of text was highlighted. "But understand that you cannot quote Hannah Arendt in a presidential campaign speech. Stick to uncontroversial American leaders—Washington, Jefferson, Lincoln. Nobody can imagine the governor relaxing in the evening with a glass of scotch and *Eichmann in Jerusalem*! It seems pretentious—never mind the scotch bit." He turned several pages. Owen could see that he had highlighted sections of the text. "I like this too: 'It is a cheap gimmick among intellectuals to equate American exceptionalism with jingoism, and then condemn jingoism. But we are indeed an exceptional people. We have been complacent in assuming that the world will understand us because we are exceptional. It is the other way around: Because we are exceptional, it is that much harder for the world to understand us. "America requires explanations," Allan Bloom once wrote, "the kind the founders gave the world."' You can't quote Bloom either. If you could find a similar quote by Reagan.... And this: 'It is difficult to be both strong and understood. The world admires strength and fears it at the same time. It appeases its fear by ascribing hypocrisy to the strong.' Hear, hear!"

He put the printed pages down again. Owen, while listening, had been strangely captivated by his own words in Stiles's measured voice. He had imagined himself again as a speechwriter for the next president. The clubby brownness of Stiles's office gave proof of his pretensions: leather, oak, and power; the large globe and the pictures framing fame; the gilded Kalashnikov—the sacraments of Washington power seemed almost to glow as Owen's careful words, uttered by Chilton Stiles, bounced off them and echoed in the room. Stiles's critique actually helped as well. He could imagine himself in the Oval Office, late at night, loosened tie, rolled-up shirtsleeves, reacting to President Romney's critique—largely favorable, but... "You cannot imagine me settling down to *Eichmann in Jerusalem*!" Then back to a cubbyhole West Wing office where there would be a bottle of single malt to drink sparingly late at night and tinker here and there with words to move an entire nation—a nation movable though not at all united.

Now Stiles was looking at him in a somehow sympathetic way, despite the brutality of his critique. "You see, in the end, this is in many ways a damn good speech," he said. "But a

143

damn good speech for your grandfather's era. Even for my era. It has a Schlesingerian ring, a Salingerian ring. Pierre, not J.D. I never liked *Catcher in the Rye*, and the fact that millions of grade-school students have read it is part of our decline and fall. But don't get me wrong, I'm not calling you a Democrat. But those were the scribes who spoke for the vital center in their time. Now we have no center, so the scribes must be either shrill or dumb to rally the vital extremes. It needs shorter sentences, more platitudes, less thinking, less history, more references to national security and the world that we fear. The fear of the big bad world is what motivates independents to vote Republican. Also, listen to how the governor himself speaks. He can handle long sentences, but if they're too long he loses his rhythm. He is not a natural speaker. So longer sentences need to be almost all iambic for him to get through them without getting lost."

Owen took out the Moleskine notebook he always kept in his jacket pocket and noted these points as Stiles made them. He noted them dutifully, but with a sense that an opportunity had been lost or he had greatly failed. He had wanted—in those long, sober hours at his father's desk—he had wanted his words to elevate America, not tailor them to America's dismal level. He was about to mention Isaiah Berlin's essay on how both Roosevelt and Churchill had used the craft of words to create a new national narrative for their countries, and by doing so united their peoples, won the war, and saved their heritage. But Isaiah Berlin was not Reagan or Will Rogers or John Wayne, so he said nothing.

"But it doesn't matter in the end, unfortunately," Stiles said gently, setting the pages on the inlaid coffee table. "Boston has decided against giving a major foreign policy speech. They've decided that this is a domestic policy election. Kennedy, that other modern president from Boston, once said domestic policy can only defeat us, foreign policy can kill us. Probably Schlesinger wrote that for him. Never mind. The idiots running the governor's campaign don't want to risk it, despite the fact that the governor's instincts on this topic are far better than the president's."

"But in politics, defeat is the same as death," Owen said, his words sounding as bitter as he felt. Stiles guffawed in his confident and exuberant way. "I hope you're wrong," he said. "They're calculators, up there in Boston, and we have to hope they're calculating soundly. They've crunched the numbers, and the governor is if nothing else a numbers cruncher. But I like your spirit. I share it. But you go into a campaign with the candidate you have. Our national tragedy—and our nation's survival hangs in the balance of this election—is that this man is one of the most decent and qualified ever to be president, and will be a great president. But people only know him through his campaign, and he is not a great campaigner, and I fear the generals of his campaign are not that great either. I'd like to tell this to the governor, but the monkeys in Boston are blocking me."

"So that's the end of this speech," Owen said, aware at how transparent his deception was.

"You have tremendous talent," Stiles said. "And I will keep the promise I made to you. If the American people have the sense to elect this good man, you will have a place in the administration. And once the lowest-common-denominator aspect of the campaign is out of the way, I think there will be a place for more intelligent speeches. Churchill, you know, reminded the English who they were in the Second World War. He practically reinvented the nation. His words alone were worth a hundred battleships. There is an excellent essay by Isaiah Berlin on that. You should read it. Hell, you should make your students read it."

"I've read it," Owen said, thinking of Churchill, who, at his own age, had been Home Secretary and Lord of the Admiralty. He felt very insignificant as he left Stiles's lonely, opulent seat of power.

CHAPTER 16

Central Park West

In the box he had rescued from his mother's storage space, he found things he had forgotten he had. He unpacked them with an archaeologist's curiosity in his Foggy Bottom studio. There were mementos from his round-the-world trip, manila folders stuffed with his early writings, some printed, some handwritten (including a 145-page handwritten manuscript he only dimly remembered writing about someone called Tom). He also found the copy of the novel he had written for Lisa, the one Audrey had asked him for. The pages of the computer printout, from one of those inkjet printers that don't exist anymore, were covered with his own red ink scratches emending the text. He did not remember ever having gone over the hard copy. The soft copy was long gone, lost on some 3.5-inch disk. Now he found his edits to be generally sound; the first draft was far worse than he had remembered it.

He had set up his laptop on the table he had recently acquired secondhand from a tenant moving out, and now set the manuscript next to it. While the laptop booted up, he poured a glass of whiskey and sat down and lit a cigarette. He began retyping the manuscript, adding in the corrections but limiting himself to those, refusing the instinct to make additional changes. Having forgotten the plot and the characters, he was surprised at the twists and even laughed at some of the humor. The badinage! Some of it was not so bad. They delighted him at times, these inventions of his youth. It was three in the morning and half the whiskey bottle was gone and nearly a pack of cigarettes when his fingers stopped typing from fatigue. He scrolled back through the document; there were many squiggly red lines where he had mistyped a word. He would correct them later. He stood and hobbled unexpectedly as he grabbed the chair to steady himself, but he was happy. "I was a writer once," he said to the empty apartment. He knew why he had done it—or, for whom he had done it. This was Audrey's now and he wanted to finish it before he saw her next, on the Washington visit. (Her texts had been vague about when that would be.) He brushed his teeth and collapsed onto his bed, leaving the last of the ice melting in the last of the whiskey on the table, a few feet away, where he would see it when he woke up and be unhappy about it.

He would continue to work on the squiggles in the morning, fortified with coffee, far more sober. He remembered that the previous night he had decided to give the manuscript to Audrey. But the manuscript was really Lisa's. Lisa had inspired it; Lisa had killed the young writer whom she had inspired. He stopped fixing the squiggles and lit another cigarette. He emptied the ashtray and took it to the futon, where he sat down and took in his lonely 400 square feet of space.

Lisa had taken full advantage of the New York apartment when they lived there. She had loved that apartment. It made her feel like one of the great New York elite. She liked giving parties. At Skadden Arps, she said, we work hard and play hard. She liked the fact that it was not only a fabulous address, but that it was the property of the once-famous Silas Stone. One night, at one of those parties, where Owen tended out of nervousness to begin drinking far before the first guest arrived, he overheard her say to one of her Skadden Arps colleagues that Silas Stone had been senile when he wrote the infamous article. Owen decided not to cause a scene at the height of the party, but he skulked around the spaces where his grandfather's memory had been traduced, turned into a bit of trivia, but a non-trivial lie! Here in the rooms where his grandfather had written two movies and his best mature novels, his grandson's wife had turned him into a cocktail topic. Being curt—or rude—to his guests, most of which were his wife's, he lurked and caught glimpses of her throughout the evening. Slim body, tanned shoulders, expensive dress, pretty hair, fake smile. Her overheard comment rang in his head. For the first time, as he looked at her, she had become ugly to him.

Owen knew he was drinking too much but still he refilled his glass and for a moment found himself staring over the night-view of Central Park thinking of his grandfather. He remembered afternoons on the terrace of the villa above Lake Como, and eighty-something Silas reciting pages of Faulkner from memory, that massive, vivid, all-seeing, all-remembering photographic memory, Scarlatti sonatas playing on the turntable inside, the old man's voice in perfect control. Call the man evil, call him a fascist, call him a visionary, call him a crank, but don't call him senile! She who floated around the place he had bought and built with his sheer intellect; she taking in the morning views of Central Park while sipping Gevalia coffee and reading legal briefs his grandfather would have hated; she, acting as if she deserved to live in this luxury but refusing to accept everything that came with it, all while playing the hostess with a distinct lack of hospitality.

He poured himself another scotch, if only to get away from
her and the crowd around her. Very few of his own friends
were there; he hardly had any of his own. He saw her glance
over at him, almost worried when she saw the expression on
his face. Then she smiled at him from across the room, as if
it were all under control. He drank and made small talk with
her small friends. There was a young man, their age, from her
law firm, James Porter, who they all said in Lisa's crowd was
one of the most brilliant lawyers of his generation. Brilliant or
not, to Owen he was always sniffing around his wife, sniffing
more avidly as the night went on. It was to Porter that Lisa
had made the comment about Silas Stone's senility.

Owen followed him around as well. How strange it
was how often she and Porter could be spied on at the same
time. Porter was a slight figure with a sharp, jutting jaw and
green eyes, a physiognomy that did not photograph well but
that demanded attention for the intelligence it radiated;
the eyes drew you in. He was attractive but not handsome;
the calm intelligence had its own pull. He was said—it
was, in fact, Lisa who had said it—that he was surprisingly
successful with women. Owen had actually enjoyed some of
his conversations with Porter, the quick wit, the vast store of
general knowledge summoned at will. When Owen had told
Porter that, during his youthful travels, just after meeting
Lisa, he had wanted to try himself against the powers of
the world, Porter had replied that Joyce was no travel agent.
Owen had been impressed that Porter recognized the phrase,
so impressed that he had been at a loss for a comeback.
Porter was, of course, like the rest of them, a committed
Democrat who had worked on the Kerry campaign. His
knowledge of American elections was encyclopedic, and he
could remember the vice presidential candidates of losing
tickets back to the Reconstruction, as well as the results of

crucial counties in the most recent election. He was one of those liberals whom Owen could talk to because he was vain enough to care more about the banter than the underlying points, to score points rather than explore points. He had, at least, the trial lawyer's virtue of being able to see all sides and argue them equally well; the client paid, after all. He seemed also to enjoy Owen's conversation, perhaps because he had never met a conservative who in his view could keep up with him. A bit of a dandy in his pumpkin-colored pants and double-breasted navy blazer that looked vintage, with a pouffed pocket square blooming out of it along with a cigar that he would smoke later. He was famous also for his knowledge of cigars. The outfit did not really suit him, except that nothing really suited him, so anything might as well, and he had a fuck-you look that somehow made it work even so. And the cigar, at that time when smoking was becoming taboo, was another fuck-you, too.

"How's your Iraq war going?" he asked Owen later that night, taking a break from sniffing after Lisa, leaning his prominent chin in so that it seemed he was grinning or offering a target for a malevolent fist. Owen, having prowled all night between trivial conversations, and having made as a good host too many "martinis" for people who thought that a real martini contained vodka, had reached that time of night and drink when he would have preferred being alone with his wife. In fact he had slowed his drinking a bit. Yet they lingered, these guests; yet they wanted to talk about Iraq, even with Central Park spread magnificently beneath them on such a clear night.

"Why do you liberals always want to talk about war?" he asked, too quickly and too snarly.

"Because all you conservatives do is make it," Porter retorted. Porter was up for this game. "It's what we call a bipartisan conversation," he added with a Harvard Law sneer.

"Aren't there other things in your life besides liberal and conservative? Besides politics? That's the real difference between us. For you, government should be everywhere, and therefore everything is political. We conservatives want government out of the way, doing the minimum required, so we can be free of politics in some other areas. We could even talk about other things."

"Get the state out of a woman's womb, and then you might be convincing with your cute little libertarian vibe. Get the state out of—"

"See what I mean? In thirty seconds you've gone from Mesopotamia to a woman's womb. Why not just smell the roses? Talk about a movie or a show you've seen, or a book you've read."

"OK. Well, you seem to have quite an interest in Gene Powell Davis," he said. "If you want to talk about books." This abrupt observation surprised Owen. He suddenly remembered that James had emerged a short while ago from his grandfather's study, where the Davis books were prominently displayed on the ancient desk, as they had been since 1953. Either that or Porter had studied his grandfather's life and knew exactly which name he had named.

"Are you trying to make a real point or just talking?" Owen hoped that his clenched fists were noted.

"You know us lawyers, if it's not one thing it's the other."

"Then I'll be a gracious host and assume it's the other."

"What's wrong, Owen? A little tightly wound tonight?"

"Just tight."

"Tight? Oh. Of course. How *avant guerre*. Still, I suppose it's better to be tight than senile."

Owen looked again at the inviting jaw, extended still, a perfect target. Then Porter removed it. "I think I'll get another drink, if you don't mind. I'm loose enough still." He walked away and suddenly Owen felt his nails biting into the soft skin of his hand. And when he turned around to watch the pumpkin-trousered lawyer ambling to the antique drinks cart, he saw his wife standing there as well, smiling as Porter walked toward her. His wife and Porter leaned towards each other to hear in the din of the lingering crowd.

When the last guest had gone, Owen, almost incoherent, told Lisa with a quiet fury: "Don't ever say to anyone that my grandfather was senile. He knew what he was writing, and the world might not have liked it, but it was what he believed."

"Don't ever say 'don't ever' to me," she replied. "You don't talk to me like that. And you're drunk. Very drunk. Drunker than usual. And it's starting to embarrass me the way you get so drunk so quickly at my parties. These are people that I *work* with. One day I want to be made partner—"

"You know what I mean: about my grandfather. Don't change the subject. He wasn't senile. If he embarrasses you then either don't mention him or don't invite your friends to his house. Go meet your friends at restaurants. This place was bought by his genius, for better or for worse. I certainly don't belong here. The only reason I'm here is because I'm the only one in the family who didn't ridicule him."

"And you keep this place a shrine to him. I want to renovate, you know. I can't live in fifties dust forever. Or we move to our own place."

"Then we move to our own place."

"I'll have to pay the rent, of course. Since you're not making any money."

"You'll have to pay," he agreed. "Because I'm not making any money."

"Stop repeating every damn thing I say," she said, suddenly shrill. She too had been drinking too much; her voice always rose when she drank too much. "And you should stop drinking. You've had enough for a night, or for a lifetime. Third-generation drunk."

It was difficult to turn away from her accusing sneer and serve himself another drink, to let her you-should-stop-drinking comment bounce off his unsteady armor and fall to a thud on his grandfather's parquet. It was difficult, one drink later, to crawl into bed and tease her thighs open and try to make babies like they agreed they should, as soon as possible, when her cycle was right. But she always seemed to anger him when her cycle was right. And when her thighs wouldn't open, and she would push his teasing hands away, he would rise again and go to his grandfather's study and open his books and fall asleep on the small uncomfortable couch that still smelled of pipe tobacco and wake up late the next morning to the smell of coffee. Lisa would be in an acceptable mood again, as if they had never had the argument. They were required, after all, to make love that morning, and why conceive in anger? She never mentioned again that his grandfather had been senile. In retrospect he wondered if what became broken later had really been cracked that night, and if Porter had cracked it.

Now, though, was another lonely drink and an unsteady toast to Audrey in his tiny Washington studio. So young and so unencumbered, Audrey, so open, so unaware of Silas Stone and, for that matter, in many ways, of Owen Cassell himself. It was the difference of generations: Lisa had been of the generation that expected everything would always improve, and all setbacks were only temporary, and that, as the Democratic party used to say, those who played by the rules would be rewarded. Audrey was the same age now that Lisa had been when she had gone to law school, when Owen had first met her. Audrey was learning to survive in an America that no longer rewarded people who played by the rules, not only because there were fewer rewards to go around, but because there were no real rules, or the ones that existed were just for the little people. Audrey was surviving; he loved her pluckiness, he loved her youth, he loved, in the end, her lack of optimism that she did not even realize that she lacked. She too seemed to dread something she did not know. Silas Stone would have understood her. Owen was drunk again, quite accidentally, and realized how much he was looking forward to seeing her.

He resolved, this time, to tell her he was a conservative. He was sure she could accept this, despite her own liberal politics, as long as he had time to prepare her, time for her to get to know him better, time in which to convince her that to be a conservative was not necessarily to be a monster, and that there were far more important things in life than politics. He began to consider a trip to New York, the two of them. They could rent a car in DC, he could show her the apartment, they could go to dinner, see, perhaps, a concert or the ballet, and he could do something wildly romantic after doing something wildly cultural and wildly civilized. All this could set the scene. Then he could tell her.

He told himself, as he faced his shattered reflection in the bathroom mirror again, that he had to reveal his truth on his own terms, after a foundation had been built. He realized then, thinking about it, worrying that she might find out by some other means, on terms not his own, that his greatest asset in life was his anonymity, his *relative* anonymity—that he was not on Facebook, that he had never blogged, that all his publications had been esoteric. He had read Leo Strauss's *Persecution and the Art of Writing* and had applied its observations to his scholarly work. It was quite an unusual thing, he thought, to be so anonymous in the 21st century, to be, effectively, un-Google-able.

CHAPTER 17

Watergate

Owen, thinking also about his grandfather, had sent an email to Stiles with several questions about his past. Stiles eventually responded by inviting Owen to dinner at his apartment at the Watergate. The apartment was on the fourth floor, and Stiles took him to the balcony and showed him the view over the Potomac with a glimpse of Arlington cemetery. A table had been set there on the balcony with a cloth, napkins, wineglasses and gilt-edged plates. They talked about the campaign over a pre-dinner martini for Owen, a juice for Stiles. Then they sat at the table while a Hispanic maid served a fig salad. Owen had spent enough time with liberals to understand why they could hate a man like Chilton Stiles, but he himself could not. He had played his cards in life fully and well and exuded a sense of knowing it. Yet the nature of his participation in history limited those he could tell his stories to. Owen, listening raptly, realized that his own relation to his grandfather made him someone Stiles felt he could talk to.

Stiles opened and poured a bottle of wine. Trying to examine it in the faint light of the terrace, Owen thought he glimpsed a 1980s vintage year.

The old man leaned forward slightly. "You want to know if your grandfather was a spy. I understand. Let me be absolutely clear. He never was, not in the sense that you mean or that might embarrass you. Of course, it eventually came out that *Remnant*, the journal that he co-edited, was financed by the CIA as part of our campaign to counter Soviet propaganda. We had picked him as our co-editor, along with Lambert Montgomery, that British fairy, because we needed left-wingers who were anti-Communist, who would be credible to other left-wingers. Your grandfather was a left-winger at the beginning, like almost all intellectuals. And when it came out at the end of the Cold War that we were the creators and financers of *Remnant*, we encouraged the belief that he was unaware at the time of that financing. And when he published that article in *Vanity Fair*, he attracted the attention of a whole generation of new enemies who played up the CIA angle. They put out the tale that he had known all along where the financing had come from and what the ultimate goal of the magazine was. So there were many false stories told about your grandfather and us. By the end, your grandfather had lived long enough to have enemies on the left and the right, and long enough for the left and the right to switch sides on many issues. He was himself, in many ways, a fixed pole, despite the stories invented by others around him."

"But you know the true story."

"I suppose enough time has passed, or I wouldn't have invited you over to discuss it. The truth is that your grandfather was intimately involved from the beginning in the *Remnant* project. He actively contributed to our attempt to make it look like he was not a part of it. In fact, the project was his idea: find leftists who were anti-Communist to attack Communism without being painted as right-wing reactionaries. Does that shock you? I expected you to look more shocked."

"I lost my political virginity a long time ago."

Stiles smiled broadly, almost laughed in the bursting way he did. "See," he continued, "in the forties, the FBI had contacted your grandfather about people he knew who were Communists. Your grandfather was already of the same view that many of us came to much later: that what came to be called McCarthyism was un-American. Unlike a lot of people on his side, though—the non-Communist leftists— he didn't deny the reality of the Communist threat, or that our government was shot through with Communists. He believed in a certain kind of America that should never be Communist. He just didn't think it made sense to go after the movie people—*trop de zèle*, as he would say. The one thing your grandfather always feared about America was that it would lose its creative nerve. He thought culture was both the most vital and most vulnerable thing in America. He quoted that famous John Adams line—when Adams said that he himself had to study politics and war so his sons could study commerce and industry so their sons could study art and gardening or ballet or something to that effect. America, your grandfather thought, was not a good place for artists because it was not aristocratic. It was not a place of sufficient leisure to produce good art, and its democratic temperament did not produce good taste. He was not a mass-cult kind of guy, in the end. Don't misunderstand me, he was not for aristocracy. He believed more in freedom than in manners, but he hoped you could have a bit of both. He saw that the threat to creativity in some ways was as great as the threat from Communism. He didn't give a shit about politicians and couldn't stand Alger Hiss. So he came to me, a former student of his, after the FBI contacted him. He knew I was working for the CIA because he had given me a reference. He told me the FBI had contacted him and he knew what came next.

"'Can you protect me?' he said.

"'How?' I asked.

"'Say that I'm working with you,' he said. 'And that should make them leave me alone.'

"'But then,' I told him, 'you'd have to be working with me. I can't lie to prevent you from telling the truth.'

"'I can work with you,' he said. 'I have an idea.'

"And that was when he proposed to us the *Remnant* idea."

Owen sipped and tried to make sense of all that. "Why not just refuse to name names and retire to Italy? Be a hero to his liberal friends. He didn't need the money, and from what I understand, he didn't much like working in movies. And he left anyway in the end. And he never came back."

"Oh, he hated Hollywood," Stiles said. "He and Faulkner, they'd drink all afternoon in his studio office or Faulkner's, hating it and loving drinking, and when the buzz wore off just enough late in the evening, they'd turn out stuff for a couple of hours to have something to show to the studios. That's why their Hollywood stuff was so bad. They were exhausted and still drunk when they wrote most of it. Lots of gems in there; no question, they were geniuses. But you had to sort through a lot of shit to find the pearls. But to your very specific and appropriate question: What do you know about your grandmother?"

"That she died when my mother was very young. Two or three years old, I think. My mother, when she was in one of her particularly anti-Silas phases, tried to find out more about her. I think she lost interest when she realized her mother wasn't a distant relative of the Vanderbilts or Rockefellers, or some European countess. My mother always had pretensions of aristocracy."

"Your grandmother was the love of his life. You can't blame him for not wanting to deal with your mother. As an innocent infant, she took away what he loved most, replaced the love of his life with a screaming baby. It seemed unjust to him, and he never forgave your mother for being born. She was a Communist, your grandmother," Stiles added.

"That would explain my mother," Owen said dryly, and then regretted it.

Stiles pretended that he hadn't heard. "The real reason Silas didn't want to testify was because Betty, your grandmother, was a Communist actress. He was too patriotic to lie to his government—or to allow the Commies to win—and too much of a man to betray his lover. It became a huge internal dilemma for him. It was cruel what we forced Americans to do back then because we wanted to save America. I say that as a man who has been responsible for a lot of cruelty in my career and I accept it. I say that as a man who is more aware than most of how serious the internal threat was in the Cold War. But Silas found an elegant way out because he was an elegant man and fundamentally a patriot."

Stiles poured more wine in both of their glasses. The maid had not appeared for some time. "We were too late, of course. Your grandfather was called before one session of the committee before we could get the *Remnant* machinery going. They asked him specifically about Gene Powell Davis and he felt he could not lie. I was there, in the committee room, when it happened, sitting in the back. I sensed the full agony of his position. But he squared his shoulders and told the committee that he knew for sure that Gene Powell Davis had been a member of the Communist party. Before the next hearing was scheduled, we managed to get approval for the

Remnant project and we made sure he was never called again as a witness. Your grandmother left him anyway. It broke his heart."

"How did she die?"

"A car accident," Stiles said crisply.

"What happened to Davis?" Owen asked, after a pause.

"After your grandfather's testimony, a few other people testified that he was a Communist. It was as if the dam had broken. I guess he got blacklisted for a while, like the rest of them. They all got rehabilitated in the end, in the seventies, and now they're American heroes to the cultural left, while those who are real geniuses and patriots, like Elia Kazan, remain controversial. A lot of them even kept writing under fake names and getting paid on the sly."

They had finished eating, and the tired maid cleared the plates. Stiles said, "I don't drink spirits anymore, but could I interest you in a scotch?"

"Between scotch and nothing, I'll take scotch," Owen said, his judgment blurred by the very fine wine that Stiles had served. As soon as he said it, he realized it sounded ungracious. He was about to apologize when Stiles beamed at him.

"Faulkner," Stiles said approvingly. He rose from his chair and went to his liquor cabinet. "My selection is smaller since I stopped drinking liquor. But I have a Talisker, a Macallan, and an Oban, all gifts from people who don't know I stopped drinking the hard stuff." Owen suggested the Talisker, and Stiles poured a generous portion into a tumbler that looked remarkably similar to his father's Baccarat set. Stiles served himself a glass of water.

"When were you last in touch with my grandfather?" Owen asked.

"We stayed in touch over the years. Of course, the world changed. As I'm sure you know, I ended up doing more anti-terrorism work after the wall fell, and it was a different kind of work. Every time I could, though, when I was in Europe, I would stop by and see him at Como. Old warriors in repose, I suppose. He, at least, was an old warrior. I had started fighting a new and harder war. I don't think he ever understood the new threats we were facing."

"But that article," Owen said. "Some people, your kind of people if I may say so, called him a traitor." The Talisker—sharp, peaty, hard; he wondered if it had overly loosened his tongue.

"I wrote him a letter when that article came out. I told him that I understood what he was saying, that we differed perhaps on what America needed to do in this complicated world to still be America, but that I understood his views and I knew he would have very few friends as a result of the article, but that I would always be a friend, that the respect I had for him dictated that I should write to him. I told him he should know that our past work together had had an undeniable impact on the endurance of freedom in our world. What most threatens freedom, he retorted in his sharp and grumpy way, were those who abused it without ever having fought for it. I think I understand the impulse of his article. But I think it belongs to a philosophy that cannot survive in our age of total data. What about you? Did you ever ask him about the article? You spent a summer with him, didn't you? In his reply he mentioned how happy he was that you would be visiting him."

"He wrote you about me?" Owen felt, beneath the peat heat of the whiskey, a chill, a sharp edginess; he felt suddenly that he was the unwitting pawn in a game that had begun long ago, but he didn't have the wit now to work out all the threads.

"He told me his only regret about the article, which he had written in a state—his words—of 'cold-blooded serenity,' was the effect that it might have on you. He said you were finishing Princeton and he wanted you to visit him. He wrote that he was looking out at his lake and its untroubled waters and wondering if it would be the last time he would see the summer sun reflecting over it. He was afraid that one effect of the article would be to prevent you from coming—your mother or something would prevent it—and that he would never see you again. You were the last of his line."

The infamous article, Owen remembered, had been published in the fall of 1996, when Timothy McVeigh, the domestic terrorist, was on death row. It had staunchly defended him, and sought to explain him by using tropes from the American Revolution. It had almost, some argued, encouraged future attacks of the same nature. Among intellectual circles it had generated a massive condemnation of Silas Stone. Yet hardly anyone at Princeton knew that Owen was Silas Stone's grandson. Owen was discreet by instinct. He had never wanted to be known for his family. When the article came out he suffered inwardly and tried to make sense of it, but he did not suffer ostracism. Nothing about the article—its vituperation, hatred of the federal government, endorsement of violence, repudiation of the idea that America could any longer keep its republic—resembled either the old man that he knew from summers spent with him in Italy, or the novels and screenplays written decades before.

One night at the Princeton library he wrote a letter to his grandfather, asking him to explain himself. But he never sent it. What was the instinct that had prevented him from sending it? Even now, staring at Stiles's weathered, blistered, and tired face, he tried to remember. He realized he had been quiet for quite a long time, and he did not know if it was the whiskey or a genuine uncertainty. "Give me a moment," Stiles said, and went inside.

Owen sipped. The Talisker still retained its peat, its sharpness, its hardness. Owen retained his sense of being not only trapped by history, but played by it. While Stiles was gone, he tried to isolate the threads and see how they formed the knot. At the same time he tried to see if there was really a knot—something designed—or if it was just the jumbled mess of events.

Stiles returned with a sheaf of pages clipped together, the handwriting of his grandfather recognizable on the pages. "I kept the letter," Stiles said. "He wrote this: 'I look over my lake and its untroubled waters and wonder if it will be the last time I see the summer sun reflecting from it.'" Stiles paused, scanned, turned pages. "There is something he wrote about you," he said absently. "I'm looking for it." His eyes scanned as he spoke. "Here it is. He just mentioned that you were a senior at Princeton and he was afraid his article would cause trouble for you. 'I fear his mother has had a negative influence on him, though I always liked his father, despite our difference in views on certain important topics. His father always seemed to me a sort of American version of Deume in *Belle du Seigneur*, though not as ridiculous. (I remember you violently disliked that novel when you were my student; you called it *Belle du Diarroeah*.) I'd like to imagine, though, my grandson as a sort of aristocrat, a modern prince. But his upbringing, while cosmopolitan, has hardly been aristocratic in the republican sense that our country was once able to produce. By that I mean an aristocracy of virtue, not birth. Now I am afraid that we have aristocracy expressed through luxury rather than virtue, and that luxury is essentially hereditary. As Montesquieu taught, this is a category error that the Republic cannot hope to survive. I am deeply pessimistic as I stand at the stage's exit. I am pessimistic about the future of our American experiment—a republic, if you can keep it!—and pessimistic about a world without America. This pessimism motivated my "scandalous" article, which was perhaps maladroit but somebody needs to notice that we are losing something that has always been essential: that the spirit of disobedience has always been somehow essential to the vitality of our laws. In any case, I appreciate your thoughtful note, your attempt to understand what I have written, though I know how profoundly you disagree. Once can only write honestly these days by writing in code. The rest of the country rumors me into insanity—or senility—and sends me to their metaphorical gallows for treason. (What do they know of either gallows or treason?) I am using my last breaths to breathe something into this dying republic, something about responsibility and self-knowledge. McCarthy, while an idiot, was in some fundamental way right. The country we love has enemies and the most dangerous of all are within, and often elected to office. What can democracy deliver when we elect our betrayers? *Et tu*, et cetera, but on a grand scale, like only America can mount. Anyway, the most we can hope for is that the old code-breakers are able to decipher the meaning, and for that I am grateful for your letter.'"

Was his grandfather, Owen wondered, as he listened to Stiles read, speaking to him across the years, and *knowing* that he was speaking to him? The book he, Owen, had published was not the same as the thesis he had presented to the committee. It was in many ways the reverse image, the knots behind the carpet. The thesis of his book, when he had tested it unvarnished to his advisor as a possible dissertation topic, had been laughed at. So he had written a thesis on state formation while at the same time writing a book on state disintegration. One can only write honestly by writing in code, and hope the code-breakers are able to decipher it. He felt colder now shuddering in the autumn chill, whipped by the muddy breeze off the Potomac.

"Back to your original question," Stiles said. "It is important that you know, whatever the purpose and the sources of funding of *Remnant*, he never edited or published an article that he thought wasn't worth publishing on its own merits, or thought that the cause was not vital. *Remnant* might have served our interests and defended our ideology, but it was never propaganda. He understood the difference. He thought that to admit to being financed by the CIA would discredit everything else he had done during that decade, and he had done a great deal. So he denied it."

"But he lied."

"You cannot live, these days, but in code, and hope that the code-breakers can decipher it," Stiles paraphrased with a short smile. "When he wrote what he thought was the truth, in his last article, that *Vanity Fair* article, he was pilloried. I think he wrote it to prove he was never anyone's tool. Perhaps it was a message in itself."

Owen allowed the silence to ferment, not knowing what to say. Stiles twisted the stem of his empty wineglass. The bottle had been empty for some time. Owen's glass still had a finger of Talisker, and his next sip was larger than the last; he felt it was time to finish it and leave.

"There is one other thing I should say and perhaps I should not," Stiles commented to the Washington wind.

"What?" Owen asked. "I suppose now you have to say it."

"Davis was blacklisted, of course. And like many, he continued writing in secret. Davis asked your grandfather whether he would formally take the credit for the scripts and pass on the money to him."

"After being betrayed by my grandfather, he trusted my grandfather with his money?"

"It is both hard to understand and not hard. I think he understood your father's betrayal and the dilemma he faced; I think he felt guilty about his own betrayal because he was also lucid enough to know, despite his socialist pretentions, that he had been lying for a long time. They, in fact, wrote in very similar styles, which helped. I think, also, Davis trusted your grandfather to remit the money to him because of the guilt your grandfather felt and because your grandfather, despite his wealth, did not care about money. Most of all, I think he wanted your grandfather to be trapped into another lie, and be forced to live it for as long as he had to, because he knew your grandfather would not refuse. Their destinies were then bound forever in mutual betrayals and mutual lies. They were both kind and unkind to each other, and the world was too complicated for them to be only one thing to each other. But that's psychoanalysis, not politics."

It was late. Stiles seemed to be drooping, his phrases increasingly telegraphic, and Owen moved to leave. Stiles, generously pretending that he would be welcome for hours more, nonetheless rose and walked him to the door. "Are you satisfied?" he asked.

"Yes," Owen said. "And grateful, and still curious."

"Your grandfather was a greater man than he even recognized. You share his unfortunate modesty."

It was an easy walk from the Watergate to his apartment, a night walk through the George Washington University campus, dotted with busts of the American Cincinnatus. He could see, a bit farther north, the cranes that were hauling up from the ground new edifices for the university. Great klieg lights illuminated the site as the buildings began to take shape. What did he, Owen, in his work, contribute to this great enterprise called America? A speech that would not be given, young minds untouched by lectures they would not remember, articles that would disappear in the slew of articles about the same thing and saying the same thing. His book, the fruit of a decade of study, travel, and observation, hardly noticed—except by one man who had happened to be an old friend of his grandfather's and who had offered him a job, a job that changed nothing about the world and contributed nothing to the great enterprise. Owen had built nothing permanent nor torn down anything bad nor even ground any flour to make bread to feed people. He had defended no freedoms. He did not have the satisfaction of an earned night's sleep. His grandfather was a book writer as well, but a man who had at least contributed to winning the Cold War, the great struggle of his time. He had been a player, a fighter, and had paid for it. And he had been successful enough that his works continued to pay for Owen's small extravagances. Owen felt very small beneath the rising buildings in the night.

CHAPTER 18

Encounter In The Library

Audrey thought she knew the woman but didn't recognize her at first. This bothered her, because she was normally good at remembering faces, but today she was tired. She worked the early-morning shift at Starbucks to earn money, then volunteered at the library in the afternoon because she was a librarian. She was afraid the woman would say something to her and she would still be unable to place her. She prepared herself as the woman approached the counter with her books, prepared herself for the embarrassment. But it did not happen. The lady looked at her with curiosity—the searching curiosity as to whether she was an interesting person, not the probing curiosity as to whether she was a person she should know. Audrey had always known she was pretty, and had long gotten used to the stolen glances of men, even their forthright stares, the jealous looks of girls her age, and the searching curiosity of older women who, it seemed, compared her with who they had once been. It was that latter look that she sensed from the older lady who approached. Audrey checked her books—four novels that were highly acclaimed at that moment. Novels, she thought, that Owen would have hated. How strange, this reappearance of Owen in her thoughts. He appeared in her imagination at the oddest times. She would look at a handsome young man, her age, and immediately compare him with Owen, and often find that she wanted to see him again, wanted to see him that instant, despite his flaws, his bad habits, his secrets, his reticence. Because only he looked at her as if she sat on a burnish'd throne, like he could throw away a kingdom for her if only he had one to throw away. It was then she realized, as the lady turned her back and walked out the library's door, that it was the silhouette she had seen in the kitchen the night that Laura had stayed over. It was Owen's mother. She checked the computer that had scanned in the books and confirmed it. The vanishing lady was Ingrid Cassell.

In the days that followed, until she saw her again, she remembered every detail. Yes, it was obviously her, the expressions were too similar, there was a certain fastidiousness in movement and gesture they both shared, as if they sensed being constantly observed and judged on the efficiency of their works. Audrey sensed obliquely that Owen and his mother did not get along, and was almost charmed by the extent to which he had, obviously unconsciously, imitated her gestures. It was the sort of thing she might be able to point out to him when they got to know each other a little better.

The next time the lady, Mrs. Cassell, came into the library, it was to return the books and check out others; she, like her son, was a reader. Audrey watched her carefully. This time she checked out a book on Buddhism. "My mother is very ecumenical in her religion," Owen had once said, when Audrey commented on the several Buddha sculptures in the apartment, the Islamic script in the shape of an eye, the sketching of Catholic monks that hung on the wall.

"She's tried them all, with equal degrees of insincerity," he had added. "Maybe not insincerity but looking in them for what any real religion will not provide—exotic beauty and convenience." Audrey had found the comment unkind but had not blamed him, sensing there was a context that was not worth pursuing.

Now, seeing the woman in person, she felt a strange sympathy for both her and her son, though she sensed it might ultimately be impossible to be sympathetic to them both. She found herself missing Owen. She had, in fact, been ignoring his messages lately—not ignoring them, she had told herself, simply unable to find a way to respond to them. She was caught, confused between the quietness of his ardor—she felt the intensity of his presence, even in the parsimony of his texts—and the clamor of his absence. Why, she asked herself, did Washington seem so far away? Why had she refused his invitations so far? She watched his mother, a small, intact lady dressed with understated taste, approach the counter. She felt a sudden impulse to say: I've fucked your son in your apartment on the twin bed in your guest room. But of course she didn't say it. She covered her mouth as if to stifle a laugh that pulled at her cheeks at the mere thought of saying it. "These are due back in a month," she said instead. Mrs. Cassell endeavored a smile, somewhere between sincere condescension and the feigned politeness to inferiors that true democracy requires. Who, Audrey asked herself, deserves an attitude between condescension and politeness? She thought about it as the lady left. A good servant, she decided. She momentarily disliked the lady and instead suddenly remembered Owen's sometimes pitiful face, his drunken default expression of determined resignation, a face that could never employ a servant. And she suddenly wanted badly to see him, and Washington did not seem so far away. It was quiet in the library, and she took out her cell phone.

* * *

Now, a few days later, came the lady again, made up carefully as usual, trying to cheat age, as usual, with age-old skills. (She had not, Audrey decided, been operated on.) She was dressed with casual elegance as usual, returning the Buddhism books and inquiring about recently published novels. She was still slightly tanned from her trip to California, and in a cheery mood. She smiled with friendliness as she approached. "I hope you're having a good morning," the lady said pleasantly, much more cheerfully than she ever had before.

"I am. Thank you very much," Audrey replied.

"It's a beautiful summer day," the lady said.

One of the novels was familiar to Audrey: *The Lacuna* by Barbara Kingsolver. Owen had said he'd read it. "I hear it's very good," she commented.

"I loved her first one. *The Poisonwood Bible*," the lady said. "Though I did not think I would. I don't think much of missionaries."

"A friend of mine read this one. He recommended it to me."

"A boyfriend?" the lady asked with a coy smile and an accent somewhat difficult to place. "A cute girl like you, you must have a boyfriend."

"Actually yes, kind of," she said, blushing, thinking: your son, actually, and suddenly imagining the three of them at lunch in the lady's grand dining room, drinking wine and hearing about when the lady had met Bill Clinton, for example, or even about her dead husband and what it had been like to be the wife of an ambassador. She would have to fake being surprised when they eventually met.

Audrey found it strange how her heart seemed to beat faster when she saw Mrs. Cassell a few days later at the library. She had never seen a woman who seemed to so own the space she walked in, tiny as she was. Audrey had discovered from one of the full-time librarians that the lady was on the board of the library, which partly explained the proprietary way she seemed to use it as an extension of her own house. But it only *partly* explained it.

"I've been meaning to ask you. Aren't you Marcia Walker's great-niece?" Mrs. Cassell asked the third time she came to the checkout desk.

"Yes," Audrey replied, surprised at the new cordiality in the old lady's demeanor.

"Marcia wrote that she had arranged for you to volunteer here. She asked me to make sure that you were fine and knew that we live in the same building. If you need anything, let me know. I'm also on the board here. We neighbors try to help each other out here in Baltimore."

"Thank you," Audrey said.

"My apartment is 5D, in the other wing from yours. But my door is always open." She smiled at Audrey. Audrey smiled back. Now she liked the lady and very much wanted to be liked by her.

A few days later the phone rang. One of the few things her great-aunt had asked of her, in exchange for staying in the apartment, was to answer the phone and take messages. Her aunt was paranoid about missing phone calls and had an old person's distrust of answering machines. Audrey picked up the phone. It was Mrs. Cassell, who announced herself as such. "Audrey," she said. "I believe I lent a muffin tin to your great-aunt before she left." She described it in some detail.

"If possible, could I come by now and get it? I'm hosting the book-club ladies tomorrow for brunch and would like to make muffins for them."

"I'd be happy to bring it over," Audrey said.

"Would you? That's very kind. Are you sure it's no trouble?"

"None at all. You're in apartment 5D, right?" The lie— pretending that she was not sure of where her apartment was—came easily, and Audrey did not like how easy it had been.

"Right," she said, echoing Audrey. "Five D."

Audrey, for reasons she did not question, after hanging up the phone, checked herself in the mirror, combed her hair, straightened her blouse, freshened her lipstick, and put on slightly more elegant shoes than the Crocs she had been wearing. She took the elevator down and walked across the lobby with the muffin tin, and waved away the concierge who asked if she needed the elevator. She walked up the five flights, regretting the heels, and rang the buzzer of 5D, shoulders straight, insides nervous. Mrs. Cassell opened the door and welcomed her in, saying with a polite smile, "I told you the door is always open. No need to ring the buzzer."

It was in many ways a very different apartment from the one she remembered. The radio was on NPR, and there were warm smells of baking as well as floral candles lit in the alcove where Audrey had once curled up and read Owen's journal. She followed Mrs. Cassell into the kitchen, still carrying the muffin tin. She was no longer the intimidating Mrs. Cassell, just a slight elderly lady doing her baking and wearing a housecoat and scooping out the Crisco to line the muffin cups. "Can I get you a cup of tea, while you're here?" she asked. Audrey, without thinking, said she would like that, and caught herself before mentioning a preference for the ginger tisane. The kitchen was ablaze with lights and smells, the countertops covered with dips and all sorts of finger food. The aromas of cumin and coriander joined with that of raisins and cinnamon from the oven. The kettle had been set on the fancy cast iron stove, and Mrs. Cassell put several spoons of loose-leaf tea into a pot while the water boiled in the kettle.

"You have a beautiful apartment," Audrey said to Mrs. Cassell.

"Thank you. It's mostly a little of this and a little of that from different parts of the world. My husband was a diplomat. But your aunt has very nice stuff, too," she said insincerely.

"She has nice stuff, but here it feels a bit like a museum you can live in. I like that."

"You're studying to be a librarian, I understand," Mrs. Cassell said, mixing the batter for the muffins that would go into the tin Audrey had just brought over. The sound of the mixer she then turned on stopped Audrey from answering the question immediately. When it stopped, Audrey said, "I have a bachelor's in information studies. I was a digital librarian in an architecture firm in North Carolina, but I lost my job. Now I'm going to get my masters in library science."

"That's good. This electronic media is fine, but nothing can replace a real book. That's why I donate to the Pratt."

The teapot began to wail, and Mrs. Cassell turned off the flame and poured the water into the pot. "Let's let it steep a little bit," she said. "This is a special tea from Russia. It has a wonderful flavor."

"Thank you," Audrey said, as the herbal smell briefly reached her and then dissipated.

"I gave my son a Kindle for Christmas. But in the end both of us prefer books you can flip through. He says the Kindle's good for travel, but he doesn't travel much anymore. He's a professor now, at Columbia University, in New York."

"I see," Audrey said. She was about to ask what he taught, but the lady interjected, "In fact, I travel more than he does these days. I have a Kindle too. I guess one day entire libraries will be accessible through machines. It seems a pity, though. I like the common space we have at the Pratt. What will happen to that?"

"I like to think," Audrey said, "that libraries are about more than storing information. They are spaces where people can meet and exchange information. And they preserve the past as well. Only a very small percentage of books are available electronically. Until they all are, which will be a very long time, I think libraries will become even more important."

"Well I hope you're right." The old lady turned and fixed her with a look of such agreement that Audrey dared to relax. "And we must preserve these great old spaces that we have, because they are exactly what you say they are: places to digest information, and to meet and interact as members of a society that values knowledge. Which I hope we still are."

On NPR someone was talking about the negotiations over the presidential debates between Obama and Romney. Audrey found herself strangely comfortable in this hearth, so strangely comfortable that—her tea finished—she felt it would be dangerous to stay much longer. She felt that the longer she stayed, the more her presence in this kitchen was a sort of lie to this nice lady who had invited her in. "Well, thank you for the tea," she said. "It's getting late."

"You don't have to go," Mrs. Cassell answered.

"Thank you," she said, descending from her stool. "It's late for me."

"Well, feel free to come by tomorrow," Mrs. Cassell said. "The book club, which your great-aunt is usually part of when she's here, meets at ten. We'll be discussing *The Lacuna*, actually, which you said you've already read. You would be most welcome."

"A great book," Audrey said, trying not to flush.

My son, thought Audrey as she left, descending the marble stairs in her heels, crossing the lobby again with its prints of old Baltimore, bidding good night to the old, stooped, white man on the night watch, who was gallant to her when she came in late, gallant almost to the point of lewdness. Now she waved him away from fetching the elevator for her, and ascended the five flights of her wing in her heels. *My son*, she thought, thinking of Owen, and deciding in the end to pour a glass of white wine. There was an opened bottle in the fridge from a few nights before. My son—and she had almost been on the verge, in the old lady's kitchen, of telling her: "Your son. My boyfriend, whose journals I've read, about the death of your husband, your son whom I will soon be seeing in Washington." She sipped the wine almost furiously, lying in her bed (in her great-aunt's guest bedroom), confused. Strange, she thought, how similar they were, mother and son, and how little they talked about each other. The same books, the same culture, the same strange American-but-not-quite-American accent. She felt somehow dirty, dishonest, for not having told Mrs. Cassell that she was sleeping with her son. She resented Owen for not allowing her to come clean. She sipped furiously again and refilled her glass in the kitchen, in the dark, using only the light of the refrigerator.

The light in the kitchen in the opposite wing was on, and she could see the silhouette of the old lady still bending to her oven, ministering to her lonely feast. She resented Owen for not himself telling his mother about her, for forcing her to pretend it was the first time she was there while she drank this woman's tea that she had already drunk, and comment on how beautiful the apartment was, as if it were a sincere and new thought. Love should not be a lie. She sipped furiously. It should not be a crime to hide the fact that she was thinking of him, and missing him more than she realized, and wanting to talk to him. She picked up her phone and texted him: "DC nxt wknd?"

CHAPTER 19

Georgetown Tobacco

The regular exercise was doing Owen good, and he had gotten up to thirty minutes on the treadmill at level six. He knew he had to give up the cigarettes and decided he would take up pipe smoking instead. He remembered his grandfather's pipes from his visits to Como. The smell of pipe smoke in fact was always entwined in his mind with his mother's hysterics, for she could not spend even a few hours with her father without one of them getting on the other's nerves. His grandfather had a temper—Owen had once overheard his grandfather castigating his agent on the phone. But he had never been anything but steely patient with his daughter. He had enough patience to let her explode first, and then she would cry, and then Owen's father would take her away to a hotel in town, leaving Owen alone with his grandfather for two weeks, his grandfather drinking martinis (when they were still allowed him) and smoking his well-discolored Meerschaums that he adored (and that he bequeathed to the gardener, who, at least the last time Owen had been there, still smoked them at Valeria's villa as he trimmed the hedges and planted the spring flowers).

It was a hot evening after work as he made his way from Dupont Circle, walking, to Georgetown, past the gay bars, over the P Street Bridge, peering down for a moment into Rock Creek, where the clothes of a homeless person were drying on a rock, as in a Third World country. Across the bridge, when reaching 30th Street, he cut down to M Street and walked along the narrow sidewalks, dodging the tourists and the pretty people, past the huge Nike store, the French restaurants, the antique stores. Georgetown, where the country's pain was hardly felt, where beautiful people strutted, but where one could sense a slight 1789 uneasiness—as if they were aware of the seething national discontent beneath them, and afraid that it could one day erupt. He stopped in front of an antique store that displayed a series of old cocktail shakers but didn't dare to go in to ask how much they cost. They would look nice in his small apartment, but so would many things and he was determined to stay within his budget. He carried on towards Wisconsin Avenue until he reached the tobacco store. He looked for Nathans, a restaurant that in the 1990s used to be a conservative hangout on the corner of Wisconsin and M Street, where he and Lisa had often dined with her father, where the New Hampshire senator had even liked to have a drink with his staff now and then. Now, where Nathans used to be, there was a sterile lavatory-like space that specialized in desserts. Why, Owen wondered, did all ice cream shops look like toilets?

Owen lived for a moment in that past that now had no monument, then entered the coolness of the tobacco store, where he had been several times to fetch a few cigars, which in those days you could smoke at Nathans. Here at least a monument remained. He was soothed by its wood paneling, the smell of smoke, and the staff who puffed on their pipes and cigars. In the far corner, where a motley collection of chairs was set up, a group of men sat and smoked cigars and chatted with some apparent familiarity. He barely glanced at them. A salesman came over and asked if he needed help and he, thinking that tobacco stores were the last commercial enterprises where real courtesy was extended, said he was interested in buying a pipe. The salesman called to someone else. "Warren is our pipe guy," he explained. A somewhat scrawny young man, a bit older than Owen, smoking a large-bowled, curved pipe, came over. He had a blond goatee and wore a worn denim shirt over faded khakis clinging to a thin waist by a once-olive-colored mesh belt that looked as if he had worn it since his Boy Scout days.

"Do you smoke pipes?" he asked. "Or are you just starting?"

"When I was in college I tried for a while. I gave it up for cigarettes."

"We have some starter pipes," Warren said, "in this basket. They're cheaper but they tend to wear out. They're good to start with if you're not sure you're going to like it."

"I'm going to like it. My grandfather smoked a pipe. I always loved the smell."

"Well," he said, tapping the glass case that separated them with the inclined stem of his pipe, "these Petersens and Savinellis are pretty good. The Petersen has a unique nib." Warren selected a few and placed them on the glass counter. Owen was listening and trying a few out for feel and heft and balance. He wanted a light pipe. His grandfather had once told him it was impossible to type with a heavy pipe in your mouth. You needed to find the light pipes to write with if you were going to write more than smoke.

"Owen?" The voice surprised him. It was followed by the movement of someone breaking away from the group of chatting men. The man coming towards him, in a suit, a nearly done cigar lingering between his fingers, a broad smile beneath green eyes. "Owen Cassell? It's James Porter."

"Of course," Owen said, shocked into recognition. "Nice to see you." Porter's shape had filled out, become more pear-like, and he had lost a bit of hair along the top of his scalp, where it lay thin and stringy, as if to say more was about to be lost. He looked older. This did not make Owen unhappy.

"What brings you to Washington?" Porter asked.

"I'm teaching here now."

"At Georgetown?"

"No. At the Institute for Geopolitical Statecraft."

"Never heard of it."

"It's a small master's program near Dupont." He was about to add the descriptive "conservative," but decided not to. He might, he thought, be outnumbered here, and was disinclined to take a stand. "And you?" he asked, as Porter drew on his cigar that had nearly gone out.

"I moved down here a few years ago."

"Let me know when you're ready," Warren interjected diplomatically, edging away from the pair. "And we can pick some tobacco for you."

"Thanks," Owen said. "I'll be there in a minute."

"I'm sorry about you and Lisa," Porter said. Owen realized that, like so many of the people who had once been a regular part of his life, he had not seen Porter since the divorce. "Hey, if you want, why don't we go down the street and get a drink. It would be great to catch up."

The offer was unexpected; welcome and unwelcome. "Give me a second," Owen said. He joined Warren where a few jars of blended tobacco stood and, since he was not focused anymore, picked the first one that Warren opened. Warren rang it all up and when Owen turned again to Porter, he was stubbing out his cigar in one of the large ashtrays set along the glass cases of pipes and cigars in all shades of brown.

As they walked down M Street again, towards the city and away from Georgetown, Owen briefly wondered why he had accepted this drink with this old rival. The bistro Porter selected was barely fifteen yards away, so he hardly had time to answer his own question. They walked in awkward silence, using the need to dodge the crowd—one going this way, the other going that, to avoid three ice cream-eating girls—as a reason not to try to have a conversation. But in these past months he had not had, except for Chilton Stiles, someone knowledgeable to talk to, to compete with. And perhaps Porter knew something about Lisa.

Porter ordered a beer, and while Owen was briefly tempted to do the same, he ordered a white wine instead. It seemed like that sort of evening. One paired wines with evenings like one did with food.

"You finished your doctorate then?" Porter asked.

"Yes. And published a book."

"Really?" He sounded genuinely impressed. "What is it called? I'll look for it on Amazon."

"*The New Medievalism.*"

"Oh, good lord," Porter said, smiling. "That really is you. I probably could have guessed that title if you had given me a minute. If not, I would have guessed something like *Prolegomenon to a New World Disorder After the Republicans Lost the Election to Obama.*"

The drinks arrived; they touched glasses, like épées before a duel, Owen thought. He tried to put himself in a jolly mood; he did not want to play the dour conservative with Porter, who was quick and always had known how to anticipate his tricks. But he realized he had been affected by his solitude; his skills at bantering had dulled. More than that, he still wondered if he had once been cuckolded by the man sitting perpendicular to him, at the corner of the bar, wiping beer foam from his still-smiling lips, quite satisfied at his last jest.

"And you?" Owen asked. "At a law firm I imagine. Or perhaps a lobbyist."

"Two very different things in this town. What would be your guess?"

"Fundamentally they are the same thing: representing any private interest at the expense of almost all public interest. But for you I would guess a law firm. Your vision of politics is too pure and exalted to allow you to go into lobbying. You fear that knowing how the sausage is made might dent your self-assured idealism, your deep faith in the goodness of the state."

"Excellent!" Porter laughed. "See, I knew there was something I missed about you. And by the way, you're exactly right—about working for a law firm, that is, but not the sausage bit. I'd like to think I'm not so naive as you suggest. Nor will I submit to the premise that a liberal attitude can only be sustained by ignoring reality. But the fact is I never really liked New York. I'm a political animal. New York was too much of everything else, and too fast to think in. In politics, you need to think."

"Is that a regular group there, at the cigar shop? You hang around and talk politics, and think?"

He laughed. "The rule is that you can talk of anything but politics. I have learned to discuss sports, even. I enjoy smoking cigars. It reminds me of my father. The little group there is rather erudite. We mostly talk about art."

"I confess I was always impressed with how much you knew about literature."

Porter gave a theatrical smile and raised his eyebrows. "And I was similarly impressed with your knowledge in general—and surprised at how far astray it led you politically."

He lifted his glass. Owen lifted his. They touched glasses again and drank. "I was always a reader," Porter said. "I guess that tends to make one a lawyer in the end."

"Or a professor."

"What is this dubious institute of yours, by the way? One of those conservative parallel institutions funded by some cranky old millionaire who hates Democrats and is sponsoring his own long march through the institutions—or perhaps, in this case, a children's crusade?"

"In a way." Owen was surprised at how close Porter was to the truth.

"Aren't you supposed to march through the institutions that actually exist, not create your own?"

"I completed a long and solitary march through Columbia. And then they spat me out."

"And you remained a conservative despite being surrounded by thoughtful, rational liberals? Lisa once told me you were brought up by liberal parents. She was raised as a Republican, but of course she voted for Obama."

"You're still in touch with her?"

"She's in DC you know."

"I had heard."

"I see her from time to time. I'll see her tomorrow night, in fact. A lawyers gathering."

Owen lifted his glass and drank. "Give her my regards," he said neutrally as he set the glass back down.

"I take it you're not in touch."

For Owen, who had not had a drink all day, it was already time for another, or it wasn't. He glanced at Porter's glass; he still had half his pint to finish. Owen tried to summon the waiter with his eyes. Then he did not want to appear as if he were evading Porter's question. "What do we have to say to each other any longer? The divorce was—not amicable but, you know, civilized. We agreed on everything in the end. The spoils were divided as among thieves—thieves of our own past, I suppose. But it didn't leave us with much to say to each other. The bone had been picked clean."

"You must have loved her once."

"Tremendously," Owen replied, too quickly and too honestly, he thought, long after he had said it. Then he thought it was an unusual comment from Porter, who had suddenly descended from his intellectual detachment to go slumming in the affairs of the heart. Owen tried to correct himself. "At least it was what I thought was love." The bartender was in front of him finally. At a nod the bottle was pouring itself into the glass, the bartender holding the bottle almost as if he were not necessary but merely there to support the bottle in case it should fall—a spotter, not a pourer.

Porter, as if himself embarrassed by his question of love, quickly—almost forcefully—returned to form. "I still don't know how someone as intelligent as you can still be a conservative. I do find you intelligent, you know, well-read, aware of history. And yet you insist on being on the wrong side of it. It must be so tiring to be you, to—what is that William F. Buckley line that you conservatives love about history?"

"To stand athwart it, yelling stop?"

"An inane line! It is glibness substituting for wisdom, like so many Buckleyisms. How can you even admire it, let alone construct your lives according to it? How can history even stop?"

"It depends what you mean by history. History is written by frustrated optimists. Why would a pessimist even write history? It would be like writing free verse, boring and obvious. But the man who believes in progress must write history. He must catalog the advances that confirm his view that we are going somewhere, and he must explain away the preponderant evidence that we are probably going nowhere. That's why he can't write history without taking sides. History is a grab bag of evidence to justify what he desperately needs to believe. For the conservative, though, history proves only one thing: the central narrative of humanity, our expulsion from the garden of Eden, is what endlessly returns. Man is vain and stupid and yields to every temptation, and because of that he is doomed to crawl through this vale of tears. I enjoy history for its narrative, its poetry, for its cunning passages and contrived corridors, as Eliot put it. But to me it confirms the tragedy of humanity and the impossibility of real progress."

"You haven't changed. In some ways it's endearing, if it weren't so frustrating, and perhaps even dangerous to the republic. A man like you in a position of responsibility could do a lot of damage. I mean that as a compliment of sorts."

"Republic! That doesn't really have a political meaning for you, does it? There is no room for something quaint like a democratic republic in your grand progressive schemes." Owen was now on his third glass of wine (the bartender, spotting him now as a real consumer, had become hoveringly attentive), and he felt the conversation had gone beyond the natural moment where it could be saved by a sarcastic comment and an agreement to disagree. It was time to go home, light his new pipe, drink a few whiskeys in solitude, and continue to work on "Leviathan in Knots." But he ventured one more comment. He had been thinking of it for half an hour but hesitated to say it. But now the topic of the right side and the wrong side of history was introduced. He thought he had scored more points. Touché! But now judgment was slipping. "There is one way," he said in a voice kept low by intense effort, "in which I am, however, on the right side of history."

"What is that?

"I'm working on the Romney campaign, writing speeches."

"Oh, good lord," Porter said, with that perfect mix of condescension and ridicule that unnerved Owen because it was so automatic and so natural.

"This is a free country with two parties," Owen said. "And the Republican party is still legal as far as I know. Why do you liberals always make it a crime to work for the other party? It's as if you're afraid your edifice will not survive anyone's challenge, even one by the supposed stupid party."

"It's not that the edifice won't withstand the stupid challenges of the stupid party," Porter said. "It's not that it's illegitimate or illegal to work for the Republican party. It's that you think you're on the right side of history by backing old Mittens. You actually think he's going to win?"

"Absolutely," Owen replied. He was about to launch into a discussion about skewed polls, massive Tea Party mobilization, a disappointed youth vote that had been for Obama in 2008 but that was likely to stay home because nothing had gotten better for them, but his instinct for diplomacy seized him. It had been too long a discussion already with a man whom he had once highly distrusted. It had been several wines. It was time to cordially end this. "We'll see in November," he said. But Porter couldn't wipe the smile off his face.

They parted on the sidewalk, going in separate directions. Porter had insisted on picking up the check, saying it had been like a blast from the past to hear Owen pronounce the same arguments he always had—but wasn't that what being a conservative meant: providing the wrong answers to yesterday's questions? And Owen replying that he admired Porter's ability to turn back the clock, and making Porter laugh. Then Porter went towards Georgetown, where he lived, and Owen began walking east back to his studio in Foggy Bottom. The night had grown dark and cooler, the sidewalks were full of nightlife people who did not watch where they were going, who stared at their stupid smartphones as they walked. Owen was a bit less adept at dodging them now, and in his mild drunkenness reminded himself to stop at the liquor store on the other side of the bridge to get a bottle of whiskey.

While on the bridge over Rock Creek Park, he admitted to himself that the reason he had accepted drinks with Porter was precisely to tell him that he was working on the Romney campaign. It had not been an accident to say it; in fact he had been probing the conversation all night for the right moment to say it. He felt inferior to Porter, especially these days, teaching at the institute. So the moment had come but it had been a mistake. He had expected Porter to be mildly impressed, but his genuine disdain—his almost sympathetic pity—had been all the more lacerating for being so automatic and honest. Now Porter was walking back to his house in Georgetown. Owen tried not to imagine what it might look like, whom it might contain (a pretty wife? precocious children?), how large it might be. He trudged back to the one thing he had earned in his life, that had not been paid for by his grandfather, his ground-floor studio in a 1950s building in Foggy Bottom where the centrally controlled air conditioner blew too cold all summer long. Everything else had been merely received. By the time he entered the clean brightness of the liquor store, not even the familiar Cutty Sark label could dislodge the sense of utter failure that coiled within him like a tapeworm.

The sense of failure accompanied him home, then was moved by drink into a sense of melancholy. He put on some of the old songs on his iPod, the songs that reminded him of that brief happy time at the beginning with Lisa. At times like this, late at night, drunk, in the right mood, he wondered if he still loved her despite everything. That was what Porter had done to him. Watching his satisfied, sarcastic face earlier in the evening, he remembered how he had once been jealous of him; being jealous of him reminded him that he had once feared Lisa's betrayal; fearing her betrayal reminded him how much he had loved her. The fact was—and he had analyzed this for weeks sitting amid the post-divorce ruin of his marriage—he would have given in on the in vitro thing in the end. He had just been surprised at how vehemently she had attacked his position, and so he had attacked her back. And the viciousness had been so sudden that it had become impossible to reset the foundation stones, repair the beams, fix the windows, and replace the roof of the house they had pledged to build together.

He finally went to bed, stumbling even in the tiny space, thinking dimly: one day I'd like to tell her that I would have given in. Why did we strike so hard and so fast at each other? They would be right now living together in the apartment in New York, with a couple of twins running around, and he would have been able to love them too and forget in the end the plastic cup and the porn DVD that had been their genesis.

CHAPTER 20
Caravaggio's "Isaac"

When he left his mother's apartment in June to move into his apartment in Washington, Owen had left a note on the kitchen counter thanking her for the use of the apartment and telling her to call when she returned. He had left, as well, a box of elegant tulips made from hand-cut, recycled, painted paper he had found in a boutique in Washington: tasteful, personal, perennial. They did not need to be watered while she was on her frequent trips. She called him when she returned and thanked him for the flowers. They had one of their stilted conversations, avoiding politics until she couldn't resist a jab at Romney, which he tried to deflect as quickly and neutrally as possible. "I suppose you're supporting him," she said dismissively. He changed the conversation to Salzburg—not telling her he was in fact writing a speech for Romney. The festival that year had featured Cecilia Bartoli singing Handel's "*Giulio Cesare in Egitto.*" She told him she was going to spend a few weeks in Baltimore and then visit friends in California and that she expected, when she returned at the end of August, perhaps a visit from him in Baltimore.

* * *

The Thursday evening before Audrey was to come to Washington, he returned to his apartment and found a note from management under his door saying there was a package waiting for him at the office. He found this strange since he had given his address to hardly anyone, nor had he even checked his own mailbox. It was late August and he had been in the place nearly three months. Only his mother had the address, because she was his emergency contact on the lease and they had contacted her to confirm. He set his briefcase down on the couch and looked at his watch. There was still time to get to the management office a block away before it closed.

The receptionist looked at the note and checked the list of packages and frowned. Then she said: "It's actually not a package. It's just that mail has been piling up in your mailbox, and when it gets full the mailman brings it here." She went to the storage room and brought back a sheaf of mail curled and held together by two thick rubber bands. Back at his apartment he went through it: mostly it was for his previous tenant—several months' worth of George Washington University alumni magazines, fliers from pizza and cable companies, credit card offers, and the usual bits of paper that circulate and accumulate regardless of whether one is dead or alive. There was, however, to his surprise, one letter, and it was from his mother. He recognized the stationery: thick, personalized, embossed envelope and paper from Crane & Co. in Boston. He sighed and opened the letter, fearing what it might contain. A letter from her signified emotion, and emotion was almost always problematic. He read the familiar, slanting, cobalt-blue fountain pen ink, briefly visualizing her Princess Grace Mont Blanc with its mother-of-pearl cabochon, and then allowed himself to be slapped by the words.

"I had expected to hear from you by now. Whether you like it or not, and I can only presume that you don't, I'm your only family left. I might not be around for much longer, but I would like to know what I have done to you..." It went on to the other side of the page in that paranoid vein, and simply reading it gave him a migraine. He poured a large drink from the scotch carafe; more than usual, but it did not help. His automatic sense of guilt then changed to one of reproach. She was supposed to have called him. He could not concentrate on anything, not even on what, all that day, had been the happy anticipation of Audrey's arrival.

* * *

He was waiting for her at Union Station, in front of the Hudson News store where the MARC passengers came out from the platform. She emerged like a Technicolor princess against the drab crowd coming into Washington for whatever it was they came for. She wore blue jeans and a colorful blouse, and sandals with a slight heel that gently lifted her shapely legs. She smiled when she saw him, handed him her canvas weekend bag to carry, and kissed him. He was surprised at the warmth of her greeting, hardly expecting it after the previous weeks of hesitance. She had always been a little bit hot and a little bit cold with him, which to him had added to the sheer intrigue of her; so young and unsure, always poised to fall yet in the end always poised. He kissed her achingly and held her thin waist as they walked towards the dark Metro entrance.

When they emerged from the Foggy Bottom station, riding the escalator up to the street, the evening sun dipping behind them, still holding her bag in one hand and her hand in the other, he glanced at her profile. She was beautiful in the dying light, as she always had been to him in the half light of night, when the sirens of the city wailed and they had made love. Then, his senses had always been dulled by his bad habit, but he had not had a drink in several days this time. The weekend bag he held seemed suddenly to him, as he walked, a totem of a deeper commitment than he had known in a long time, than he had even expected.

"Hungry?" he asked.

"A little bit."

"I thought we would eat at home. I prepared a little something."

"You cooked?"

"Sort of. The kitchen's very small but I've mastered a few dishes."

"I can't wait."

"It's a small place."

"I'm not a big girl."

He kissed her.

"This is it?" she said, when he opened the door to his studio. It had only taken her a moment to realize that there was not much more to it than what she saw from the front door: the bathroom, the closet, and the small kitchen. But she had not said it in a mean way. She had said it with the satisfaction of arriving. He watched her do her quick assessment of the place before she sat down on the futon.

"It's very you," she said, glancing at the bookshelf, the prints on the wall, the bar with the crystal carafe of cheap Cutty Sark and the other bottles he had recently bought.

"I have to heat up a few things, but can I get you a drink in the meantime?"

He had stocked his bar with whatever he thought she might want—white wine mostly, but she also sometimes drank vodka martinis.

"What are you having?"

"I think I'll start with a Campari and soda. I haven't had a drink in days," he added, and then felt self-conscious about admitting it.

"Do you have vodka?" she asked.

"Of course."

"And tonic?"

"Assuredly."

"Then I'll have that." He made the drinks, put on some music from a playlist he had prepared for this weekend, and she joined him in the tiny kitchen while he made the final preparations for dinner. He had made a fig salad and orange snapper fillets and had marinated vegetables that he now put in the oven to roast.

There was enough room in the kitchen for a small round table in the corner and two chairs. He sat down and clinked his glass with hers. She placed one leg on his knee when he sat down, and it seemed like the most natural thing in the world.

"You've lost weight," she said.

"I've been trying not to smoke, and to exercise a bit more. There's a small gym in the basement, and I've been doing a little bit every morning. It helps when you don't drink—at least during the week I try not to drink. I'm getting back into my fighting form."

"For me?" She was suddenly frightened of the changes he was making to himself.

"For whom I think you deserve."

"You don't have to. I've dated athletes without a bit of body fat, so they said. They had nothing else to say, though, and were always staring in the mirror. That's not what a woman wants in the end."

"Exercise helps me pass the time that I used to spend drinking and smoking. It tires me out after work. I come home, work out, shower, cook something healthy, do a little work, and go to sleep. I find myself looking forward to those clear mornings. I had forgotten for a while what it was like to wake up sober."

"That's great. All I'm saying is, don't do it for me."

"But why not?" As soon as he saw her face, he wished he hadn't asked the question. It had come out harshly, as if he were daring her to tell him to go to hell. She was quiet for a while. "You change yourself for someone," she said, "and you end up being someone for someone else." Her reply melted him. He only wanted to lean over and kiss her and tell her how wrong she was. He was thinking, the silent seconds creating—he sensed—a massive misunderstanding. "Audrey," he said. "I do it to become the man I think you deserve. And that's the man I want to be. Apart from anything else, it's good for me. Take it as a compliment, not as an act of dishonesty."

She accepted that and smiled, and he said, "I've planned a perfect day for tomorrow." He asked her if she had heard of Caravaggio, which she hadn't, and he began to describe the exhibit and where he thought they would go to brunch.

Audrey sought, in the openings of the conversation, to find a way to mention that she had met his mother. None of the openings seemed big enough, right enough, so she didn't mention it. He had opened a bottle of white wine to go with the fish, and they finished it. When they went to bed he was still very sober and explored her lithe body with an unusually light touch long after they had finished and she had gone to sleep.

* * *

They woke up late. They made love again, turning to each other without discussion or inhibition. Afterwards, he showered while she gradually woke up. She was young enough to need her sleep and slow to become herself in the morning. He made coffee while she showered and gradually made herself up as she got used to the unfamiliar space and the tiny bathroom he had just cleaned. It was sunny and hot that morning, and they walked to a healthful restaurant on Pennsylvania Avenue for brunch, a few blocks from the White House. She noticed that he didn't drink and was for some reason glad. Then they took the subway to the National Gallery, as he had planned.

"One day," he said, "I have to tell you about my grandfather. He was the one who introduced me to Caravaggio. This exhibit compares the paintings of Caravaggio and Rembrandt. Both of them were extraordinary masters of light." Then he added, "I'm so glad you texted me about coming down this weekend, because this exhibit is closing in two weeks. I had thought about asking you to come to see it, but I didn't want to put any pressure on you."

"I wanted to see you," she said. "For a while I thought that maybe we shouldn't see each other, and that it would be easier in the end, since I'm going north in a few weeks. But I wanted to see you." He squeezed her hand and didn't ask any questions. She leaned her head against his shoulder and smelled the cologne she had smelled in the bathroom that morning, after he had showered. It was now decayed and mingled with his particular smell that now lacked the hangover of tobacco. She held herself against him agreeably while the Metro car shot through the tunnel.

The exhibit was crowded because it was a weekend, but they found their spaces in front of the paintings. She loved him more, she realized, for the exhilarating passion of his commentary. He tried to be fair to the two painters, but he could not hide his preference for the Caravaggios. But she loved that he tried to be fair; she loved that he cared enough about her to share this, with her; she loved that he respected her intelligence so much that this was how he would spend the day, his arm around her shoulder, his warm voice in her ear, that nowhere accent describing things that mattered to him. And everything about him, she felt, was a desire to share what was most important to him but that he would not dare to reveal to just anyone. She could almost feel the quickening of his pulse in the hand that she held, that she would not let go of.

Here he explained this use of light, that thickness of brush, this point of anatomy—the muscles rendered perfectly, learned on an illegal slab of a Florentine morgue—the surprising accessories that he painted with stunning reality. Caravaggio had been the first painter to say that it took as much skill to paint a fruit correctly as it did to paint a saint. The point was to make it real. He loved the cocked-head attention with which she listened to him, that she asked intelligent questions, that she sought the source of his amazements and even had amazements of her own. It seemed to confirm to him that he had found some sort of gem.

She was thinking to herself, as she listened to him discuss this Caravaggio, how much like his mother he was. They had certain of the same mannerisms, the same not-quite-American accent he had once described as "international-school English," and that had made his mother sound almost foreign to her the first time they spoke. And they both seemed to her, in an exciting way, almost too engaged in these things of culture. It was not that she found something wrong with it, it was that she wanted to be more like them, like both of them, and she wanted them to like each other more than they seemed to. And so she listened carefully to this strange man who was probably just a little bit too old for her, who probably couldn't quite give her what she would eventually need, but who still seemed to be able to pull her towards him.

Both Rembrandt and Caravaggio had painted Abraham about to kill Isaac, and the curator had placed the two side by side. Owen stood far enough back to contemplate them both, holding her hand. For these two paintings he offered no commentary. They were the same scene and yet they were stunningly different. Rembrandt's Abraham seemed relieved when the angel knocked the blade from his hand; his other hand held over Isaac's face, shielding his son from what he was about to do. Caravaggio's Abraham, though, seemed frankly annoyed at the angel's interruption, as if he distrusted the angel and his message, and was half ready to dismiss it as a heavenly hoax and slit his son's throat as first instructed. The palm of his left hand was pressing into the nape of his son's neck, the knife moving in, while the angel seemed almost desperate to hold it back. The mouth of Caravaggio's Isaac was open in what seemed at first like a scream—a last-gasp plea to his father. His grandfather had pointed out, many years ago, that when you look at the precise position of Abraham's thumb on Isaac's mandible, the scream was probably a silent reflex gasp that seemed to separate parent from child as cleanly as death would have. From the side of the painting, a ram looked on with curiosity and relief, as if thinking: there but for the grace of God...

He had made reservations at Morton's in Georgetown for dinner, early, to get a table. They went by taxi, freshly showered and perfumed, holding hands through the long wait of DC traffic lights, watching the jostling army of pedestrians crowding the narrow sidewalks of M Street, waiting for the signal to attack, and once he could not resist leaning over and kissing her. She turned to him and smiled, and he wished right then that he had a camera to capture that smile. He had told her to pack for a nice dinner, and she wore a summer dress that was white with slanted navy stripes and the white-heeled sandals she had worn the previous afternoon. She looked gorgeous to him. He himself had taken care in what he chose to wear: light, almost white linen slacks, a new pair of supple leather moccasins that had cost shy of two hundred dollars from his slight savings, a white shirt, and a Brooks Brothers seersucker jacket he had found on Craigslist and bought for forty-nine. He felt regal, like Hollywood royalty, but sober, following her as she followed the maître d' to their table, watching her from behind, watching the others in the restaurant watching her, remembering the first time he had seen her silhouette that rainy night in Baltimore when she had been afraid of him and he had fallen in love with her.

He ordered a whiskey sour and she, feeling happy and comfortable and beautiful, picked a negroni from the cocktail menu.

The cocktails arrived. They talked about the exhibit. He wanted to know what she thought of the paintings. They compared the Isaacs. His points to her were rendered in a sort of detail that she almost found unappetizing. Something else, though, was on her mind, which she had thought about before coming down. It was something she had begun thinking about the previous night, after they had made love, and it had hardened during the day, as they had held hands and looked at the paintings, when she had realized not only that she loved him more than she had realized, but that he seemed to need her more than she had believed.

"Summer is almost over," she finally said. "I'm leaving in a few weeks. I'm going to Syracuse for two years. You're here. How does this end?"

"I don't think it needs to end."

"You're being romantic and I'm being real. You must have noticed that I've been hesitant about answering your emails and texts recently."

"You must have noticed that I kept sending them. And you finally texted me back about this weekend."

"I don't know what to do. I don't know if this can work or not."

"Do you want it to? That is the only real question. I know I do. I can't get you out of my mind."

"I don't want to want something I can't have."

"Imagine," he said as the waiter appeared to pour the wine. "Imagine that I was a wizard who could make it all work if you wanted it to. Just for the sake of things, imagine I could move to Syracuse and find work near there, either teaching or a contract for a next book, which I'm working on anyway." He tasted the wine and told the waiter it was fine. "Imagine that I could support myself decently while you studied, and we were together while you studied. And after you graduated we could make other plans, depending on how things went for both of us. If all of that were possible, would you take it?"

"We hardly know each other."

"How else will we get to know each other? Audrey, I'm not rooted to any place. What I do, I can do in a lot of different places. I have, as well, some resources of my own, despite what it may look like by the way I live. And I'm not saying marry me, I'm saying give us a chance to not lose something that might in the end be something that can't be replaced. I'm crazy about you."

"What do you see in me?" she asked, sipping deeply from her wine and then wiping her mouth because she felt she had drunk too much. "I'm not like you in so many ways. You've traveled, you've experienced things. I'm just a girl from Carolina who lost her job and ditched her boyfriend and thought you were a rapist when I first saw you."

Owen dropped his head and let his shoulders droop and then wished he hadn't. He had dropped his guard. The gesture reminded him now that he had to be on guard against his reflexes. The reflex had been normal; how does one answer a question like that? "You beg the question," he said.

"What do you mean?"

"When you say, 'What do you see?' you assume that it's about what I see. You're young and beautiful and fresh, like eight girls on the Metro every morning, like six girls in my classes every day, like twenty on the sidewalk when I walk to work. It's not about what I see. It's deeper than that, and harder to put in words."

"You sound now like how you wrote about Lisa fifteen years ago."

He had forgotten she could use his own journals against him. He had not wanted this dinner to turn into this chess match, requiring the application of mental energy, the evaluation of positions, the hedging tactics of lovers unsure of themselves. He understood her distrust and was aware of the insufficiency of his answers. Nothing he could say to her could be any different from what he had said to Lisa fifteen years before. And she was where Lisa was fifteen years before. Perhaps Audrey deserved her Prince Charming, and not the recycled chump that he was. She had played her trump card, and it was all he could do not to drop his head and let his shoulders sag again. But he did not; he held himself up straight and looked at her, as if unaffected by her piracy of his past.

"What Lisa taught me was that there are no guarantees. I was at an age when I thought there were guarantees, and I believed in a sort of love that worked just because it was love. But people drift apart, and it's the hardest thing in life to learn how not to drift apart. I'm not offering you guarantees. I'm offering you myself, for better or for worse. That's a deal that Lisa wouldn't take."

"I would feel terrible to make you move to Syracuse. It doesn't make any sense. You have your job here."

"Also," he ventured, "I might have an opportunity, later in the year, depending on the election."

"Do you have a chance to work with the Obama administration?" she said. "That would be wonderful! Oh, you couldn't come to Syracuse. It's too big of an opportunity for you. I would visit you here, though. You could take me to the White House."

"Well," he said, heeding the inner coward again, "nothing is for sure. Let's wait for what must happen to happen." There would be another time to deal with this issue, he thought, sipping his wine. He simply could not risk it in this moment, though the evasion left him feeling more like a spy than a lover. For the first time, he realized, she did actually have strong opinions of her own. He had thought—or had wanted to think—that she wore her political positions casually and that he would one day be able to nudge her towards him. To tell her who he was became suddenly more necessary, but radically more dangerous. This was not, he thought, the place or the evening for it.

"We don't have to decide it tonight," he said. "I just wanted you to know that I was serious. I think you might be the last person I ever love." He did not know why he said the last sentence. He knew he had thought it, and he believed it; he just couldn't believe it had come out of his mouth.

"Oh God," she said automatically. "That's too much responsibility." He watched her with the look of a chess player who had just taken his hand off his queen and seen on the board he had lost her. The rest of the evening was awkward small talk, a quiet cab ride back to his apartment, and two bodies on separate sides of a queen bed, not touching. With knowing dread Owen began to hear, through the walls, the slow-rising moans of the neighbor's orgasm, mysteriously induced by the silent lover. To hear that and feel the warmth of Audrey's body, young and lithe beside him—it was hours before he finally slept, hours aching to touch her.

The next morning he woke before her and made omelets and coffee and baked fresh croissants that came in a tube. He prepared it all, imagining the perfect weekend. There was nothing left to do but follow the plan. The smell of pastry and coffee filling the studio woke her up. She emerged from the shower wearing exactly what she had worn when she had arrived at Union Station thirty-six hours before: her traveling clothes. Her leaving-him-behind clothes, he thought. He had lain awake most of the night trying to find solutions. He had written in his mind screenplays of the conversation they might have. He had barely slept and hardly remembered the dialogues that had robbed his sleep. Now, out of the shower, her perfume was summery and her wet hair fragrant with shampoo, and for a moment her soapy female presence in the kitchen overwhelmed the smell of baking. He took the croissants from the oven and put them on a plate and served her the omelet. "I could get used to this," she said. He didn't say anything. His offer the previous night was precisely for her to get used to this. "This is my grandfather's recipe," he said about the omelet. It had tomatoes, asparagus, and pecorino cheese that he had specifically bought at the Whole Foods near Foggy Bottom station. "Delicious," she said. He wondered if last night's unpleasantness, the non-resolution of their future, had been totally forgotten or was simply being ignored.

"I'm sorry about last night," he said.

"You're mother's back," she said at the same time.

"I know," he responded automatically. Then he looked up at her. "How do you know?"

"I saw the light in her apartment."

"You still look over there?"

"I saw the light go on. For a minute I thought it was you."
He nodded and said nothing.

"You haven't gone to visit her?" she asked.

"You were coming here this weekend."

"She's been back for a few weeks."

"We have a complicated relationship," Owen said. "She called me when she got back, but said she was going to California to visit friends for a few weeks, and for me to visit when she gets back. In the meantime, I've been busy."

"I think I'd like to meet her," Audrey said, uncomfortable with her lie, fidgeting with her fingers under the table.

"She's a tough judge of people," he said unthinkingly, thinking of his mother more than of Audrey, realizing his mistake too late.

"You mean I wouldn't pass?" Audrey accused. "Why would you say that? Am I too dumb for your brilliant family?" A squall of anger darkened her face; an eyebrow remained arched afterwards. The truth was, he thought, his mother probably would dismiss this girl. She was too young. She was a librarian, not an intellectual. She was a bit too provincial for his cosmopolitan mother. She, like Lisa, was from the south, which his mother distrusted. The mood in the small apartment had suddenly darkened and now Audrey was spoiling for a fight.

"She places great weight on how much of the world people have seen," he tried to explain. "She's a bit of a snob." Even Lisa, he remembered, had had a hard time, despite coming from a wealthy Washington family and having once summered in Europe and spent a semester abroad in Argentina. With Lisa it hadn't helped, of course, that her eminent Washington family was Republican. But he realized that Audrey was

206

angry, angry in a something-to-prove sort of way, and he wished she were not so young and he had not been so stupid.

"Well, I think you should visit your mother," she said.

Later he took her to the station and they left it at that.

CHAPTER 21

Doldrums

The last two weeks of August were the least busy time for the institute. Dean Cernic went to Florida, leaving the dreary building in Owen's hands. Owen looked forward to a relaxing few weeks. He would teach, the following semester, the two courses he had taught in an accelerated fashion over the summer: Introduction to Strategy and Statecraft, and Historical Patterns of American Foreign Policy. He was comfortable enough with the material for both classes; the texts were classics and didn't need to be updated. His notes were already prepared and easy to lecture from. He had already planned, while Dean Cernic was away, to spend most of the time doing research on his grandfather. Perhaps there was a biography in there. His last conversation with Stiles had given him the idea.

He worked at the institute from eight in the morning until two. He ate a light lunch while working—still trying to lose weight anyway for Audrey, though he had not heard from her since her visit. He would arrive at the Library of Congress by three, and be able to read there under the large dome for several hours. He discovered that no biography had yet been written about his grandfather. The library's collection did have an unpublished dissertation about his fiction, which included some details on his life. The dissertation had been written in the 1980s by what appeared to be a conservative PhD candidate. This was, of course, before the infamous article. At that time, the two criticisms of Silas Stone, mostly from the left, had been for his decision to give Gene Powell Davis's name to the House committee in the 1950s, and two decades later, for the revelation that *Remnant* had been funded by the CIA. It was the latter charge the PhD candidate sought to defend. In doing so, he also tried to exonerate him of the former.

But at least three books had been written about Gene Powell Davis. Among them was a memoir by his daughter, which Owen opened one afternoon in the Library of Congress. This was his favorite way of working: reading, taking notes by hand, his fountain pen drawing ink on good paper, losing himself for hours in the thoughts of the writers he was reading and the thoughts that gave birth to themselves as he wrote and commented. Like this he could lose hours of his life and not even need a drink.

Sylvia Davis, Gene Powell's daughter, narrated her teenage years in 1950s California: daughter of a successful novelist and screenwriter, privileged student at a Beverly Hills high school, in love with her father and intimidated by the remote beauty of her mother, a mother who was a fading actress trying to resurrect her career by writing a memoir (never published but available to her daughter), and who was indifferent to her daughter, whose youth, even her lesser beauty, was a reminder of all she was losing. Of course the parents were separated and awaiting a divorce that in those days, before no-fault, had to be schemed: faked adultery in a hotel room, private investigators, the judge shaking his head, the press running the story for good measure. There was no such thing as irreconcilable differences; in those days most differences were presumed to be reconcilable, or vowed as such. Owen, reminded of Lisa and the ease of their divorce after the quick erosion of their vows, pushed past this line of thought and moved on. Teenage Sylvia, then finding her own writing voice (she would go on to have some success as a teleplay writer in her own right), disparaged her mother's cracked and keening prose and ridiculed the late-career flings with faded stars and failing producers. She adored her father, his wisdom, his concern for the fallen world, his desire for global justice, his faith in the Soviet Union as the promised land of the New Man.

With those sentiments in those days it was only a matter of time before the FBI would come knocking at Gene Powell Davis's door. She described with moving pathos the persecutions that began, petty at first, then more intimidating, then decisive. She described with particular vehemence the hearing at which Silas Stone had named her father's name. Just like in the *Lacuna*, she provided the transcript of the hearing, annotated with perfect little barbs of acid logic. Owen could not blame her, but it made him want to write a defense of the old man. He began to write that defense, leaving her book aside for a moment, filling sheets of his ruled paper. But there *were* Communists, but they *did* infiltrate the government, but the Soviet Union was not in the end the utopia of the New Man, who in any case had never been born. And what might the daughters of those who perished in the Siberian gulags have written of this Davis, who had defended before the world the system that had stripped them of their dignity and later of their lives? And Davis had broken the law, as imperfect as it was. And Davis, for all his daughter's admiration of him, seemed even by her account a stubborn, selfish, pretentious man. When Owen looked at his watch he found he had spent nearly an hour on the defense—filled nearly six pages with tightly written script, legible practically only to himself, that went all the way to the margins—and that his head ached. The library would close in an hour.

He took up her book again, laying down his own notes, reading quickly, skimming the bits about what seemed a meaningless summer romance with a young writer who was also a handsome lifeguard at a nearby pool. It was the stuff of vapid teenage diaries, the embarrassing idiom in which first loves are always described, the prose always reading the same, no matter the quality of the writer, no matter the quality of the lover. (He recognized it in himself from his early journals.) But these pages read as if they were merely spruced-up versions of her adolescent diary entries, then interrupted by actual citations of her diary. He cringed at them. He skimmed the flushed retelling of being picked up in the lifeguard's convertible for economical dates on the shore with cheap fried chicken and moonlight, and heavy petting, and his teenage loveliness, and the rivals for his affection among the other girls from school who also went to the pool. Owen skimmed faster, wondering when it would end and wondering why anyone would publish this drivel, let alone write it. And then he turned the page and stopped, and read slowly.

She had somehow gotten pregnant. Somehow the heavy petting—she had never confessed to anything more—had led to some sort of miraculous meeting of his semen with her eggs even though he had never penetrated her. This was 1954, a year after her father had been blacklisted, when he was out of work, had sold his home, and was living in a small apartment in Venice Beach, drinking in the unconstrained way that a man with nothing left to live for drinks—or, if you're Fitzgerald, the way a man with everything left to live for can drink, if he is a drinker. It was painful in those days for her to visit him, to

211

see this lion caged, this object of her adoration almost giving up on everything he said he had fought for. Owen looked for the first time at the front matter of the book. It had been published in 1994, when she was nearly sixty. He returned to the text, where she was telling her mother she was pregnant; she had reached the point where it could not be concealed any longer. Her mother, unsurprisingly aware of these things, made arrangements.

She described how she went away for a weekend, a weekend she was supposed to spend with her father, telling him instead she was spending it with a friend in Malibu who was celebrating her birthday, but that she would see him on Sunday after the party. Instead she went by bus to the house of a woman who did that sort of thing, in Ventura. (Very much, Owen thought, *not* a birthday.) She took the bus to the specified stop and was met there by a man, the woman's husband, who recognized her immediately, presumably from the bulge, and drove her to what she described as a run-down house in a cracked and weedy neighborhood. The woman, whom she described as a "witch doctor," told her to take the pill she had been told to buy before arriving. She took the pill and when the pill had finally relaxed her the witch doctor shoved a hose up her vagina and injected fluid. That was Friday night. She was to return to her father's on Sunday, but by Saturday evening the baby had still not been induced. It was terrible for Owen to read of those hours, when the dead fetus would not be expelled, the witch doctor who yelled at it through the flesh of the womb, calling it to come out, like some exorcist—thirty-six hours of waiting, of pushing, of agony, of fear, of holding herself over a bedpan, the witch checking the fluids. Then, finally, she felt it slithering through her organs and dropping with a pulpy flop into the tin bedpan, with the witch picking through the fluid to find the lump, cutting it

212

up with tweezers, and Sylvia Davis looking down and seeing a bit of tiny leg amid the pulpy red. *I'm sorry, baby,* she thought to herself. Owen looked up suddenly to the grand dome of the Library of Congress reading room. This, he thought, was some excellent writing.

In that moment, the horror of the abortion so well-described, Owen, the liberal-cum-conservative, dared to believe that she also might have become a conservative in the end, or at least pro-life, or at least tolerant of those who were. It would have been a stunning climax to a book filled up to then with all the intellectual clichés of the genre: the bookish girl who thought too much, whose uniquely fascinating life was impossible to comprehend by her peers—those bubble-gum-chewing masses who had few inner anguishes beyond wondering what skirts to wear in the morning and what beer to drink in the evening, who had no true understanding of the world, because they were merely uncritical consumers of whatever news was placed before them, unlike her, who at the tender age of sixteen did not care about skirts but truly understood the world! But there was no stunning climax. The abortion was done, the boredom and the pain were endured, the mission was accomplished, and it was "I'm sorry baby" and then off to live the superficially examined life and write for television. And she would use her freedom gained by the expulsion of this pulpy mess to the full. Seven years later she would marry a young and promising movie director who would become an older, philandering has-been, but who would give her a son who would in his own right become a minor actor Own had never heard of but could search on IMDB.

But first she must return to Gene Powell Davis's apartment in Venice Beach, late on Sunday, much later than expected. He is washing dishes in the grimy kitchen of his small apartment, a glass of whiskey beside him on the sink, wearing an apron, his gaze indifferent, revealing nothing of what he might have been thinking as he washed mechanically—this being what the House committee had reduced him to. Perhaps he was thinking of the plight of the oppressed of the world, perhaps the sight of a woman's breasts, perhaps the means of procuring another bottle.

Owen found it almost quaint to imagine the great Gene Powell Davis in an apron, washing dishes like a working man, his grandfather's best friend, his grandfather's sad nemesis. He looked up from the book, closed his eyes and tried to imagine the scene as the daughter came in the door, cured from her unfortunate tumor. As he was imagining the scene, the chimes rang, indicating the library would close in half an hour. Soft echoes of shuffling paper filled the grand space as other researchers began to gather up their things. Where did they go? he wondered. He would go to the nearest bar when this was done. He had begun drinking again, far more since the weekend with Audrey. But meanwhile, Sylvia, in the dingy Venice Beach apartment, was standing in front of her father and his soapy hands. He stared at her and then finally said, "You shouldn't have done it. You should have talked to me first." And she felt, for the first time, a great resentment for the father whom up to then she had only admired.

Owen, glancing at his watch, five minutes to closing, skimmed the epilogue while blindly collecting his papers. The grand reading room felt empty, and he could feel the wardens bearing down on him. Sylvia, he skimmed, went on to live a wealthy life in California, living off the producer's alimony. She published her memoirs whose epilogue he was rapidly trying to finish. Her father killed himself seven years after the abortion, precisely when Catholics say intelligence would have entered his grandson, had he lived. It was a bullet to the mouth from a revolver she always knew he had carried. They both had died, leaving her alone, but she refused to accept it, neither that she murdered her baby nor that her father murdered himself. She returned to the moment of her father's suicide. He was not that kind of man, she wrote, not after all he had endured at their hands, and all he had gotten through, just when he was beginning to emerge from his alcoholism, and write again, and speak again in the name of the poor and the downtrodden. Not when the blacklist was about to be lifted, and in any case he had begun making money again as a script doctor and had received an advance for his memoirs of McCarthyism. Why would he do it then, at the beginning of the end of his despair? Why then, she wrote, "when he was just beginning to enjoy being the grandfather of my son"? She could only believe that it had been done by someone else on behalf of someone else, because all through his life there had always been people who wanted to kill him. Because all through his life he had made himself a nuisance to those who oppress others, and oppressors by definition have the will to kill as well as the means. Owen shuddered suddenly when he read those words. They seemed rather familiar. But a security guard was standing over him telling him that it was time to go, that the book would still be there tomorrow. The library was closing.

* * *

It was not difficult, these days, to find out who Sylvia Asher's son was. Dan Asher, of Malibu, was born in 1960, the year of his grandfather's suicide. A glance at his credits on the IMDB database revealed that in the brief moment he had been moderately famous on TV, Owen had been growing up abroad. Asher had also been attached to some fashionable political causes: anti-apartheid, abortion, gay rights. In 1998 he had overdosed on drugs and was found dead in the Malibu bungalow he had inherited from his father. With him had gone the line of Gene Powell Davis, just as with Owen himself would go the line of Silas Stone.

* * *

On one of those August days, Owen left the Library of Congress early and went home. It was around 2 p.m. when he reached his apartment. For a moment he felt he didn't recognize it, and then he realized it was because there was no smell of cooking in the hallway. It was too early. He realized he had never been home on a weekday at this hour. He glanced at the door where the smells of food and the sounds of sex regularly came from, paused for a moment, and then opened his door. It might have been too early for a drink, but he poured himself one anyway. He sat down on his futon and opened almost at random one of the books he was using for his Leviathan essay. He would have one drink, he thought, and read himself into a nap, and then he would work late into the night.

He was suddenly very tired and felt sleep coming over him. He closed the book for a moment, his finger marking the page where he had stopped, and shut his eyes, waiting for sleep, the drink half-drunk on the flat, wide arm of the futon. And then the familiar sound began, the creaking of the bed, the rhythmic pants, and her familiar grunts. Afternoon sex; it was impossible for him to sleep now. But then a new note sounded through the walls. A deeper grunt in counterpoint to her alto gasps, each filling the space the other left, like clapping in flamenco, but slower, with longer spaces in between, but growing faster, with shorter spaces in between.

What? Owen thought. Had he at last learned to speak? After having listened so often to her solo performance, her aria of pleasure silently induced, this tenor punctuation seemed wrong, out of place, deceptive, treacherous, not written for this opera. He looked at his watch: not yet three, on a weekday, not the usual hour. Then a terrible thought struck him. She was with someone else, she was betraying the silent lover of previous nights—husband, boyfriend, roommate, the one for whom so many dinners had been planned and cooked, the one to whom she had said: "I'm coming, baby. Are you coming with me?" The brute tenor quickened his pace, their efforts mingled for several bars into a single rhythm. Then came her familiar moans building to the moment, and afterwards the long, hungry-cat whimper. It was over much faster than normal. The whole sequence differed from the once-predictable concert he had grown used to. A dead silence followed—interrupted less than five minutes later by the bang in the hallway of a closing door and the switch of the latch inside, then the screech of the faucet and the running of water through shower pipes that seemed to course above Owen's head. He could neither sleep nor read now. He stared at his own walls, stunned at the betrayal of the man he didn't know by the other man he didn't know, and despising the woman he didn't know whose lusty moans he did know. From behind the wall he heard a kettle whistle. She must have showered and now decided to have a cup of tea. Finally Owen finished his drink and gave up on the idea of sleep.

* * *

The Republican convention was held in the final days of August. Owen did not have a television or an internet connection in his apartment, so he stayed late at the institute to watch the proceedings on the TV there, foot up on the desk, the leaves of the trees of Dupont Circle waving outside his window in the night heat. He thought, when Romney gave his acceptance speech, that a line in there had been taken from the speech he had written for Stiles. He wrote it down and reminded himself to check later. He had enjoyed watching, as well, the commentary of Fox News political expert Melvin Jackson. Jackson, after graduating from George Mason, had become a firebrand investigative journalist for a right-wing news magazine in the early years of the Bush administration. Then after the Iraq war he had turned against the Bush administration first, the Republican party next, and finally conservative ideology. He had gained some fame in liberal circles with his memoir on working for a right-wing magazine and the dirty tricks they used to trap liberals. Owen had been disappointed at Jackson's conversion, he having converted in the other direction around the same time, but nonetheless found him enjoyable to listen to. You could tell he still detested the left as much as he did the right. He detested, Owen surmised, political America. Now here he was on television saying he would hold his nose and vote for Romney because he now believed that neither of the two parties should be able to inflict their damage on the country for more than four years at a time.

CHAPTER 22

Tea In Baltimore

Audrey found herself again at Mrs. Cassell's apartment, chatting about books, about baking, about what she planned to do with her life. Audrey could not help but open herself to this lady. It was not only that she was flattered by her attention (this woman who had met Bill Clinton!), but that she seemed like an informed ally in a still-unfamiliar place. Her eyes were so similar to Owen's, and she would think of him more and more fondly as she chatted with Mrs. Cassell. At the same time she understood less and less why Owen would not talk about her. She noticed that she, Mrs. Cassell, hardly talked about Owen. There were a few photos of him in the apartment but fewer than one might expect of the only child of a widow. Mrs. Cassell had spoken of him only when asked about the photos. Otherwise, he was not part of her general repertoire of curry recipes, liberal politics, fashionable fiction, and tales about life as a Foreign Service wife.

Only once had she mentioned her son unbidden, and it was when Audrey had commented on the elegance of the tea trolley. Mrs. Cassell had responded that her son, when he was a boy, used to love to set up the tea trolley for her ladies' afternoons, that he knew which spoons to use, which knives went with which cheeses, and the difference between a wineglass and a sherry glass. "I don't drink anymore," she said. "Unfortunately I sometimes wonder if my son learned a little too well which glasses went with which drinks. He seems to use them all, but that's another story." Audrey suppressed a smile at this little anecdote, imagining young Owen knocking back a sherry or two before wheeling out the tea trolley, then feeling sad that all this mother knew about her son was that he was an alcoholic. Audrey changed the subject back to books, not daring to ask more about this comical, drunkard son, afraid perhaps that questions would somehow reveal her own subterfuge, which increasingly bothered her. She resented both of them for putting her in this false and uncomfortable position.

They were sitting in the kitchen as Mrs. Cassell was cooking. "One of my beaux just gave me an iPhone," Mrs. Cassell was saying that evening. "But I don't know, it seems so complicated to use. Do you know how to set the time? It's stuck on Cupertino, wherever that is, and the weather in Cupertino is obviously not Baltimore weather."

"Let me do it," Audrey said. "It's really easy." She took the phone and looked at it. "I've changed it to automatically adjust the time wherever you are. Cupertino is in California, the Apple headquarters."

The old lady took the phone back. "Well this technology is something. It would have been useful in the old days, when we were always traveling. Back then you had to set your watch manually. Once we missed a train to Cannes because my husband forgot to change the time after we had come in from London. For a diplomat, he was so careless about some basic things like that."

"Wait," Audrey said. "Does that mean you have an iPhone charger? Mine's nearly dead. If I could borrow yours for just a half hour..."

"Of course. Let me go and get it." She went to her study. Audrey looked out the kitchen window, across to her aunt's darkened apartment, looking at it as Owen would have during those evenings at the beginning, imagining him imagining her.

"Is this it?" Mrs. Cassell asked, holding the familiar white cord with the USB on one end and the familiar plug for the iPhone on the other, dangling it from her manicured hand extended from her Chinese-silk sleeve.

"Yes that's it. Thank you." She plugged her phone into the charger and the charger into the jack on the counter near the door of the kitchen. Mrs. Cassell had turned to her stove, where she was deep-frying samosas, and the smell of cumin and coriander was pleasantly filling the kitchen. "I'm spending the day in Annapolis tomorrow," she said. "Old friends of ours have a sailboat. I decided to make samosas as a snack. I put them in little plastic bags so they don't get wet. But you can eat them quickly; they fill you up." She went to the door to the fire escape and opened it to let out the smoke—the fire escape, now just a plate of steel, where Owen used to sit and smoke, Audrey thought. Audrey could not help but imagine the three of them here—her, Mrs. Cassell, and Owen—talking and cooking and making plans for future travels, telling stories about past travels, about Owen as a boy, planning a sailing trip. She could not help, even, thinking of grandchildren running around in this kitchen. She held back a smile, whose source she could not yet explain to the lady. She thought of what Owen had said to her about coming to Syracuse. She began, as the older lady described seeing the Taj Mahal at dawn back in 1965, thinking about all the things she wanted to say to Owen. Yes, you can come to Syracuse. I'm sorry if I doubted you. They had not been in touch since that weekend. Now, a letter composed itself in her mind, and

the kitchen was warm and smelled of hot oil and exotic spices
and family.

Mrs. Cassell made a pot of tea, and they took it into
the salon off the main living room. Audrey sat on the couch
where she had read Owen's journal that night, the night,
perhaps—she realized now—that she had probably fallen in
love with him. Mrs. Cassell mentioned that her friends with
the sailboat in Annapolis were big-time Democratic donors.
"I used to sail on Lake Lucerne," she said, "when I was in
boarding school, growing up. My father hated boats, even
though he lived on a lake until he died." She said this almost
to herself, as if assuming that Audrey would understand why
she hated her father. "My son is a good sailor, though I don't
think he does much of it anymore." Then she was back to
her friends with the sailboat, as if the parenthesis had never
been opened. They were very concerned, her friends, that
the Republicans, with their voter-ID laws and other tricks,
were intent on stealing the election. They had contributed a
lot to the Obama for America PAC. She, of course, had done
her fair share, but her real contribution would be a car pool
she was setting up with some friends to help underprivileged
Democratic voters go to the polls.

Audrey listened and drank her tea thinking how strange
it was that Owen, the intellectual, who could talk about
anything, hardly ever talked about politics, yet what a
political education he must have had around the dinner table
with a mother like this! She felt oddly comfortable in this
apartment, where she had once come to Owen, where she had
slept with Owen, where she was now friends with Owen's
mother, whose exotic cooking smells filled the air. It was really
two apartments, she thought, Owen's when Owen was there
and his mother's when she was here. Still, she almost felt, as
she was leaving that evening, that she was leaving home. She

wanted it to be home. She tripped away down the stairs on that side of the building with a sense of destiny, desperate to call Owen and discuss what he had said about joining her at Syracuse. She suddenly realized she wanted him with her if he would still go. It was only when she closed the door behind her in her great-aunt's apartment that she realized she had forgotten her iPhone charging in Mrs. Cassell's kitchen. His number was on her phone. She looked quickly over the familiar space from her kitchen and saw the light go out in the apartment on the other side and the shadow of Mrs. Cassell going to bed. She would call him tomorrow then.

* * *

He had reached a modus vivendi with his mother: visits on her birthday and Thanksgiving. At Christmas, when he was married to Lisa, he would visit Lisa's parents. Since the divorce, Christmas had not been negotiated between them. In recent years, he had preferred to go to mass, dine alone, and go home to a book and a drink. On both her birthday, in March, and Thanksgiving, she arranged elaborate dinners at her apartment, mostly with Baltimore grandees whom she had met through the Pratt board, or retired Foreign Service friends. Many diplomats had brought retirement property in Baltimore. It was close enough to Washington for the occasional consulting assignment, but much cheaper to afford on a government pension than a place in Washington or its suburbs. His mother was always surrounded by friends and, if not friends, people very much like her. But this post-divorce, late-summer visit that was suddenly required by his living in DC demanded a new protocol. He wanted, as well, to see Audrey. He proposed brunch and then said that he had planned a dinner with a friend in Baltimore. He hoped to be

223

with Audrey for most of the night. His mother's handwritten letter had made him even less inclined to spend time with her. Clearly the old wounds that he thought had partly healed in fact were still too raw.

"Brunch?" his mother replied on the phone. "Aren't you going to stay the night? Why not stay for dinner? I was planning on having the Allens over. You remember them? They served with us in Indonesia. Their son was a year above you at the international school."

"I was planning on having dinner with a friend," he said.

"A friend? In Baltimore?"

"Yes."

"Well, invite him over. Unless he's...well, even if he is. I suppose you Republicans are a bit more bearable now that you're out of power."

"Why don't I come for brunch, have an early dinner with my friend. And then I'll be back in time for dessert with the Allens."

"I don't care one way or the other," his mother said, in a tone that told him she was disappointed as usual but too tired to fight about it. "I'm buying wine for the Allens. They still drink too." He realized she thought he didn't want to stay for dinner because he would not be able to drink. Perhaps she thought he had invented this friend.

"It's not that," he said. "Let me see if I can change my dinner plans."

* * *

After she hung up the phone, she felt the usual twinge of discomfort that had long followed a discussion with her son. This was, however, merely an old problem getting worse. She had learned, on the advice of a therapist, to establish a distance, treat him more like a diplomatic guest—an official, for example, of a dictatorial Third World regime where her husband had been posted—than a member of her family. It had worked at least in keeping the peace, but it was, she thought sometimes, an unhealthy peace that could not last. At another time in life she might have been furious at his coming only for a brief visit and using her apartment like a hotel, so he could visit *friends*, although probably just go out drinking, and she would have made her fury known. But now she accepted it as something that happened, rather than as a situation she could do something about. But the diplomatic pretense was just that and sometimes something else was required. He had not even *mentioned* her letter, let alone *answered* it, though she had stated her feelings in the strongest terms. She did not like to wear her emotions on her sleeve; they had never been that sort of family, but if one *must* let out a *cri de coeur*, at the very least a response was due.

She was angry, quietly furious, but she sat still and tried to allow her sour mood to run its course. She would, however, find a way of letting him know when he was there that his ingratitude was inappropriate. And yet another part of her was relieved that he would not be staying long. When they spent too much time together they either ended up in a political discussion and disagreed, or talked around politics in a way that was so artificial that it bothered her because she knew he was hiding the native intelligence she had done so much to cultivate during his youth. Now and again the artificiality infuriated her so much that she would try to bait him into a political argument. At those moments, though, he was too much like his father: compulsively even-handed, adept at sliding out of the corners she tried to put him in, shy about conflict, ultimately afraid of her. He was not, like her own father, for all his flaws, a fighter. Her son's lack of courage, more than his fascist politics, disappointed her. She would have preferred him a fighter, no matter what his views. He had all the talents and the pedigree to raise the family name. Instead, he was likely to be, like his own father, her deceased, alcoholic husband, something of a comfortable American failure.

* * *

The next day Owen tried to reach Audrey several times to arrange dinner but she didn't answer. He imagined she was at the library and had turned the ringer off. He tried again in the evening and she still didn't answer. He put on Chopin and poured a whiskey and tried to imagine her next to him. While conducting the Nocturne with his drunken gestures, he knocked the whiskey glass off the arm of the futon; it broke and he didn't really have the energy then to clean it up.

* * *

When she left the apartment at 6:30 a.m. to go to her shift at Starbucks, Audrey asked the black lady at the desk if Mrs. Cassell had left. "She left a half hour ago, honey," the lady said, in her blue uniform with its patches and epaulettes loosely tailored to cover her large frame. "I think she said she was going sailing."

"Shit," Audrey said, frustrated. It would not be until late that evening that she could get her phone back.

"When is young Mr. Cassell coming back?" the lady asked.

Audrey blushed. "I don't know," she said and left the building feeling guilty, and feeling she had something to be guilty about, blushing furiously that the whole building staff seemed to know of her liaison. She resented the intrusion on their privacy and yet wanted to see him more than ever. She needed her phone back. She had not expected Mrs. Cassell to leave so early.

After her shift at Starbucks, she went to the library, where she had promised to do some reshelving. She wanted to return home at seven, when her shift ended, but there was a speech and a reception for Madeleine Albright, who had just written a book, and her supervisor had politely requested that she help set up the room and break it down afterwards. Audrey listened politely to the tiny former secretary of state's speech and mingled at the margins, thinking intermittently about her phone and about Owen, but gradually giving herself over to the venerable charisma of Albright. She then had several glasses of wine from the refreshment table she had helped set up and was flattered by several young men who approached and asked about her interest in international relations.

It was after ten at night when she returned to her apartment, but the lights in Mrs. Cassell's apartment were off. She finished by herself the rest of the white wine, the bottle she had opened the night before, and decided she had nothing better to do than to write Owen a letter by hand, the old-fashioned way, the way she thought he might appreciate. She began to write, and she imagined giving him the letter. He would say, when she gave him the envelope: What is it? She would answer: It's a letter—to you, from me, in my hand. He would give her that little look, that look that showed his fear in believing something good might happen to him. He would ask her: Should I read it now, or is it something that I don't want to open? She would kiss him. She wanted badly to kiss him now. She would say: Read it when I've fallen asleep after making love to you. With this consummation in mind she began to write it, honestly, freely. She had never written like this before. Like this: as if to a future husband. She astounded herself at the decisions that seemed to have made themselves in the back of her mind as she began to write and think of him. She felt, in writing, a tranquility and sureness about her thinking that made her feel as secure in the world as she had ever felt.

* * *

It had been a long time since Owen's mother had spent a day on a boat, and she had forgotten how much it exhausted even a younger body. The relaxation of sailing was precisely in the way the hard sun, the constant adjustments, the hauling of sheets, exhausted one gently. It led to the best night's sleep. It was hard to stay awake on the solitary drive back from Annapolis, and she stopped in Pasadena for a cup of coffee and a break. Sitting in the brightly lit uniformity of the McDonald's she suddenly felt, as she sometimes did at unprovoked moments, the desolation of her widowhood. Her husband had been a failure in many ways, but at least he had been a husband. Her father had been an outsized success in literary ways, but he had never been a father. Her son appeared to be a failure and yet not even a son. She had not been able to bring herself even to read his book, dense and academic, above all so terribly pessimistic when life had been so good to him. He had dedicated the book to that stupid, Republican, Catholic hypocrite who had not even been able to stay married to him.

She felt herself about to cry, so she took her coffee with her and sat in her car. She turned on the radio in the dark and while trying to reach the volume hit one of the pre-selected stations. It was a modern pop ballad, compelling for a moment, but not the sort of music to quell her tears and certainly not one of the stations she listened to. She listened to the song for a moment, wondering how it had gotten onto her programmed list of stations. Then she turned it off and began to cry anyway and pulled off the road. She cried for a life without mothers and daughters. When she was done crying, she finished her coffee with defiance and drove home.

She arrived in Baltimore shortly after nine, found a good parking spot around the corner from her building's entrance, allowed the concierge lady to drive the elevator up to her floor, opened the door to her familiar apartment, and made a pot of tea. She was suddenly not as tired; the coffee and the cry had given her energy. She changed into her nightgown and turned on the TV to watch the news. During the first commercial she went into the kitchen to make a tisane. Quite unexpectedly she heard a song, a ballad. It was the same one she had heard in the car. It came with a strange buzzing, a vibration, and she realized after several bars that it was a phone. She suddenly remembered that the young girl, that Audrey, had left her phone to recharge. She must have forgotten it. She glanced at it to be sure, wondering what to do—to answer and explain that the owner was not there, or simply to let it ring? She looked at the phone, whose screen was now luminous, and then she looked again, and almost dropped her teacup. The screen said that Owen Cassell was calling. She almost answered it then, suddenly wondering if it was her son calling her on her phone. But the iPhone was still plugged into the jack, and it had a little pink cover that was definitely *not* hers. It was a young girl's thing, the *cutest little thing* in a tacky Hello Kitty sort of way, a bauble that even she, as a young girl, would never have chosen. It was a tasteless plastic thing warbling an insipid disposable ballad. But the screen said that it was still her son calling, and the plaintive love song went on and on, while the phone vibrated and buzzed as if it were her own son prancing like a puppy before some unworthy master. She stood there, clutching the kitchen counter, gradually understanding.

* * *

Owen called Audrey shortly after nine thirty, wanting again to tell her he would be in Baltimore the next day, that he would have brunch with his mother and spend the afternoon with her, and wanting to have dinner with her and perhaps more. Again the phone rang and she did not answer. Again he feared how much he loved her, because her refusal to take his call filled him with such fear.

He put his phone down on the table in his small space and poured himself another whiskey. He put his playlist of favorite ballads on, already a sign of resignation. He would drink his way through them. Alone in his space, with the lamps on and the overhead lights off, with his solitude circumscribed within familiar walls and more familiar cones of light, he sat back in his solitary armchair, feeling the chill of the central air conditioner shaving the back of his head, and he thought of that weekend when she had come to Washington. I came on too strong, he thought. I scared her with that talk of moving to Syracuse. I did not respect enough the fact that she is moving into a new phase of her life, graduate school, new people, maybe new boyfriends, and all I am is an older guy who she thinks wants to put her in a cage. No wonder she's not answering, he thought. She needs her space and time to think about things. I have no space, much time, time at least for another drink, another ballad, or maybe Bach's Chaconne and its arpeggios.

An unthinkable sadness came over him—the familiar dread but more. It was not, he thought, a sadness about

Audrey herself. That was a sadness he would have to deal with separately. It was a sadness for who he was and who he would never be. Somehow he thought of Lisa and the breaking of that vow between them, and perhaps his failure with her was a curse over everything else. Audrey had awoken him from the dull coma of Lisa. But Audrey was there, alive, beautiful, and had come to him that night, chastened and unbidden. She had taken a leap of faith. His eyes searched the small, barren apartment around him, and she was there in every nook and cranny. And one of the new ballads from his iTunes library, one that Audrey had said she liked when they were driving back from Annapolis, was playing. He almost forced the tears to his eyes. It felt good to be drunk and to weep. But he wondered if he had lost her forever. He had come on too strong. The arpeggios consoled.

* * *

He took a morning train to Baltimore, arriving at the station a bit after ten, walking down the still-familiar Charles Street. The under-construction University of Baltimore Law School building had made progress since his last visit; part of the street was still sectioned off to allow for the construction, and he crossed the road.

The daytime concierge let him in again, saying it had been a long time and how much his mother must be looking forward to seeing him. He wished for a moment that he lived the life she must imagine he lived, and then was ashamed of his self-pity. "I'll take the stairs," he said. "Thank you, though."

The door to the apartment was unlocked, as it always was. Inside he smelled the baking of muffins and heard from the kitchen the American folk songs his mother still loved. He dropped his weekend bag in the foyer. "I'm here," he said. He went into the kitchen just as she was coming out and pecked her lightly on the cheek.

"You've lost weight," she said.

"I've reached that age where I thought I'd have to develop a few good habits or just let myself go."

"I hope one of those good habits is to stop drinking." She had been a catastrophic drunk at his age.

"Unfortunately it's not." Why did she have to start with that? She was carrying a tray of muffins to the table in the salon. There were already crackers and cheeses and a pâté set out, enough food for ten.

"You're too old for me to tell you what to do," she said, setting the tray down. "Not that it ever did any good anyway. But just remember that that's what did your father in—killed his career first and then killed him. You can stop. I learned to. It's a question of willpower."

Owen sat down on the sofa in the salon, exactly where he had sat that first night that Audrey had come. Her image formed in his mind. He wondered if his mother was deliberately baiting him or if she just couldn't help it. He could see the spot where they had begun their rupture, the day of his father's funeral. He looked at his watch, but he was glad his mother had turned her back and headed towards the kitchen when he did so. "Now that you're here," she said, "I'll just put on the tea. I'm sorry I don't have anything stronger."

"By the way," he said, "I *can* stay for dinner tonight. My friend in the end couldn't make it." Audrey had never called him back.

"That's nice," his mother said. "I'll set an extra plate for you. The Allens will be happy to see you. They were rather disappointed when I said you could only join for dessert."

232

He wondered where Audrey was now; perhaps not far away. He sighed. The first conversational gambit with his mother had already tired him, or rather, it had reminded him of how tiring the day was going to be, and that was enough to keep him in his seat, staring at the harpsichord his father had built, sober surely when he had fitted the joints together, strung the wires, carefully adjusted each pick that plucked the wire when the key was pressed.

"Earl Grey OK?" his mother asked from the kitchen. She had turned the music off; it had been medieval-sounding string music, some madrigal.

"Yes, perfect."

"Milk?"

"Sure."

"You're not on any crazy diet are you? I have pâté. I brought it from France."

"I see that. No, I'm not on a diet. Just generally trying to be more careful. I don't have pâté every day, though. I'll certainly have some today."

The kettle started to scream, so he wasn't sure if she said anything back to him. Then she came in with the tray again, bearing the tea.

"What happened to that tea trolley that you used to have?" he asked.

"In the dining room," she said. "But I have that nice embroidered tablecloth from Limoges over it. The surface was getting scratched. Why, do you want it?"

"No. I don't need it. My place is just one room and I hardly ever have guests, and don't really host teas."

"That reminds me," she said. "I just want to call a friend. She left her phone here the other day, and yesterday I left very early to go sailing and couldn't give it to her. I'm sure she's missed it. She's quite young—a neighbor. And you know how kids are these days: They need to have their phones all the time. She's probably dying without it, poor dear." He barely registered what she said. He was relieved that the conversation had been rescued from the topic of his drinking. She must have been pleased, he thought, that he had decided to stay for dinner. He began to relax.

He poured tea into both their cups as his mother went into the study to make her phone call. He thought it was a bit of luck that she had gone sailing. That was something to talk about that might take up ten or fifteen minutes. She returned to the room. "Oh, you've poured. Thank you."

"How was the sailing?" he asked. "Annapolis or the Eastern Shore?"

"Annapolis. The Joneses retired there. We served with them in Mexico. Big sailors, even back then. They bought a boat in Acapulco a long time ago and sailed it through the Panama Canal and back up the Chesapeake. Forty-seven feet. I still do love to sail, even though I mostly sit there at my age and cling to the guy lines. Robert, though, Robert Jones, you remember him, always the top of the tennis ladder at the Jakarta American Club? He can still manage a boat quite well when the wind isn't too much."

The doorbell rang and his mother got up to get it; she got up, Owen noticed, spryly for her age and almost skipped to the door. "Oh do come in," she said. "While you're here, let me introduce you to my son."

And in a second, practically tugged into view by his mother, like a recalcitrant pet on a leash, there was Audrey, standing in the foyer. Owen stood up; they stared at each other, a moment of mutual indecision. Owen walked over and held out his hand. "Pleased to meet you."

"Yes," she answered. "I've heard so much about you."

"I'll get your phone," his mother said and disappeared into the kitchen, leaving behind a smile that Owen could not decipher. Owen and Audrey stared at each other, his hand still holding hers in a guilty handshake that they pretended was innocent until she pulled it away. Her gesture was harsh. The look in her eyes was taut panic. He could not imagine what his face looked like. Audrey thought: This was not how I imagined this would be. When his mother returned with the phone, Audrey thanked her in a weak and arid voice.

"Stay for tea and muffins, and some pâté—if you like goose liver. It's not to everyone's taste."

"Oh I really can't."

"Nonsense. Sit down." And Audrey found herself sitting down next to Owen, on the same couch where she had read the journals that had made her fall in love with him. Owen was beside her, leaning back and almost sunk into the puffy cushions. She could almost feel him thinking his way out of the room.

"Audrey works at the Pratt," his mother explained, pouring a third cup of tea. "Her great-aunt is my great friend. They live in the other wing." For the first time, Owen noticed that there were three cups of tea, and three plates, and three spoons, as if another guest had always been expected.

"Are you all right?" his mother asked, far too cheerfully. "You look like you've seen a ghost."

"You must know that I have," he replied.

"Whatever do you mean?"

"I really must go," Audrey said. "It was nice to meet you." She turned to Owen to offer her hand, but he knew that it was too late and didn't extend his.

"Audrey, my darling," his mother said, "don't insult my intelligence. My son at least has figured it out."

Audrey turned to him. He looked back at her. "She knows."

"What do you mean?" Audrey asked.

"An unlikely couple," his mother said, sitting back, comfortable, almost satisfied in her armchair, holding her teacup like a contessa. "A bit of an age difference to start with. Then again, my son always did like them younger."

"I couldn't tell you," Audrey said to Owen, apologetically, hand wringing hand, eyes close to tears—tears first of embarrassment. Perhaps other kinds of tears would follow later. Owen, for his part, couldn't move if he wanted to.

"Why should you have?" he said stiffly. "There are things I haven't told you."

"Sunshine is the best disinfectant," his mother said cheerily.

"You didn't have to do it like this," Owen said to her.

"Well," his mother answered in that same cheerful tone, "I'm just surprised. I rather liked Audrey and we've had some wonderful conversations. In many ways we think alike despite our different...our different experiences. And of course I love *you* like a mother should, and wish the best for you. I'm just surprised she can stand your politics."

"What politics?" Audrey asked.

Owen looked up at her, hardly believing that it was happening.

"You don't know?" his mother said, pausing. Owen suddenly realized how carefully she had thought this through. Now he was watching Audrey, who stared at his mother and now turned to look at him. This time he knew the look on his own face: It was the resigned diplomatic stare, the concealed shock of a chess player who has just noticed he's left his queen exposed, hoping vainly his opponent won't notice, but knowing she has and the match is over.

"Owen, my dear son, is a Republican. A conservative Republican. For all I know he's working on the Romney campaign. That's of course his right as an American, but I was just surprised at what you could possibly have in common. Not age, not politics, not background. Is it only sex? I would find that so disappointing—in both of you!" She was looking at Audrey, who was looking back at her. Audrey was the only one standing in the room, but, it seemed to Owen, she was about to collapse.

If only to break the tension and change the momentum or simply end the agony for Audrey, he said, "As a matter of fact, I *am* working on the Romney campaign."

"I don't care how you waste your time," his mother said, snapping at him, suddenly a mother again, scolding, and he suddenly a child again.

"Why didn't you ever tell me?" Audrey said, turning to him, shoulders squaring, standing firmer. At least, he thought, she now had something to blame him for. "I thought you were going to work for Obama if he was re-elected. That's what you said."

"Really," his mother said. "Did you go that far to get into her pants?"

"No, it's what I didn't say. It's what I let you believe for a while. Until—"

"Until what?"

He looked at her stunned face. He now realized it was not his politics that generated her gathering fury, it was that he was a liar. He knew then, staring at her features set firmly in anger, that to her he would always be either a hypocrite or a coward; the moment had come to choose. "I thought a better moment would come to tell you. Then today happened."

"A better moment? When? After we had moved in together in Syracuse? When? When Romney wins the election and you leave me to work for him? I might not be as refined as you two are, but at least I know what I believe and don't hide it!"

He exchanged glances with his mother. She said nothing. Her glances shifted between them now, as if she were watching a tennis match, intrigued by the angles the players were finding, the desperate lunges as they tried to stay in the point. Her teacup remained poised in her hand like an afterthought. Owen looked at Audrey and she back at him, telegraphs vainly passing each other in a silence that was finally broken by his mother's chirpy voice.

"Move to Syracuse?" his mother said at last. "Good god, how extravagantly you throw away the brilliant opportunities you have been given."

"It's not about the politics," Owen said, his voice resigned, unconvinced, knowing that he had already lost Audrey and everything. "It's about..."

"You two are terrible people," Audrey said, her posture resolute, finally sure that she was the wronged one, clutching her phone, turning and leaving, her sobs echoing in the marble staircase, the clack of her heels seeming to hang and echo in the landing long after she had disappeared.

Owen stood up. "You're not going to chase her, I hope," his mother said. "You know it would never work in the end. It's not your different politics or your ages. It's that you have nothing in common. I'm not trying to be a snob. She's a nice girl. I think I did you a favor. It would never have worked, just like the one you married. And I warned you about her. You have no sense for women. Trust your mother for once."

"It was an awful thing to do," he said. "And I don't think I can ever forgive you. You set out three cups. You planned this. You wanted not only to destroy it, but to do it for your pleasure!"

"You deserved it," she said, but she seemed surprised at the fury compressed in her son's clenched posture, as if he were about to strike her—a fighter at last. Perhaps that was what surprised her. He reminded her, for a moment, of her father. Now *she* seemed to huddle in the cushions.

Owen looked down on her, tall above her small seated frame, his eyes first angry, then hard and sad. For the first time he sensed his mother was baffled by her own design. She could play these games, he thought, because she was secure in her life and had once been loved. But Audrey didn't have the security and he didn't have the love, though he still believed with a tightening heart they might have made it together, he and Audrey. Now he knew it would never happen. He was standing over the cooling tea and the untouched pâté and muffins and his mother who stared at him with an expression of silent pain he had never seen before. "I think, Mother," he said, "I think this is probably the last time we will ever see each other."

She stared back at him, her mouth dropping. He picked up his weekend bag from the spot in the foyer where he had left it and walked down the stairs and across the lobby.

"Poor Miss Audrey," the concierge said as he crossed the hall. "She was crying about something; she didn't say nothing, and just ran up the stairs on the other side."

He went up to her apartment and knocked on her door. He shouted inside for a while, saying I need to talk to you, I need to explain, I love you—platitudes that she endured for a while until finally shouting back, "Go away, you sick fascist bastard!"

He waited a while in the hallway, hoping that she would change her mind, and then picked up his bag and went down again and out the door. He started walking north on Charles Street. It was a pleasant, early-fall day, and he walked across

West Madison against the red light because it was Sunday and there was no traffic.

CHAPTER 23

Election Day

He walked on that Monday evening before Election Day from his apartment to the Foggy Bottom Metro station, carrying the same light travel bag he had brought to Baltimore that weekend and wearing a raincoat, feeling the insistent evening chill. The massive hurricane that had lashed the East Coast for several days had left behind shifty winds and light rains, a sort of chastened attitude after the destruction it had caused, the same personality only calmer now and contrite. The Metro had just started running again after the storm, but it was running slowly. He had left his apartment with plenty of time to spare. This was not a train he wanted to miss, and he knew he had been lucky to get a ticket.

The orange-line train at Foggy Bottom came surprisingly quickly, and he rode it for three stops and got out at Metro Center and went upstairs to get the red line towards Glenmont. He felt a curious relief as he thought about the next day. He had survived the Obama era. Four more years of Obama would change forever the nature of what it was to be American: on the dole, on meth, on the take, others hoarding guns and provisions and waiting for the next civil war. He briefly imagined himself as the foreign secretary of an insurgent movement, negotiating the terms of a peace settlement with the once-federal government, re-establishing freedom.

He waited on the platform at Metro Center, checking his watch. The digital sign said the next red train was in three minutes. There would still be plenty of time to make the Northeast Regional to New York, and there might also even be time for a drink at the Center Cafe. Well, yes, now he may as well drink. When the train arrived it was crowded with people in Capitals jerseys. It must have been a game night, he thought. They were standing, filling the aisles of the car, mingling with each other, talking about defenses and offenses. Owen was able to find a vacant seat. The hockey fans were excited and anyway were getting off at the next stop, the Convention Center. Above the joshing and joking and pre-match commentary, he tried to continue his imagining of the Romney administration and his role in it. Speechwriter, he thought, for the president on foreign policy, and he imagined himself in the Oval Office making points in a debate about the position the government should take on some foreign crisis. Some of the fans were young; he was surprised at the number of young women among them. One or two reminded him of Audrey. A few days earlier he had written a letter to her that was philosophical and contrite; he had tried to explain things. He had addressed it to her program at Syracuse. But instead of mailing it he had thrown it away in a trash can that was not for recycling.

At the next station Owen was only half aware of the hockey fans getting off as he stared at his reflection in the train window, thinking about the words to explain a more rational foreign policy to America, thinking sometimes about Audrey, thinking that in this reflection in this light he was actually not unhandsome. The subway car moved again and he sighed thoughtfully, tiredly in fact, thinking about the train journey ahead, thinking about New York again, the unique smells of the city and the familiar comfort of his grandfather's apartment. Finally he turned away from the window and settled his gaze into the empty space in front of him.

She must have been staring at him for a while, and now he stared back at her. She was sitting three rows away, facing him from across the space where the doors were, where the Capitals fans used to be. They were maybe ten feet apart. He thought he could have fallen in love with her all over again, like he had before, on another subway car. Older, lips pressed into a tighter line, eyes warier, eyelids heavier, worry lines on her forehead that never used to exist, still beautiful, very beautiful. But there was also something very tired about her. As he stared at her and she stared back, neither smiling nor speaking, he thought that what seemed tired about her was himself. He was the part of her life that had etched her pretty face with those thin lines, the face that had once smiled as she'd pulled out a copy of *A Confederacy of Dunces* from her handbag in a different world and on a different train. Now she stared at him with a gaze that asked nothing, forgave nothing, consoled nothing, offered nothing, cured nothing, yet remembered everything. A gaze that held together all the nothings they had left and spat them out, a red pulpy mess of regrets, a gaze he could not break. He stared as they rushed through the tunnel, not even wondering what his gaze said to her. He was merely absorbing the stillness of her eyes on his. The train pulled into Judiciary Square and she got up. Without leaving his gaze she walked towards him to the door and turned to it, waiting for it to open, her high-chinned profile indifferent to his mute gaze. They were five feet apart, the unmistakable bump of pregnancy pushing through her dress. The doors opened and she left the car. He stared in front of him where she used to be, staring at nothing as the doors closed and the train moved again. When it finally jerked into motion, he turned to look out the window again. She was still standing there on the platform, in front of him, waiting for the next train, a train without him, and he saw that she remained slim and high-chinned, dark-eyed, with wonderful legs, her hair pulled back, a woman who was still of phenomenal beauty, if only to him, if only forever. The train pulled away from the station and the window went dark.

* * *

There was time indeed for a glass of wine at the Center Cafe. Owen asked for a Malbec, as usual. He recognized the bartender, who didn't recognize him. "A man walks into a bar with a slab of asphalt," the bartender said. Owen pretended absently that he had never heard the joke before. The Capitol was nearby, sensed in its granite immensity but invisible. There were Senate races too and perhaps the next day, on Romney's coattails, the Senate would also turn Republican. Yet he felt dull. Finally, on the cusp of something real, there was no one to share it with. The image of Lisa's insistently indifferent profile shone from the circle of wine in his glass, from the reflection of his eyes in the bar mirror, from the zinc of the bar.

He stood in the stupid, snaking line in the departure hall for the Northeastern to New York, the wait endured by labored fantasies of a destiny fulfilled. Stiles as secretary of state. He, Owen, as his chief of staff. But who do you come home to? He found a seat in the quiet car and put on his iPod with his Scarlatti sonatas, staring at the landscape as it passed him by—New Carrollton, Baltimore-Washington International Airport, Baltimore itself, the too-familiar station. This

Northeast Corridor, much maligned by conservatives, was also the embryo of the nation. From Washington, through Delaware, to Philadelphia, past Trenton, where Washington had crossed the Delaware, to New York, where he had bidden farewell to his troops at the Fraunces Tavern near where the towers fell, the tavern where drinks were still served and the whiskey collection was superb. There was nothing else for Owen to do but love this country, despite the row upon row of derelict houses in Baltimore, the prison outside Wilmington, the emptied factories that had once produced bicycles, paper, wreaths, machine tools, the massive mound of discarded fridges and bathtubs just north of Philadelphia. But everything to him seemed renewable, like the very spirit of America itself.

* * *

The apartment, despite the storm, had suffered nothing. It was far enough north in Manhattan, and on high enough ground, to have escaped the fist of wind and rain that had punched southern Manhattan. The electricity, heat, and water all worked. He felt, inside the apartment again, both a familiar comfort and a terrible double discomfort: for his grandfather who had never returned, for his marriage that had begun to die there. He still could not walk these spaces without thinking of Lisa. He turned on the lights in every room, wandering through the museum-like spaces, both the curator and the only visitor. And when he reached the study, and saw the first-edition novels of Gene Davis Powell in their place of prominence on the vast desk where his grandfather had left them, he finally removed them and cleaned the spot where they had sat for fifty years, scrubbing with a paper towel and Windex. He put the books into a box and decided he would sell them. The debt had been paid, and everyone to whom it might have been owed was dead.

He could hardly sleep. The image of Lisa on the Metro kept him awake. He thought: They had said more to each other in those two minutes of silence on the train than they had ever said in words, and everything was too late.

* * *

The lines were long the next morning at the polling station on the West Side, where he was registered to vote. There was a clear and early sun that November 6, with enough chill in the air to make the walk pleasant as long as you had an overcoat and a scarf. This was weather he loved. On the street a large number of people walking towards him had little stickers on their lapels and shirts, with a red check, saying "I voted." He too had voted. He walked with his weekend bag back to Penn Station, to take the 10:35 back to Washington, and watch the returns.

About The Author

Scott Seward Smith lives in New York City. *Red Line Blues* is his first novel.

Learn more about new and upcoming titles at

LibertyIslandMag.com